MY C . .
LITTLE PLACE

ADVENTURES in the QUEST to find ONE'S PLACE in LIFE

STEPHEN PAYNE

Chalk Stream Books

Stephen Payne asserts his moral right to be
identified as the author of this book.

Published by Chalk Stream Books
www.chalkstreambooks.com

ISBN: 978-1-917056-00-7

This book is not trying to portray exact events of history,
nor its characters in perfect accuracy.

The use of any lines, paragraphs, chapters, parts or the
whole novel in any and all of AI, artificial intelligence or
ChatGPT-type training exercises is strictly and expressly
forbidden and prohibited. This will be enforced and all
necessary prosecutions will be pursued. We reserve the
right to use artificial intelligence (AI) to track perpetrators.
Attempting to load any part of or all of this novel into AI risks
damaging your computer system. We take no responsibility
for your actions or any damage that may be incurred.

For permission requests, write to the publisher,
addressed "Attention: Permissions Coordinator",
at contact@chalkstreambooks.com

Printed and bound in the UK.

This book can be purchase at chalkstreambooks.com/molp

www.facebook.com/profile.php?id=61556713946264

Author's Note and Preface

⋙◐◑⋘

The future can only exist
because of the present.
The present can only exist
because of the past.
History is our pedestal.
By it – we rise or fall.

Author – October 2023

To live life to the full, we have to take the lid off conventions. There are no confinements. Life these days, for all of us, it seems, knows no limits.

The storylines here, as in real life, know no limits; they go wherever life takes them.

Adventure – in all aspects of our existence.

This book is the first of the trilogy of the "Quest". It is naturally and modernistically extending the boundaries of literary conventions. And, it must be said, this is necessary and timely for humanity and for life on this planet.

But, rest assured, volume one is climactic in itself!

Refreshingly, this is verging on the rebirth of the Modernism style.

Compartmentalising thinking typically restricts writing to one genre. It seems we have here an essential new genre – a "Whole of Life" quest. With these multi-genres, it is legacy.

The adventures will be in a variety of locations; some may be in different eras.

Please note: There are characters and accents here of Irish, American, Arabic, Russian and youthful origins. Grammar will not always fit standard practice in places due to the characters' eras and traits. Hence the accents and the grammar may be stylised for these particular adventures.

The quest starts off in Part 1 by laying down its concepts and forming the small array of storylines – the groundwork of elements for the later main storylines. The strands are all then gradually drawn together. This culminates in the key storyline in Part 3, which is over half of the novel!

This book has been written for continuous, in-depth readers. It is not for skimmers, scanners, or cherry-pickers. All of whom will be missing out on both the true essences of the novel and on the culminations to selections of plots and endings. They will have missed the point, and hence wasted their time.

Where some scenes change plot or direction rapidly, points of view will adjust accordingly.

But don't worry! The narrator will cover you where necessary and keep you in touch with what's going on.

(Bronagh wouldn't want you to miss out on anything now, would she? ... to be sure.)

"Who is Bronagh?" I hear you say ...

You will be needing sustenance. The narrator will kindly provide you with slots for the occasional tea and biscuits.

With thanks to and for

Mark Thistlethwayte

Simon Brocklehurst

Spike Travers

Wendy

Liza and Oliver

The American guy in Lancaster, California, who transformed into Ezra

Emily

Neal

Michael Richards

Colyton Grammar School

Adrian Notter at Design Image, and Lhea, illustrator

Duncan Potter at Riverside Publishing Solutions

Catherine Dunn, editor

Mark Butler, mentor

Glenn and co. at PR for Books

Ken Walker of Jellyfish Solutions, printing

John & Joan

Karen

PART 1

Places

⌒⊙⊙⌒

There is a place for everyone … but
the job of finding the right place
requires very special techniques.

As adventures unfold, all is not as it seems –
learning for the present and for the future.

Chapter 1

The View from the Wing

⋞◌◍◌⋟

Bronagh, a twelve-year-old Irish schoolgirl, is on holiday by the coast. She looks into the distant seascape and surf of the long sandy beach, musing. Bronagh is no longer the happy girl she once was. Her eyes are wistful, and a splash of salt water spray gradually crystalises on her cheek. She is unsettled, distant and very seriously disappointed and upset with the way things are in her life right now. She thinks to herself …

If only … if only … she imagines herself as a very, very far-away bird.

In the unrelenting, torturous and cold contusions of the Southern Oceans that are whipped by the Roaring Forties, where sight of land is more rare than a glimpse of the sun, the thread of survival is based upon the resources and features of one's blessings.

I am hearing the music of Mendelssohn as I fly through this. A strong but light body, covered in watery spray and rain, on chill-proof streamlined mottled feathers and a wide and long wingspan of three metres (that's ten feet!) tussles with the wind. This secures the lengthy durations of expansive and even global exploration in this inhospitable and hostile environment.

Circumnavigating the globe in forty-six days like this – with stop-overs in a very special place occasionally –

is the regular and normal way of life; it may be even ten thousand miles on a single non-stop leg.

Humans often marvel and are in awe of what I am, what I can do and where I do it.

I mean, I don't actually make a wing beat – only very occasionally. Why waste the energy when you can angle your wings appropriately and use the free energy from the mighty resource of the natural atmospheric wind systems?

This marvelling and awe-inspiring is something they, people, can learn from. What can they learn? Well, I don't know; it is up to each of them individually – or collectively, through communication – to determine what principles or attitudes or techniques are relevant and useful to them.

Why do I do this existence? What drives me through it all? What do I have to look forward to? What is my relief? I think of this all the time but, thinking about it, not thinking about it for most of the time; so that must be in my subconscious, then, an innate lure. Yet this is a drive that my consciousness doesn't allow me to be aware of, lest it distract me from my dynamic flight skills that permit me to thrive in this solitary existence and live this life.

It is 2,579 miles between South Georgia and Antarctica, 1,093 miles to Tierra del Fuego, 836 miles to the Falkland Islands.

Ahh ... there it is! At least I thought I saw it; was I mistaken? That could have been it, that so rare first glimpse of the dark, rocky outline of South Georgia ... home.

It will be a while yet. My thoughts are flooding my mind quickly now, the subconscious rising to the conscious. Images and feelings fill me and warm me throughout, from feather tip to feather tip, from beak to talons. There is a mounting overwhelming feeling in my heart. Sharp eyesight, now, is crucial for the final navigation and flight path approach. All the senses are coming into play for the fine tuning and alignments. My heart is now all of a flutter and bursting almost as the images of and feelings for my lifelong partner engulf me.

Yes, I see those images in my mind of the meeting, the embrace, the callings, the exuberance, the mutual and deep affection … before it actually happens.

I wonder, would it be too far a stretch of the imagination? Is it possible that humans achieve a parallel with this experience in their own human lives? "Life could be so simple if you do it this way. Why not follow your instincts and go with the flow?"

Seeing this flight in her mind's eye had the immediate effect of triggering the rising of the phoenix in Bronagh's soul. It provided her with the inspiration she desperately needed.

Chapter 2

Closer to Home

જ⊙⊙⊙

Finn is eight years old. He is walking down a country lane in Dorset near where he lives. He looks through a hedge, as he loves nature, to see … and thinks to himself, as if in the robin's mind's eye …

Hopping about on the garden fence, looking here, looking there. Delicate chirping music serenades me. Checking behind, flitting here, flitting there … who is that looking out of the window? Oh, it's the owner. What is that wriggling under that leaf? Oooh! Could be breakfast … yes! I'll have that! *Gulp!* That's better. Now I'm ready to survey my territory once again.

I will deal harshly with any unwelcome intruders, be warned. Oh, okay … except those that are smaller than me, but I will still let others know that I regard them as unwelcome and hope to suggest to them that they should find the door. Of course, my red chest will be displayed prominently to signal my displeasure.

With work now done, I must find more food for those hungry new little mouths. You know it takes ages, flitting around here and there to pick up any kind of morsel to bring back for those permanently open beaks of theirs, but it does give me a deep satisfaction; this is my family and my cosy home. I selected it, as it was the best place I could find for security, shelter and peace. I know, I know, one day they will have grown too big to stay here and will fly the nest ... but I will be so proud. I will even return to this same nest, if it remains in good shape. They may also then be somewhere nearby as my family.

Do I feel a sense of resonance of this with human family life? No, I don't, but I'm beginning to feel that I should ... and I should have empathy.

Chapter 3

Further Away

⚗

The aim of military training is
not just to prepare men for battle,
but to make them long for it.

— Louis Simpson, *War: An Anthology*

The real man is a maze of a million
notes: the label is all one note.

— Hilaire Belloc, *A Conversation with an Angel*

A loud and close *Crunch! Crunch! Crunch! Crunch! Crunch!*, precise and rhythmical, penetrates your being from the polished black high boots goose-stepping in clinically straight and repetitive columns in an expansive parade and civic square rally in Nuremberg. Emblazoned with red, white and black drapes, banners and flags, the atmosphere is harsh, sharp and disciplined – purposeful and thick with realism.

In the distance, on a platform, is a short, forlorn, solitary figure in a peaked cap, unlike the helmeted thousands upon thousands now at attention.

His short neck is swollen, pulsing and tensing to produce visceral and complex, overwhelming and overpowering commands and addresses, striking at the souls of all. Forcefully strident, the barrage and tirade streams to the silent assembled masses.

Those bellicose rantings couldn't fail to stun.

But I hear Holst, *The Planets* suite, Mars …

Hence now journeying to Kehlsteinhaus, Obersalzberg, Berchtesgaden, in the Bavarian Alps …

That same short figure, without his peaked cap, baring a short, greased hairstyle that adds nothing to fashion, sits in a garden chair looking out over the panorama that has become his bequest. I am hearing Beethoven- and Strauss-themed music. Before him is a backdrop of multiple layers of snow-peaked, serrated mountain ranges, depreciating in sharpness and clarity into the horizon.

To the fore in the valley are, by contrast, swathes of lush green pastures. He is looking at nothing in particular except for what he sees in his mind. This is probably a bigger picture, in actual fact, than what he sees even with the clear blue sky adorning the vista before him.

He actually sees a map of the whole of Western Europe, of Eastern Europe, of North Africa, of Mediterranean countries, of Russia … there is no limit. What he sees on this map, he sees as his.

This location is the Eagle's Nest, in southern Germany. For someone, this is a place of peace, of solitude, with space and time to think without interruptions. To think of new ideas, new plots, new plans, new tactics … and above all, cunning ways to execute his strategies. So, you see, a place such as this, with the solitude, the freedom, the stillness, is the place of both restfulness and inspiration. Whoever you are, it is essential to have such a place as this in order to succeed in your quests.

Chapter 4

Far-Reaching Implications?

∽◈◈◈∽

I don't like authority, at least I don't
like other people's authority.

A. C. Benson, excerpts from the letters of

Lord forgive them, for they
know what they do!

Karl Kraus, in *Karl Kraus* by Harry Zohn

Word was out of that solitary man's reflections, thoughts, intentions and plans.

Meanwhile, back in Poland, the people and the churches prayed. Back in England, the people and the churches prayed. Back in France, the people and the churches prayed.

The people in England and in Europe and the British government, quite rightly and reverently, thought that enough was enough regarding World War I. The nations and people were still in recovery mode from the deeply troubling and traumatic effects of that period.

There was much talk, discussion and exploration in debate about how to deal with this emerging threat from Hitler and the Third Reich and the Nazi movement. Worry was great and prevalent. The health of the nation and the nation itself were at great risk.

The obvious and natural solution to this dilemma was to put a peace treaty in place as quickly as possible. The great and the good travelled to and interacted with many in Germany in order to liaise on building positive relations and attempting to negotiate a binding peace treaty. As time went on, it became troubling that in spite of these energetic and determined efforts, any forward progress seemed to be gradually countered by fresh and increasingly negative assertions by Hitler and the Reich.

Demoralisation began to set in, and the feelings of a forlorn nation became apparent.

Out of an extreme crisis, however, and through continued prayer within the British people and the nation, some positive stirrings started to occur. A new voice was starting to be heard, which was resonating with more and more people and being listened to more carefully in government and in a new light. A new positivity and strength could not be held back. It gathered pace. This was the birth of a new conscience and character for the whole of the British nation, the Commonwealth and beyond. It was the creation of a dynamic new government around a new leadership — that of Prime Minister Winston Churchill.

He had clearly thought very deeply and profoundly on this predicament that faced Europe.

For some reason, or by way of a distinctly different mindset, or by way of getting his inspiration from elsewhere, he had seen a different vision for Europe.

He had also managed to share that vision with MPs, with some other European and international leaders, and with an adequate number of British people. He had then been able to move all of them, obviously including the necessary military leadership, to act in a cohesive, coordinated, positive and secretive direction that would lead to and seek to achieve fulfilment of that vision. No mean feat in itself, and so dramatically different … it became contagious.

Elsewhere – but what of Bronagh?

I expect Bronagh had now settled down into school life and work again after her holidays …

No, she had not!

Bronagh had entered her teenage years. Her behaviour and attitudes were much the same as those of any adolescent. Except that in her case, she was already unsettled. This resulted in further turbulence in her life – fiery interactions with her parents and with the nuns at her convent school. They all despaired of her.

"Bronagh!"

"Yes, Sister Mary Concessa?"

"Come with me, would you?"

"Do I have to?"

"Bronagh! When I say 'Come with me', it means 'Come with me now'!"

"Oh, you people are so outrageous …"

"Bronagh, what's gotten into you? Don't tell me! I know, I know the answer to that one myself, don't I just? It's precisely the reason I'm calling you into my study.

"The fact that you don't learn the catechism, you don't say the Hail Marys and you don't respect any of us here enough is precisely the reason that the Devil has gotten hold of you, so he has, and has gotten into you and controls everything you do and say!"

"You really believe all that stuff, don't you? So how would you know? Do you sit up and chat with the Devil every night to see what he's been up to?"

"Bronagh! Enough! We're going to seriously wash your mouth out with soap, recite prayers and take Holy Communion over you *all day* tomorrow, so we will!"

Chapter 5

Back at Home ... Quintessentially

∽⊙⊙∾

The art of reading is in great part that of
acquiring a better understanding of life
from one's encounter with it in books.

Andre Maurois, *The Art of Living*

Meanwhile, in the rest of England, in the country,
a background ambience generated by Handel's
"The Arrival of the Queen of Sheba" surrounds the
quintessentially English impressions of a British country
house, set in the unspoiled and undeveloped rural
countryside of southern Hampshire. As it has very close
associations with an adjoining village, all its needs in
terms of provisions, staffing, estate farm materials and
workers, blacksmith, timber yard, brewery and more
can be met from its environs. Typical village, farm and
rural life are all harmoniously tied together in daily
life ... The baker provides for the regular daily craving
for his mouth-watering crusty fresh-baked bread;
the regulars chat and gossip as they queue for their
turn to get as close as possible and sniff the golden rows
of loaves; the postman is always smiling as he greets
everyone whilst going about his deliveries; a horse and
cart slowly pass through the village streets, loaded with
sheaves of hay; the squire, Colonel Evelyn, slowly and
carefully drives his latest new black and shiny motor

car back from town and passes the church, waving and smiling to every parishioner.

The colonel enjoys his return along the snaking drive, past the lake and up to the house; he parks on the gravel standing. An adjacent gathering of farm labourers touch their caps as he does so. All is very well, and hey, just in time for lunch.

Nothing in the wildest imaginings could touch or spoil this perfectly idyllic demonstration of country community life in 1930s southern England.

(The colonel has already bought this country house, and the whole estate, from his nephew, from whom he had been renting the place. Circumstances had been such that it might have had to have been sold off – a close shave indeed.)

Elsewhere – but what of Finn?

Yes, Finn eventually ended up being schooled in the south of England. The trouble was, he found it difficult to concentrate adequately on the academic side of life, as he was always preoccupied by the anxieties of his early years.

What was to become of him?

Chapter 6

Meanwhile, Unseen ...

Until it is kindled by a spirit as
flamingly alive as the one which
gave it birth, a book is dead to us.

Henry Miller, *The Books in My Life*

There is something strange in the
modern mind, by which a material
cause always seems like a real cause.

G. K. Chesterton, *All I Survey*

However, up above all of this – above in spiritual
terms, as in the normally unseen realms, in what
might also be termed a "parallel universe" – there has
been much stirring and frantic disturbed commotion,
all unseen to those on Earth below. Long dark dinosaur-
like creatures, jointed wings flapping powerfully,
with a number of legs trailing below, fly in aerial
combat with one another. Blood-curdling screeches
and cries fill the air as threats, warnings and intense
anger are exchanged between the creatures. Hot fumes
and gases, sulphurous vapours and flames issue forth
from their mouths as they dig their numerous sharp
teeth into the nearest passing opponent, who responds
in kind.

This has been going on for a while now.

These are not Earthly creatures but what would seem to be representations of devil images, devilish and satanic creatures fighting ... and black angels. This is the unseen spiritual warfare in distant realms that manifests and tries to influence the direction of human life on Earth.

Not all humans can or will be influenced by these dark forces, but there are some individuals predisposed, perhaps, to be vulnerable to their evil intentions.

The British Army had been fighting Hitler's forces in northern France during 1940. It was close to defeat and was trapped at Dunkirk.

During a national broadcast on 24 May 1940, King George VI instructed the people of Britain to plead for divine intervention. Together with members of the Cabinet, the king attended Westminster Abbey on 26 May for a National Day of Prayer, whilst literally millions of people across the British Isles flocked to join in prayer, seeking deliverance.

Nothing like it had ever been seen before in England or indeed in any other country, with people queuing to get into churches, pleading for help.

The result? Astounding.

Hitler stopped his general advance.

A storm of extraordinary fury grounded the German Air Force on 28 May.

A great calm settled over the English Channel for several days, enabling 335,000 men of the British Army to be swiftly evacuated from Dunkirk.

Defeat and the invasion of Britain were averted.

From then on, people referred to what had happened as "the miracle of Dunkirk".

Looking back, Dr H. A. Wilson wrote, "If ever a great nation was on the point of supreme and final disaster, and yet was saved and reinstated, it was ourselves … It does not require an exceptionally religious mind to detect in all this the Hand of God."

Four days after he became prime minister in May 1940, Winston Churchill – who had approved the National Day of Prayer and, upon hearing the news of the successful evacuation of the British Army from Dunkirk, himself become an enthusiast – officially appointed Sunday 9 June as a Day of National Thanksgiving and went on to approve two further national days of prayer in each of the next three years.

> Dunkirk was so absorbing that for days we could think of nothing else. An acquaintance of Hubert's took his motor-boat there and says it was the finest weekend he ever had in his life. He came back with the boat riddled with shot.

Evelyn Underhill, *The Letters of Evelyn Underhill*

Chapter 7

The Quintessential Home Again

❦

The year is 1942. There is a sharp rap on the front door of the house, with a very positive and purposeful tone. The doorman attends.

"Good afternoon, sir. Are you expected? Do you have an appointment?"

"No, I'm afraid I don't – bit of urgent business and all that. Is the squire in? I do need to have a chat with him rather urgently, if it's not too much trouble?"

"I understand, sir. I will see if he's available to see you. Who shall I say is here to see him?"

"Ah, yes – just say it's the Chief of the Home Office … from Whitehall."

"Right away, sir. Won't be a minute."

"Sir, it's the Chief of the Home Office from Whitehall to see you. I'm afraid he doesn't have an appointment, but he says it is rather urgent."

"Oh, good Lord, that's unusual. Whatever's up? Would have thought he would have written first. All right, show him into the drawing room, would you, old chap? Thanks awfully. Oh, and better prepare some tea."

The doorman shows the chief through, past the grand staircase, and they enter the drawing room, where they are received by the colonel.

"Good afternoon. It's awfully good of you to see me at short notice, but … look here, I've got something that I really wanted to talk with you about in person ..."

Colonel Evelyn asks his other guests to leave the room and looks at his visitor. "I say, would you like some tea? I will get some brought in right away, and then we won't be disturbed." He looks at the doorman, who nods.

They sit in very comfortable drawing room chairs, surrounded by large paintings of various members of the house's sequence of squires and the colonel's family history, facing the tall central window.

The Chief of the Home Office is clearly agitated and wants to get on with things. "Now look here, I'll come straight to the point, as time is of the essence. Clearly you will be aware of the difficulties we are facing in Poland and France from the hostile advance of Hitler's Third Reich forces."

"Yes, of course."

"Well, this is totally top secret, and I must insist that you give me your word that you will not divulge any of this or discuss anything I have to say with anyone outside these walls, with the exception of your wife. I have to ask you to give me that assurance before I can discuss this matter with you any further."

"Good gracious. Well ... what can I say? At these times this must be extremely important, and I feel I must give you that assurance right away."

"Good fellow. That's what I like to hear. I must also say that the house is surrounded, but very discreetly – none of your staff or workers would notice – so that if there were any potential information leaks, the military fellows hiding in the woods would have to deal with things on the government's behalf, shall we say."

"I'm dumbfounded. This is so extraordinary. I mean, we already have some of those damned chaps from the navy living here with us. What's the problem? Give me a moment, please." The colonel sips some more tea, very thoughtfully, and is by now nervous and deeply moved.

"I see. This must be terribly important … and sensitive, of course. I assure you that I won't risk breathing a word of anything here with anyone. I assume you'll need me to sign something, would you?"

"Good chap. That would be most helpful too."

"I am here on the express command of none other than the prime minister, Mr Churchill himself … who has also had words with Eisenhower, His Excellency Charles de Gaulle the President of France, and Field Marshal Montgomery, who is also in on this."

"My goodness me, you don't mess about, do you? I do believe your credentials!"

"Just wanted to make myself clear right from the outset."

"Right, then let's get down to it."

"I appreciate that this might come as a bit of a shock to you, but you're man enough and you appreciate the seriousness of the convictions of all who are behind this."

"Yes, of course," mulls the squire, now increasingly attentive and tense and eager to find out what it's all about.

"The government, Winston Churchill, General Eisenhower … and the War Office have sent me to tell you that, in the interests of the country and the western world, your house is going to be used as a command centre for allied forces. This will entail the government, the War Office and the military taking over the entire house.

"To all intents and purposes, it will still look like a normal country estate from the outside, if you see what I mean, but the house will regularly be occupied by all levels of command hierarchy at various times. I can't say more than that at the present time. Of course, you and your family will need to seek alternative accommodation, but discreetly. We hope to make amends with you, but of course at a much later date.

"Do I have your word, sir?"

"You mean this is a requisitioning? I'm speechless … wait a minute, but this is forcible removal! So I have no other options, do I? This is a fait accompli? But … uhmm …yes … but I shall need to discuss this with the family …"

"Good man. I knew you were the sort of chap who would see this straight away. Right, must be off – got to get back to London. My chaps here will stay with you and do a little bit of appropriate paperwork and start to make the arrangements. Any questions?"

The colonel is keeping his cards close to his chest.

"No … ah, no, of course not. It's all perfectly clear … ahh, and thank you for coming down."

Chapter 8

Oh Dear

⋄⋄⋄⋄

Every man contemplates an
Angel in his future self.

Ralph Waldo Emerson,
Journals of Ralph Waldo Emerson

A good indignation brings
out all one's powers.

Ralph Waldo Emerson

The following day naturally sees a sombre disposition falling on the immediate family members at Southwick House, those that are very immediate having been made vaguely aware of the foreboding situation. An immediate family gathering is called.

The colonel outlines.

"This dastardly government, by their shameful deviousness, and its navy, who clearly have a hand in this by all accounts, have been gradually trying to lever us out of our dear home. Good God, they have even been so bold as to plant the British Navy Navigational School here for the last year!

"Now I must tell you that yesterday I had a very high-level delegation come down from London to visit me, and they leave us in a dire situation, with uncompromising terms and, I fear, no options …

"I am saying that, I am afraid, the British government, nonetheless, is requisitioning this house, formally and with immediate effect.

"It means that we are in effect now homeless. We shall, of course, find some other very fine accommodation in the short term, so do not worry yourselves; after all, we are not penniless, not by any stretch of the imagination.

"We may have to accept almost anywhere in the short term, but I will find for us something more in keeping with this place in due course. It may take a while – after all, there is a bloody war on; we have a lot of work to do."

"I hope they are paying you a goodly price; this is such a splendid place!"

"Such matters are not currently for discussion, such is the nature and urgency of the situation."

"What do you mean? Why do they want or need this home so badly and so quickly?"

"I am not at liberty to say or to discuss such matters with anyone, and the same goes for all of us here present. Is that understood?"

"Oh gosh."

•◆•

Sunday arrives, and it is time and an occasion for seeking solace. The estate is still in the ownership of the colonel. It has within its confines, jurisdiction and estate chattels an elegant but charmingly and quietly isolated small church and churchyard. The church building is partially screened from the nearby small country road by a line of trees wrapping around it.

One of the trees, a yew, seems particularly old – in fact, very old. It also has the unusual characteristic of having, believe it or not, a hollow trunk at ground level, which one can even enter. The trunk then encloses itself to form a roof over the chamber within. This tree is so close to the church as to be virtually touching the stonework – a curious and wondrous feature and a naturally occurring creation.

Inside the small, quaint, well-appointed church, with all the hallmarks of a fifth- to tenth-century Saxon origin, at the front of the nave's left-hand pews is a beautifully crafted square booth with seating and its own door. This is the designated booth for the squire of the estate and his immediate family – their own little place.

The colonel – the squire – and his family take their due seats in the booth. The sombreness of the atmosphere is fitting for the reflections now circulating in their minds, which may continue to circulate for some time. The colonel, now in his eighties, will undoubtedly reflect in an even deeper way, praying and appealing to God, perhaps, for comfort and solutions for himself and his family. Although wise and having the benefit of maturity, the colonel may still suffer more torment than most in his personal dealings with his predicament.

The searing sounds of the engines of a roaring flight of Spitfires overhead interrupts the peace.

Chapter 9

When Times Are Hard

⚜

The year is 200 AD, prior to the building of the Saxon South Boarhunt church. This site may have been identified as a place of worship by those who saw meaning in the perceived significance of the yew tree. The yew was important in Celtic times as symbolising the process of death, as well as encouragement for birth and rebirth or resurrection. From an archaeological perspective, there may have been a small neolithic wood henge, a gathering of stones, a small stone circle or a barrow on this site.

This specific yew tree in question has been dated to 150 AD ... one would have seen this tree here in 200 AD.

The year was 1400. A period of significantly different weather patterns had now cloaked Britain. Due to the housing, working and sustenance conditions at that time, no one, absolutely no one, could help but notice the fresh cruelty of the winters, which seemed to be becoming even more harsh by the year. "Times was hard," times were harsh, food was hard to come by. If you had little or no income and a family and were moved on by your previous landlord, you were in the most desperate of times. Your life was potentially on the brink, as were those of thousands of others. In this wild countryside and in cruel and uninviting towns and cities, with no direction and no hope before you, what were you to do as yet another autumn and winter of biting winds, lashing rain after lashing rain, and alternating frosts froze you to the raw bone? That was before the snows and blizzards arrived.

Part of the answer to the delicate puzzle of tentative survival lay in the new art that you found in your brain via the caring drive from your soul. That was the art of searching. Searching for what? Searching for the slight signs of protection that your imagination could afford that you could see in any, any slight covering or shelter that you could seek anywhere, absolutely anywhere. Hunger and cold made this job all the more uncomfortable, challenging and dangerous. How much longer could you keep going? How much longer would your hope and vision last?

Best to leave the family huddled somewhere temporarily. The best you could find was in a rough-hewn farm cattle shelter, perhaps, in with the animals, to share their warmth until they were needed.

Wet, cold, seeing your own breath, wrapped in your wet coat, scarf and wet clothes, you see a small church, which unfortunately is locked. Your soul-driven search and imagination allows you to see in your mind's eye a potential miracle. Before you stands a large wide yew tree adjacent to the church. On closer inspection the enormous trunk reveals an opening – an opening to a hollow inside the yew tree. The circumference is a clear six feet across, covered overhead and with few openings to the outside … and it is clean!

With renewed vigour, you hurriedly return to your cold, lost and forlorn family to enthusiastically break the news of your find. They reluctantly follow to just another of your "miracle" finds.

To your joy and fulfilment, they all approve of your latest new find and can all see the cover, protection and dry, sheltering features afforded by this place, their new home for the winter. The hollow trunk of the yew tree shelters them from all the storms that winter could throw at them. This is their own little place – a secret, private space, providing security that becomes sacred to them.

I am sensing that this searching process can also turn into a further yearning ... for more searching, possibly for things yet unknown. This addictively becomes an exciting process of further searching, if done in the correct set of ways. After all, I see that when done in these ways, the outcomes are seemingly good for me ... why shouldn't I want more?

With the knowledge of how to go about this and a template of how to do it, everyone will want to achieve the best for themselves that they possibly can.

If only I could find further directions ... and guidelines ...

Elsewhere – and what of Finn?

With all the difficulties he encountered in early life, how on earth could he progress? Perhaps that was the making of Finn. Progress his life he did.

College life suited Finn. He also made great progress at living independently, even in the London area. This was a very big scary challenge for him, eclipsing everything that had gone before, but he made it.

Chapter 10

It Appears We Have Visitors

✎◈◈

Bronagh was an avid learner. Coming from Ireland, and with a religious background, that was where she felt comfortable progressing her learning – religion. If the truth be known, Bronagh was not at all happy or satisfied with the way things had been going at her Catholic school. As a consequence of her experiences there, she was left hungry and clamouring for a broader education. She wanted to put all her knowledge into context historically and geographically.

Her school was visited once a month by a van. This van was driven by a Mrs Doyle, of the County Library Service, the mobile library. Over time, from Mrs Doyle's regular visits, they got to know one another. Mrs Doyle was a prim lady in skirt, blouse and spectacles, her hair in a bun. Bronagh liked Mrs Doyle, and, learning about Bronagh's frustrations, she got to know exactly which books to look up and bring along for her next visit to Bronagh's school. As Ireland is part of the British Isles, events in England sometimes formed the basis of what might later unfold in Ireland.

Bronagh was keen to get to the bottom of some of this. Her thinking and findings went like this …

"In part of the Roman era of occupation of Great Britain, Constantine came to Britain with his father, the emperor Constantius, in 305 AD. Constantius died in July the following year in York.

"The system of succession at the time demanded that another Caesar should become emperor, but the soldiers in York immediately proclaimed Constantine their leader. It proved to be a pivotal moment in history. He is known as Constantine the Great for very good reasons.

"After nearly eighty years and three generations of political fragmentation, Constantine united the whole of the Roman Empire under one ruler. By 324 AD he had extended his power and was sole emperor, restoring stability and security to the Roman world.

"Constantine also abandoned Rome as the most important city in the empire, but not completely abandoning it – building a new capital modestly named Constantinople (now Istanbul). In the next two centuries, Rome and Italy became vulnerable to barbarian invasions. The much more easily defendable Constantinople lasted for another thousand years.

"Finally, and perhaps most famously, Constantine's strong support for Christianity had an incalculable impact on European history. He is said to have been converted to the faith in 312 AD.

"At the time, only around ten per cent of the Roman Empire's population were Christian. The majority of the ruling elite worshipped the old gods of Rome. Constantine was the first emperor to allow Christians to worship freely, helping to unite and promote the faith. He went on to instigate the celebration of the birth of Christ that we now call Christmas."

Chapter 11

But No One Knew ...

⋯⊙⊙⋯

1944, springtime.

For reasons of security, diversion and camouflage, in the woodland surrounding Southwick House gardens you will find Nissen huts and caravans providing accommodation housing for … General Eisenhower, the Supreme Commander of the Allied Expeditionary Force, Europe. This would reduce the risk of him being killed by any bombing or attack on Southwick House at night.

One morning, in the springtime of 1944, Ike notices, in the trees over the caravans and huts, peaceful-looking birds accumulating and roosting.

He enquires, "What are those birds?"

"They're collared doves, sir."

… musing and reflecting …

"Really?" replies General Eisenhower.

After a crucial day in the map room in Southwick House, having had all the crucial military and intelligence reports presented to him for consideration for his monumental decision-making process – a decision that will potentially change the course of history – he stands alone, looking out of the dining room central long window … and ponders; he ponders heavily but alone.

Unbeknown to Ike, in the spiritual world outside the window and above him are flocks of doves and of angels ... hovering ...

6 June 1944, D-Day.

For days now fever had been building. The weather had been judged to provide a window of opportunity that morning for the combined forces of the Allied invasion of Normandy to act at that precise moment.

Hundreds of thousands of hours and men had been prepared for a decisive blow to be struck against the Third Reich and Hitler's occupying forces in France and beyond.

Ferocious fighting at sea, on the beaches and in the hinterland ensued that day, with terrible loss of life on both sides.

An identical battle raged far above in the spiritual domain between demons and black angels against white angels and all the angelic realms. There were extreme forces at play. The stakes were high and one faction was going to win – and it was seen to it that one side did win.

Elsewhere – and what of Bronagh?

We very clearly get the picture of her suffering. Bronagh had had enough of the convent and convent school life by the age of sixteen, and she persuaded her parents to let her go to college in Dublin. She would also need to persuade her parents to support her financially, so she had to learn to play it carefully. And she did.

Chapter 12

Meanwhile, Back Home

⋙◈⋘

Back in southern England, the business of the continuous loading of supplies for the replenishment of the Allied troops making headway through Normandy was the order of every day now. Bustling streets and ports loaded ships, ensuring a flow of food, equipment, medical supplies and military hardware to what was now the largest active port in Europe – the Mulberry harbours created at the Arromanches beachheads in Normandy.

Meanwhile, the former occupants of Southwick House were in animated discussion, and concerns were still running high. The family were conversing about their plight and taking stock of the situation.

In 1941 the government had assured the family that they could get the house back after the war. However, further changes were afoot for the family. Colonel Evelyn died in 1943, possibly resulting from the considerable distress he had suffered at the quandary presented by the loss of Southwick House. In a further twist, he left the entire estate to his nephew, Hugh Borthwick.

In yet another unfortunate twist, Hugh Borthwick died in 1950, his widow taking over the management of the estate. His widow was Mrs Borthwick-Norton, a socialite who was friends with Wallis Simpson, the American divorcee who forced the abdication of King Edward VIII.

In 1950 the government paid them £40,000 for the house, well below the going price. It is believed that it was not made clear to them whether an option to buy it back at a later date was in place. This option had been a normal and expected feature of similar previous cases.

Twist of fate? Fortuitous?

Mrs Borthwick-Norton died on 27 February 1988. She had no children of her own to leave the estate to. There was then a revelation in her will that the entire estate was to be left to ... the original Thistlethwayte family!

From 2002 to 2007, there were government plans for fourteen new "Garden Cities or towns" – 80,000 new homes which were to be in south Hampshire, including in the Fareham Borough Council (FBC) area, 10,000 of which were to be on land to the north of Fareham. This land happened to be owned by the Southwick Estate, now run by the new squire, Mr Mark Thistlethwayte. He formed Buckland Developments Ltd in 2005/6. His company objected to the 10,000 proposed homes of the FBC plan on the grounds of diminished quality of life, quality of social life and environmental infrastructure. They wanted to minimise car use. Southwick Estate had developed solar farms to power electricity needs for the Welborne development, as it was to be known.

Curiously, in 2016/17, the government announced that it planned to offload the original Southwick House for housing development – contrary to their statement in the 1940s where they had said that the

Southwick Estate would get the opportunity to buy the house back.

In 2018/19 the government and Hampshire County Council gave the go-ahead for Welborne, saying in 2019 that the "construction of elements [was] to begin right away".

Elsewhere – but what about Bronagh?

Well! Major surprises for Bronagh and new additions to her life experiences record. She found both college life and the freedom of Dublin euphoric when compared to convent school life – as you might have imagined. She proved to be popular there and attractive to a string of suitors, one of whom went so far as to chance his luck and ask her to become engaged. But, of course, our fiery Bronagh wasn't having any of that sort of nonsense.

And what about Finn?

A major achievement! Getting an acceptance at a major and prestigious drama school in London. You have to try these things, and Finn did. But it's not always the right time, and alas, this wasn't the right time for him.

Chapter 13

People and Places

There is a time for war,
and a time for peace.

Ecclesiastes 3:8

Ukraine/Russia border area, February 2022.

Mr Zelenskyy has his own little place. It is called Ukraine and he is happy with it.

It had been noticed by various friendly states of Ukraine that over a period of time there had been a build-up of military hardware and troops along great swathes of the Russian side of the border, rising originally from 80,000 to eventually over 120,000 Russian troops. This had been discussed in the West and in the press and media.

This information was also shared with Russia itself and especially with one Mr Putin.

He declared, "Oh, it's only exercises" – i.e. no need to worry yourselves; nothing more sinister; we're not like that; after all, though, we have to be prepared to defend ourselves from any potential aggressors.

Mr Putin has his own little place too, of course, but he is not a happy bunny.

After a while it transpires that Mr Putin actually had a conceptual ambition … he exercised it and called it a "special military operation" – i.e. not an invasion of Ukraine.

What about the Ukrainian people? They live peaceably in their millions of little places and homes throughout the towns, cities and countryside. They have no axe to grind.

"Si vis pacem, para bellum."

"Igitur qui desiderat pacem, praeparet bellum."

"If you want peace, prepare for war."

Very high up above, and unbeknown, a conversation ensues between two very high- ranking angels. "If humans can get through this and survive, it will be a miracle!"

September 2022, Her Royal Highness
Queen Elizabeth II.

The sun shines down every day and the miracle of photosynthesis takes place ... every day, because of the perennial sunshine.

This has repeated for centuries and centuries, and all other forms of life function because of this too ... until one day, against all expectations of the universe, Her Royal Highness Queen Elizabeth II of the United Kingdom of Great Britain was declared to be unwell. Her doctors expressed concern for her health; she passed away later that day.

In Wales, Lloyd George once declared the Ceiriog Valley to be "a little piece of heaven on earth". This comparison will be clearly appreciated by anyone who has had the good fortune to explore the Ceiriog Valley.

So too the comparison can also be made that the life and reign of Queen Elizabeth ll was also "a little piece of heaven on earth". She also enjoyed the location of Balmoral, in the Upper Dee Valley in Scotland, which was her retreat in life and her escape.

This inevitable but very sad event took place on Thursday 8 September 2022; there followed eleven days of official mourning in the UK.

From that day, there was felt by many, many people a sense of the outpouring of the Holy Spirit. This was clearly and visibly evidenced in the way in which media presenters were touched and by the way in which King Charles lll rose to his sudden new plethora of duties and was so clearly emotionally touched and spiritually strengthened too.

The new Prince of Wales, William, responded positively to try to repair rifts with his brother, evidence of the Holy Spirit in play and in effect.

Additionally, many other mortals were also touched, moved and emboldened by the latest new move of the Holy Spirit, starting during this particular week.

This event was, of course, well known in advance in the celestial and spiritual realms. The smoothness of the accessions was also conceived and managed from there, and, as we observed, with perfection befitting the occasion.

The spiritual realms organised a reception for Queen Elizabeth II befitting the caring, humble and triumphal person that she was. Choirs of angels were aligned in banks and arrays, all singing as harmonised choirs … it could be imagined to be like the choral rendition of the King's College choir on a very special occasion at Westminster Abbey. This would be an experience that lifted all human spirits to great heights of emotional upwelling and a tear down the cheek, leaving long-lasting feelings and memories of warmth in the heart and soul.

These experiences were repeated at the Coronation of King Charles III.

Elsewhere – and Bronagh?

Bronagh had now had enough of college life and of Ireland – for the time being at least, actually as a result of the engagement scare.

She decided she needed a new life, and that was to be in London.

And Finn?

Finding work in London was now Finn's dedication. Being a supermarket check-out clerk worked for him, as did training as a teaching assistant. He dovetailed both of these together. His long-term goal was still an acting career.

Chapter 14

How Do I Find My Place?

A nd life begins to unfold for Bronagh.
What begin'th at charity?

Unbeknown, and high above, there is an audience looking down on someone … a host of life specialists to rely on. So, introducing:

Camael: Archangel, Leader of the Powers, one of the Dominions, whose specialist areas are strength, courage and compassion.

Gamaliel: Cherubim and archangel, whose specialist areas are protection and strength.

Raphael: Archangel, Leader of the Virtues, one of the seraphim, whose specialist area is all manner of healing.

Finn is twenty-one years old and now lives in a small flat in London. Due to his background (he had had a tough upbringing down south), he is, unbeknown to him, "shepherded" by Camael, Gamaliel and Raphael.

Angels can speak in a language of their own and have the ability to project it so that their listeners and readers can understand.

Camael: "Finn is going out looking at charity shops today. What have we got for him? He needs something really, really inspiring for a change."

Raphael: "I agree. He needs a boost to lift his spirits."

Gamaliel: "I've seen just the thing! It's in Bromley Road. I will set up some signs and signals for him.

A bus headed that way at just the right time would be a good start. He will think, 'Oh, I might as well take this one.' I will put two attractive girls at the getting-off bus stop for him – a signal he can't miss! – and the shop is only a glance from there."

Raphael: "A good plan."

Camael: "Okay. I will keep an eye on him."

Finn leaves his house and walks up the road, wondering exactly where to go. He sees a bus coming, headed towards Bromley, and thinks, *Oh, I might as well take this one.*

The bus stops, and he gets on.

After ten minutes, approaching Bromley, he sees a row of likely looking shops, but also two rather attractive girls!

Finn thinks to himself, *Well, why don't I just get off here, then?* He gets off.

A few minutes later, after the girls have gone, he glances over and notices a charity shop that is different from the usual type he visits. He has noticed things and coincidences already this morning.

A slim, attractive and fit Irish girl with longish dark fiery red hair is already in the shop. She is Roman Catholic but doesn't admit it or talk about it with others … but she actively prays regularly to God about her past, her dreams for life and her desires, with God's approval and as part of His plan.

She has felt frustrated by a lack of fulfilment in the past.

Shelves of books, tables of trinkets … pottery, ornaments, jewellery boxes, sundry small furniture items and racks of clothes are in front of her. She heads for the books first and tilts her head in order to read their titles, eager to find a strong thread of interest. She side-steps along the row, looking, reading and digesting as she goes.

"Ooops! Sorry," she exclaims, feeling dreadfully embarrassed as she accidentally steps on someone's foot, as she has not been looking where she was side-stepping.

By good fortune or by bad fortune, it is Finn, who had been similarly browsing the bookshelves from the other end of the row.

"Oh! No, it's okay," says Finn. "I am so sorry – I was not looking where I was going. I was so engrossed in searching through the books and with my head to one side."

"Me too," says the Irish girl. "I feel so foolish. It was my fault entirely. I do apologise."

"It's perfectly okay," says Finn. "These things happen. So, what books are you looking for?" he asks helpfully, moving things along. Finn, all the while, is thinking to himself, *My word! That was a stroke of luck! What a cracker!*

As his eyes gaze up and down her, he can't help noticing the appealing slim figure and sharp features of this, to him at least, stunning girl.

Their eyes meet and he finds that she is smiling at him! Finn's pupils are now dilated, but he easily manages to smile back.

"Oh, I don't know, really: I suppose I was looking for something to be inspired by."

Not being one to miss a trick and being a quick thinker, Finn immediately replies with a broad smile, "Well, you've come to the right place, then!"

She giggles in response. Finn interprets this as a positive sign and follows up with, "Well, look, there's a section of well-read holiday reading books. You can tell if they are any good by how thumbed and worn they look – the tattier, the better."

He looks at her for a reaction ... she smiles, he smiles. So, swiftly moving on to engage her interest still further, he says, "And over there are loads of Harry Potter books and next to those, self-help books." He looks backwards and forwards at her to try to maintain eye contact and tries to monitor her body language and facial reactions.

All good. Finn sees her listening carefully to his every word with an enthusiastic big smile on her face.

"I'll buy every book you suggest!" she says. "You're such a good salesman! Do you work here?"

"Well, thank you, how kind," says Finn, also with a smile on his face. "No, I don't work here – just browsing too ... and also looking for inspiration!"

"So what are you specifically trying to find?" she replies inquisitively. "What would interest you today?"

Finn thinks, *Is this a very smart move by her to draw me in even more than I am already drawn in?*

He decides not to say what he would really have liked to have said(!). "Something that is mind-stretching or brain-challenging," he answers, philosophically and hence safely.

"Oh, you don't want to be doing that now on such a bright and gorgeous day!" she says in her warm and jolly Irish accent, which Finn already loves to hear.

Finn is now in a euphoric, dream-like state in his head. His ability to do anything, think or move has been suspended, and you could have knocked him over with a feather.

Bronagh senses this, and to snap him out of it, she says, "Would you like to go for a walk?" There is a flurry of activity inside Finn's head at the sound of her voice again. His heart rate is heightened. His voice is now beginning to emerge again from his dry mouth.

"Uh … yeah, that's a great idea … lead the way!" He moves his head and arm to gesture, ushering her towards the front door for the walk to begin.

Unbeknown and high above …

Camael: "Well, I think we've got a lot more than we bargained for here!"

Raphael: "Yes, I am absolutely amazed how positively Finn is responding."

Gamaliel: "He clearly feels safe, comfortable and open: I think it's that soft, warm Irish accent which is new to him, intrigues him and is making a breakthrough with him."

"What's your name?" enquires Finn as they stroll briskly, probably towards a park.

"Bronagh," she replies.

"Wow! That's a very nice and interesting name; how do you spell it?" exclaims Finn.

"B-r-o-n-a-g-h … pronounced Bro-neh," exudes Bronagh in her warm, colourful and engaging accent.

"Does it have a meaning?" Finn shows further interest.

"It's after St Bronach, an Irish saint," she replies.

"How cool is that!" He confirms his further appreciation.

Bronagh has a strong background, through family history and from living in rural Ireland, in her blood and genes. This is a rich Celtic endowment of which she is very proud, and she celebrates it as such whenever she can. It brings a warm glow to her heart and to her face, which is something Finn has tuned in to.

"So, young man, tell me, do you have a name?" Bronagh figures it's about time to ask.

"Finn," he replies.

"Finn! What kind of a name is that? I don't see a fin on the top of your head!" She guffaws. Finn laughs too and smiles.

Chapter 15

In London's Fair City

Unbeknown and high above …

Camael: "This is now a situation where Finn should ideally look upward to the skies, raise his hands and arms too, take a deep breath and say, 'I feel great!'"

Raphael: "Finn is finding spiritual direction at the moment. He also has a lot of healing going on; he is moving on internally, past his fixations and hurts of the long past. Where is he getting this spiritual direction from?"

Gamaliel: "Partly direct from us and partly from an increase of the Holy Spirit, probably as a consequence of that book he was given [*The Imitation of Christ* by Thomas à Kempis] and partly from what seems to be coming across from Bronagh's natural spirit."

Inside the park entrance, Finn and Bronagh spend a few minutes in silence, looking upward into the sky, engulfed in a timeless fuzz of sensory uplifting.

"I feel great!," exclaims Finn as he raises his arms in the air.

Bronagh admires this. "That's truly terrific, Finn! Well said, and funnily enough, so do I." She raises her hands and arms too.

After a few minutes, lowering their arms slowly to their sides, Bronagh breaks the moment by saying, "Finn, have you ever been to Ireland?"

"No," says Finn. "Never have."

"You must go sometime. I think you'd like it."

"Well, yes, one day I'd like to go. I haven't been anywhere much, really … only Dorset, where I'm from, and Devon, and London, of course."

"You must get out more!" says Bronagh teasingly and jovially, smiling broadly, looking at Finn for a reaction. He smiles back, pleasantly amused.

"So, what are you doing in London?" asks Finn.

"A good question. I think I wanted some big city life experience outside of Ireland, so what bigger place can you start?"

"True," says Finn.

"I love Ireland and a whole variety of things there, but I wanted to compare with something else; after all, the world is a very big place."

"Yeah, it is. I don't have enough money to explore it, that's the trouble," says Finn slightly forlornly.

"Oh well, there's plenty of time for that," says Bronagh reassuringly. "And Finn, may I ask what brings you to the fair city of London? Do you drive trains, rob banks?" She laughs cheekily.

Finn sniggers. "No, neither of those! Nothing as exciting as that, unfortunately. I do three jobs, though, actually. Teaching assistant, supermarket check-out and an acting course."

"My word, Finn, you are a dark horse! All that talent hidden away all this time … So you're in the city to make your fortune, then?"

"Well, I hope so; that would be nice … but I don't know how that's going to work, exactly," says Finn with a degree of realism.

"Well, at least you've started your journey – that means you have a chance of arriving!" says Bronagh positively.

Finn senses that this appears to be a major new development in his life. He is not used to this sort of thing – major new developments. He has always been highly anxious about considering anything new, let alone actually doing it. Finn has always needed lots of encouragement with many things in his life.

However, he has also learned, more and more, that when he does take the initiative, it often seems to work out for him.

He is now feeling nervous because he doesn't know if he can get any help and support this time.

"So tell me a bit about you, Finn," enquires Bronagh pleasantly.

Chapter 16

Deep in Thought

❦

Before answering Bronagh's question, Finn recognises that at this point, in this situation, he is suddenly being dictated to by his old former self … his childhood memories are flooding back to him. These are in the same language as when he experienced them for real.

⋯•⋯

I was born in Dorchester hospital to a family who didn't hold themselves up to much … on benefits, in a council house, not working, living by more needs than their worth. What you're born into affects a young mind. My family were already on the radar with Social Services, and they took all my siblings away after my sister told Mum she was touched up by her neighbour. This led to Mum going to the house and beating the neighbour up with a weapon. The people came and we all got taken away into foster care. About a year later all my siblings went back to my mother when she came out of jail … but not me. I was given to a foster family aged one. This was supposed to be temporary but turned into a permanent placement, as they thought I suited the family.

We get to about age seven or eight, when I was introduced to my real mother. It was supervised at first, but then that turned into unsupervised, as my mum showed good behaviour.

I want to add that the files at the time stated that my mother didn't come to the meeting with her social worker, and potentially she was still taking substances … but I still got to have unsupervised visits!

Of what I can remember, it was nice but different. The foster family didn't sit at the table together; they sat wherever they liked. It was messy – toys everywhere. My mother had a pet cat, two dogs, two rats, two birds and a squirrel named Sparky, which she had rescued as a baby when it fell out of a tree. I have four brothers and one sister. The older brothers would tell me to do horrible things to the foster family I was staying at and tell me how that wasn't my real family and that they would never love me like they did.

I would eat a lot of junk food, as my mum always wanted me to have a good time. She was sweet, but it was so different for me, and as a child I was scared every time to go there, like it was a really horrible job I had to go to. I'd watch the clock sometimes. Even though my mum was the most beautiful person ever, I just couldn't see it then. I guess it's conflicting having two mothers – one who does everything, puts you to bed, reads to you and takes you to school and one who wants all of that but hasn't been able to get it, but has the most remarkable and beautiful ideas and thoughts. The most loving person crippled by pain and hate from the ones she loved the most. It was hard to see those emotions when I was so young, and it was hard to be going to school at the same time.

I never really had any friends, and sometimes I wasn't even popular. The kinda kid who was just there, known for not living with his real parents. It's weird how even at that age, they want to let you know out loud the situation you're in, like it's a category you have to stick by. My behaviour started getting a bit more erratic when I was about age nine to twelve – running away, hitting my foster family, destroying their house, peeing in their car, throwing hot water on them and making them feel horrible. They would regret this, but maybe not in the obvious ways. My foster dad would hit me with the slipper – classic! – and the belt – old school! They would sometimes try and be more tactile, recording me and saying they would show my school and all the teachers.

I once threw food at my sister, so my foster dad grabbed me by my face and pushed it into my dinner and held it there for five seconds. Felt longer! I was fighting my sister and she was trying to restrain me, and I jerked my head back and hit her eye, giving her a black eye. This is when I think everything broke down. My foster dad was shouting he wanted me out – how could I do this to his daughter? I was never a part of the family … all understandable things. My foster mum rushed me upstairs, as I could hear my sister crying so loudly. I said to my mum that I didn't want to leave. I really didn't. I said, "Please don't put me into a care home." She said she wouldn't! I went to school the next day. My foster dad woke me up saying, "If you don't go in there and see what you did to my daughter, you won't be coming back." I went into to my sister's room. She looked at me with half her face black and bruised. She had a party due that week, but would she go now? She was the strongest individual I know, as she still went and wasn't camera shy and didn't once say that her brother did this. That made me feel ill.

My social worker came the following week to say that they were going to take me to another family for a bit so this foster family could have a break. I loved this family. This was my home. Why I did these horrible things I do not know. Battling two mindsets, I didn't know where I belonged. I was ten at this point, and I was taken to a house in Devon with a small family with a nice house, two boys and a girl. One of the boys was also fostered. It was nice for a while. The dad used to take me quad biking and I would go out with the mum to do the housework. I didn't go to school during this time. After about two weeks it started to change. The sister and older brother would force me to fight him upstairs in the attic, with the other brother watching, playing Xbox. He would hit me so hard and not care, like he knew I wasn't going to stay a long time. I tried to frame some of the hits, but I would be trying to escape and lock myself in my room, as the mum and dad were out and I was left alone with the siblings. The foster brother went back to his mum for a while, and I knew it was my time to exit.

I ran away in the middle of the day and stole a clipboard and paper. Whilst knocking on people's doors, I was saying I was a charity worker asking for donations. Obviously I was ten and didn't look like one! They would question me, saying where was an adult? I would say it was my mum and I was just doing these houses while she did the others … a lame excuse. Some believed, and I managed to get £4.50 altogether after knocking on about fifteen houses. I hid my rucksack of clothes so they wouldn't be more suspicious of me. The mum saw me from her car and drove past me, saying, "Good luck trying to get anywhere, mate. You have no idea where the deuce you're going," and drove off.

She was right. It was Devon, no buses or trains coming. I knew nothing at age ten. I went back with my £4.50. I thought I might have to do what I did before, go out and be the most destructive person I could be to get back at that foster family who I didn't want to be with. It makes no sense, but I guess you chance the things you're comfortable with. That family was all I knew. I woke up and began walking downstairs. They made me breakfast … it was nice of them, they were nice people, but I said to them, "I'm leaving today. Social Services will be picking me up." They smiled and said they hadn't heard anything, so it was unlikely.

I said, "We'll see" and picked up the breakfast they made me and smashed it on the wall. They weren't that shocked, to be honest. They just called me an idiot.

That was when I kinda knew that it was going to have to get personal to crack them. I went into the living area and started to smash their picture frames. The dad grabbed me and said, "No, not these."

So it was clear that there was a lot that was not safe in the house. Stage one is to make them concerned so they have to keep a visual on you. I went mad and broke a lot of stuff. In the end I managed to escape the house and run away.

They called the police, and it was a "hunt for an underage runaway" malarkey. This didn't take long, and the police took me to the station to ask me why I smashed up their house. I didn't reply. The cool "no comment" line, I thought.

I was the one, a ten-year-old boy being questioned by the police – what a loser. I became more aggressive towards the police and grabbed the key card from around the neck of one of the officers. It was a strap-release lanyard, and I got out of the room and began running around the station. It was big, so I managed to hide from them for about an hour. It was a lot of fun for a ten-year-old, I guess.

I got found and restrained. The officer was bending my thumbs back and not letting me move. I guess he was letting out the frustration of having to look for me for over an hour. The carers came and took me back. Was it worth it? I don't know. They said to me that I didn't need to smash up the house, but I got what I wanted. They were giving me to a new family and taking me to a new placement in two days, but not back to my old foster family. I was pissed off.

I knew that at the next place I went to, I had to do the same. The way they passed me on to another family was … in a petrol station, no social worker or anything. They just said, "Hi, this is Finn" and put me into the car. It could have been anyone! It was a man and woman, no kids, just a dog and them in a bungalow. I instantly felt bad knowing what I was going to turn into.

Mini tip – always be good on the first night. You need to know what you're in for!

The first night we watched a programme about how they take apart slot machines to see if it's a scam. It was nice …

[To be continued: see Appendices.]

•◆•

"Oh, you know, the regular issue school days, which I enjoyed for the most part. It's important to have a good school, though, isn't it, Bronagh?" replies Finn, trying to get the attention off himself.

Raphael: "This is interesting. Finn has consciously chosen not to reveal the emotional, tense details of his past. I suspect he may reveal some of it to Bronagh in the future, if and when appropriate. He is displaying mature emotional intelligence. I think he could make it."

> And I will pray this to the Father,
> and He will give you another Helper,
> that He may abide with you forever – the
> Spirit, whom the world cannot receive,
> because it neither sees Him nor knows
> Him; but you know Him, for He dwells
> with you and will be with you. I will not
> leave you orphans; I will come to you.
>
> John 14:16–18

"Yes, it certainly is, Finn! I know all about that," says Bronagh with a degree of emphasis, meaning and hinting in her voice. Then, hesitantly, "I was put through a Roman Catholic convent school."

"Oh, okay," says Finn, with not a clue what that meant or what it involved.

"Hey, Finn, do you realise how far we have walked?" says Bronagh, attempting to change the subject and realising that time and distance have drifted on.

"No. How far?" wonders Finn.

"Probably time for us to head back – that's if you were planning on returning to the shop that I dragged you from," Bronagh suggests cheerily.

"Yes, you're right … I mean, probably time to head back, but no, I don't regard you as having dragged me from the shop! I came voluntarily, of my own free will." They smile.

Back at the shopfront, they stand looking at each other, smiling.

"Well, thanks for today," they both say over the top of each other and laugh.

"Hey, Finn, if I don't tread on your foot again, would you like to meet up for a coffee sometime?"

"That would be great," says Finn, laughing, who then initiates an exchange of phone numbers. They wander off.

Chapter 17

The Park

⋆⊙⊙⋆

A few days later, the phone rings.

"Hey, Finn, do you remember me? Bronagh."

"Ah yes, that woman that treads on people's feet!" says Finn engagingly.

"Glad I made an impression, then, but not literally, I hope! Do you fancy that coffee we spoke about?"

"Yeah, that would be great," says Finn.

⋆◆⋆

They meet later near the original charity shop.

"So, Finn, how's the relationship life going?"

Finn, slightly startled, says, "Well, I think it may have just begun."

Bronagh ponders and reflects for a moment. "Really? That's interesting. So, you mean you have recently started some relationships in your life?"

Finn concentrates his thoughts and says, "You said 'relationship life' … I take that to mean the only current relationship I know of."

Bronagh pauses. "So you know of one. Knowing of one is good."

"It may seem sketchy or wishy-washy to you, but it is actually you and me. I regard this, as it is already meaningful and special to me, as a relationship just started."

"Wow," responds Bronagh. "I like that idea and I like your focus there; good one, Finn! Actually, I am of a like mind on that, as well you know."

There is a pause, but with a lot of thought and feeling going through hearts and minds; they both seem to wear their hearts on their sleeves.

Quite a long pause, actually.

"So, what shall we do now?" wonders a bemused Finn.

"Let's talk about Ireland. I'd like to take you there and travel around a bit, exploring."

Finn is taken by surprise. "Sounds an intriguing idea, and I have noticed you are very absorbed and enthusiastic about Ireland – quite naturally, I guess."

"Sorry, can't help it … I love it and am driven by it! I hope some of it rubs off on you too," says Bronagh very warmly and heartily.

"I can certainly be up for that," says Finn with a smile. "Where and what do you have in mind?"

"Have you never been to Dublin, Finn? No, obviously not! Oh, you'd love it! Guinness like fresh cream … loads of Irish bands, singers and fiddlers in pubs … and the Book of Kells! And that's just Dublin!" Bronagh is clearly very enthusiastic and selling it well.

"Okay! I get the picture. So Dublin is where you start?" says Finn, eager to hear and know more.

"Yes, as you know from the song 'In Dublin's Fair City' … and there's the statue of Phil Lynott of Thin Lizzy. Anyway, I'm glad you like the idea."

"So that's one day – so what do you do for the other days?" enquires Finn.

"Oooohhh, dear Finn! It's a big city – it will take several days there to properly absorb those things. Then it will be onward to Cork, in southern Ireland, and then to County Kerry. Oooooh, it's lovely there, Finn; you'll love it! You'll need two weeks minimum."

"What? Two weeks?" exclaims Finn. "That's more than I could afford, and my holidays don't come up for that long until July anyway."

"Okay, Finn, let's do it in July," says our enthusiastic Bronagh.

"So where do I get enough money from for that? I barely make ends meet here as it is! Have you not found out yet the cost of living in London, Bronagh?"

"Dear Finn, yes, I have found out the cost of living in London; I had heard about it before as well ... so I came prepared and brought enough money with me to see me through. In fact, I have enough money to take you with me to Ireland – and, what the heck, to cover us for trips to anywhere, anytime ... okay, yes, you guessed right – I have independent means." There was a short pause. "Would you like another coffee? Here, let me get this one."

"Yes please. I think I need it!"

"Ahh ... sorry, Finn, here's me ranting on ... what sort of things do you like? Do you like the outdoors, countryside, wild places, or just cities?"

Their coffees arrive.

"I like the countryside, farm animals ... I liked Dorset and Devon. I do like the New Forest areas, forests ... winter as well as spring and autumn."

"Oh, that's good – sounds lovely. I've never been to the New Forest. Will you take me there, Finn?" Bronagh pleads.

"Sure. Another thing I like to do is fly fishing for trout."

"Really? Oh, there's lots of fly fishing and trout fishing in Ireland, and salmon and sea trout fishing … all sounding good."

"I'm hungry," recounts Finn, so they have lunch.

Another walk ensues, to another bit of the park.

While walking along side by side, arms swinging as they go, their hands accidentally brush. Bronagh takes this opportunity to take Finn's hand. Finn does not object.

They stroll on together, hand in hand.

They stroll a long way for a long time like this, without anyone saying anything.

They are getting used to this new closer contact world, with all of its sensations of touch and warmth, and are enjoying it, and are glowing.

They look at each other and smile occasionally; that is enough; it says it all.

The park has well-tended gardens displaying shrubs, but not in much leaf yet, and crocuses, daffodils and neat grass edges. A wide variety of trees intersperse the landscaping, together with the occasional bench and play area.

This proves a golden moment for Bronagh to enjoy a ride on a swing, being pushed by Finn.

A slower walk back begins … but there is a sudden stop. They turn to each other, embrace and hug. A strong gaze into each other's eyes ensues and continues. Their eyes scan each other's faces, hair, head and back to eyes again.

Their heads move closer together … warm breath confirms the closeness. It is perfectly obvious that their lips are being moved closely in range for a first kiss ... and it happens.

And it lingers.

The embrace continues. Why move?

They affectionately appreciate each other with touches and words for a while.

It becomes time to head back once again, and they return, each to their own home.

·◆·

A new dawn, a new day ...

"I will cook a meal for us tonight, Finn. Would you like to come round?"

"I would love that. Thank you very much for the invitation."

"Oh, Finn, you're a very polite boy, so you are."

Chapter 18

A Door Opens

⚜

He who is outside the doors
has already a good part of his
journey behind him.

Dutch proverb

This invitation to dinner had fired something up – something that Finn had had lurking and swirling in his mind for quite a few days now. It had been preoccupying him and taking up too much of his personal energy in trying to process it.

Finn had, for many years, had the unshakable belief that, due to his too-well-ingrained knowledge and awareness of his past and upbringing, he was not good enough. He felt, due to his too-well-programmed thoughts, that he was not valuable – that he was damaged irreparably and had no chance of a "normal" life or a "normal" relationship.

These thoughts had undermined Finn for years and had held him back from doing or even trying lots of things he might have wanted to do.

This was now in full focus in his mind, for obvious reasons. Here he was at a potentially key stage in his life and at a key stage in enjoying his growing and magnificent relationship with Bronagh. He was having great problems in his mind trying to square off this positive new swathe of experiences, feelings and emotions with those old anchoring mindsets and memories.

What was a fella to do?

Should he tell Bronagh all about it? To do so ... or not?

What would she think of him? What would be her reaction?

Would she end it? Or would she think about it ... and then end it?

Or would she do what Finn thought was the most unlikely outcome – understand and accept him for all that he was?

No answer was coming to Finn. *Oh no, not having to live with this all again!* he thought to himself ...

Ding-dong! He rang the doorbell of Bronagh's apartment.

The door opened and there she was, looking radiant, gorgeous and beautiful ... and with an even more pronounced profile of her figure seductively defined and silhouetted against the brighter internal light of the hallway.

Oh my, fantastic! thought Finn. *But yet more pressure.*

They embraced and hugged and pecked each other on the cheek, and she invited him in.

The dining room was set with low mood lighting and candles. Dinner jazz was playing softly in the background. The table was immaculately decorated, including small vases of arranged flowers at each end. The room had a few modern art paintings on the walls.

They settled in to a wonderful three course meal, including water, wine and coffee.

Finn thought it was unfair – and would seem unfair – if he did not tell Bronagh about himself at this early juncture. He felt he could be accused of misleading her if he told her later or, worse still, she found out somehow sometime later.

Finn realised that he had to grasp the moment … seize the day … *It's now or never.* He felt the time was right, so he told Bronagh the story of his past and his upbringing.

Bronagh cleared a few plates and dishes, then encouraged Finn to slide through to the lounge and the sofa. She snuggled up beside him.

She put on the appropriate masterpiece for the occasion and set the stage for the evening – the peacefully serene and intimate, noble tones of Nora Jones.

After a while of drifting away, Finn reflected, "Wow, this is so peaceful and relaxing … I have a totally clear and uncluttered mind. It's as if I have a brand-new self."

"You have, Finn … you have." Bronagh kissed him on the cheek slowly, fondly and reassuringly.

They kissed, softly and slowly … and lingered.

•◆•

Later that week Bronagh told Finn again that she was so grateful to him for being man enough to tell her all about the full detail of his early life – about his difficulties with it all and how he had, through thick and thin, managed to endure, survive and prevail.

She thinks he is a huge person and admires him more than anyone she knows … and tells him so.

They move on. They spend much time at Bronagh's flat but also occasionally spend time at Finn's. Bronagh's flat is better equipped, more spacious and, crucially, more comfortable, with a sense of *gemutlich*.

They also give each other space, which is healthy, spending time in their own abodes too.

> Happiness is not a matter of events,
> it depends on the tides of the mind.

Alice Meynell, *Prose and Poetry*

Chapter 19

And So to the Emerald

⋘◉◉⋙

Certain books come to meet one,
as do people.

Elizabeth Bowen, *Vogue*, 15 September 1955

No one ever reads a book. He reads
himself through books, either to discover
or to control himself. And the most
objective books are the most deceptive.

Romain Rolland, *Journey Within*

July has arrived.
    A few years before … in the middle of the night, outside in the Irish countryside …

The eerie, lonely, haunting, single plaintive hoot of a lost – in the expanse of the mountainous and wild countryside – owl … under the dark, cloud-cloaked cover that billows between mountain, hill and vale. This frail claim to existence in the darkness, pitch black, was heard and noticed by, firstly, an even more distant respondent, who must have been cheered up. This would have raised their spirits no end. Then, secondly, it must have been heard by a nearer but higher-pitched respondent, this suggestive of a responding potential mate. Success of the plaintive cry achieved.

This was, perhaps, symbolic, a prediction and a parallel of Bronagh and Finn finding each other at a later time.

•◆•

Things unseen have a light of their own.

Raoul Plus, *Living with God*

More recently, regularly, each day for about a week, two large black crows had been present in the trees beyond the back of the house. Their presence, of no consequence at first, had grown more conspicuous by the day and more ominous with time. The regularity was noticeable but became a kind of normal … but a worrying normal. It appeared that these two, encroaching daily, were the monitoring presence of some ill-intending over-watchers … but who or what exactly?

•◆•

Following the days of absorbing the delights of Dublin, Bronagh and Finn navigate to the west coast of Ireland. On the Ring of Kerry, with, looking out to sea, MacGillicuddy's Reeks behind them and a moderate wind blowing onshore, gulls wheel around, gliding smoothly from salt to sky and back again. Their plaintive cries, so typical of harbour and beach memories, pervade here too. The sea spray in places is almost seamless with the low mistiness of the cloud bases. There is a continually moving cycle of flows this way and that way, building and collapsing energy interplays.

I am hearing … background music: "Cry of the Burren" by the Kilkennys.

"This is just out of this world. I had no idea you could travel like this and see so many different types of countryside," said Finn in awe as they sat on the steeply sloping green swathe that was the safe cliff edge. The spray from the crashing waves below blew up and over continuously, leaving a salty taste at each lick of the lips. "It's so beautiful … and wild, and natural."

"Finn, this is how I see life, perched on that island rock – that one over there." Bronagh pointed. "I find it interesting and fascinating. It takes your mind and imagination vividly to incredible places of existence.

"The finest example of an early Celtic monastery is on Skellig Michael, a rock pinnacle. Its isolated and almost inaccessible position and the absence of frost have contributed to its preservation. The monastic settlement there is enclosed by stone walls. Despite its isolation, the community will have been largely self-sufficient in its food supply. They would have fished, and the trapping of seabirds would have been aplenty. Goats to supply milk, herbs and a few vegetables may have been grown in small plots protected by stone walls on the sheltered eastern side of the rock.

"A movement to island sanctuaries, like this one, appears to have begun and reached its peak during the seventh and eighth centuries. But none of the islands is so severe in its isolation as Skellig Michael."

"That is so bleak! Sounds okay to set it up, but to live like that for years?"

"The disappearance of the Christianity of the Celtic Church was inevitable, owing to the absence of central organisation, but it is impossible to reach the end without a feeling of regret. A Christianity so pure and serene as that of the age of the saints could hardly be equalled and never repeated. It had begun the habit of wandering – and more on that later, Finn – which is one of the most remarkable features of the Celtic religion and of which the island sanctuaries are the most unique and remarkable testimony. No one can visit the Skelligs without being overawed and overwhelmed, as you have been, by the type of devotion that could choose these bare rocks as a habitation, nothing to look out upon save sea and sky and the distant hills. This is the true spirituality of the Celtic Church."

Finn was open-mouthed. "That is so awesome – what amazing people. Can you imagine the lives of those guys, day after day, living with these winds and storms too? That's extreme dedication!"

Looking out approximately eight miles towards the very distant horizon, Bronagh pointed. "You see that island out there? That is Skellig Michael," she observed.

"Finn, listen … I am going to tell you about something stunningly amazing. A mysterious alignment connects seven monasteries from Ireland to Israel – yes, Ireland to Israel! The seven sites are very far from one another yet perfectly aligned. Is it just a coincidence? Legend says that the line represents the sword blow inflicted on the Devil by Archangel Michael to chase him off, but I don't know.

"That mystery alignment, known as Via Sancti Michaelis, includes the three most important medieval monasteries venerating St Michael in Europe: Mont-Saint-Michel in Normandy, the Sacra di San Michele in Piedmont, Italy, and Monte Sant'Angelo in Apulia, Italy.

Not only are the three sanctuaries located on a perfect alignment, but they are also at the same distance – about nine hundred kilometres apart.

"Incredibly, four other St Michael monasteries lie on the same straight line: Skellig Michael in Ireland, which is exactly where we are now, St Michael's Mount, Cornwall, the Monastery of St Michael on Symi Island, Greece, and then Mount Carmel in Israel, covering a 2,000-kilometre pilgrimage route."

"No way!"

"Lines like this axis are believed to be a system of 'highways', possibly at some locations exuding kinds of natural spiritually strengthening energy to some. Perhaps, as an analogy, with a similar purpose or meaning as the chakras and acupuncture meridians in the human body, emulating lines of natural energy."

"This is interesting – these natural energy-strengthening ideas."

"It is inspiring, the beauty of these centuries-old buildings. Often perched on impossible mountains and rocks, they are in many cases isolated and erected where the living conditions are extremely difficult."

"I see, and so that's why. Wow, Bronagh, you must have done a huge study of this! That's amazing … but how can that be? I mean, that's preposterous … what are the chances of places being developed in lines like that in those days? How did it get organised?"

"Take it or leave it, Finn, that's just the way it is. Will we ever know the answers to your questions? I don't know. But I do know one thing that you should know – that you need to know … It's a bit of a secret, I think, because some people have experienced this energy thing at some locations for themselves." She paused. "I have too, you know."

"What – really?" exclaimed Finn. "How? Or what?"

"It's difficult to explain, but once you experience it, or something, you will know." Finn listened, dumbfounded. "Hey, come on – listen. Why don't we try it out for you?"

"Uh, how, exactly? What am I getting myself into? Bronagh, you're scaring me!"

"Where's your sense of adventure, Finn? Let's go somewhere."

"So how do you know all this stuff?" enquired Finn.

"Okay, I had to tell you sometime; it might as well be now. You may remember … I don't know what you remember about what I've said …"

"I remember everything you've ever said," interrupted Finn, and she looked at him and smiled before continuing.

"I said I was put through Roman Catholic convent school. There is a reason I put it like that. My family, going back some, are staunchly Roman Catholic and traditional. I don't know what you know or have heard about Catholic upbringing or schools, or convent schools especially? In general, it's dour and it's tough. The Roman Catholic religion, in my view, is so dogmatic, so unbending and so unforgiving that one can hardly breathe. I mean that, Finn.

"It was also a boarding school, so you have little contact with your own family members during the year, which made it all even harder to bear." Bronagh sighed. "My childhood could have been so much more joyful and energetic and sociable ... but they squash and squeeze it all out of you.

"And they just don't realise what they are doing – how it hurts, how destructive it is. It was soul-destroying. At a time when I was supposed to be enjoying my childhood and having fun and exploring the countryside ... No!

"You are not allowed to enjoy yourself or laugh. You had to learn and recite all this biblical stuff and psalms and hymns and verses – 'Dominus' this and 'Dominus' that, and if you didn't, you were told off or even beaten. They also made mental threats on you about if you didn't do this, then this would happen, etc." Tears spill from Bronagh's eyes. "Don't get me wrong, Finn, I'm not saying that all the convent schools here are like this ... far from it ...

"When I was ten years old, I thought there's got to be more to life than this ... there's got to be a better way ... but I kept those thoughts to myself for fear of more retributions. There are things that you don't dare talk about, even with other 'inmates' ... they could easily tell on you ... saw much of that ... the horrors!

"There was a visiting van library once a month. One day I found a book in there all about Irish history, pre-history, the Celts, folklore, myths and Irish culture. This was an eye-opener to me; once I started reading it, I couldn't stop. I couldn't put it down ... It gave me a great joy in my heart. Here was an alternative way of thinking and of life. I became so excited about it, but I knew I had to keep it secret and certainly not tell anyone there. So I had to have a plan ... and do you know what, Finn? God forgive me – I know He shouldn't, but I think He has – I stole that book, Finn! I stole it ... that's how important it was to me." A big beaming smile was evident all over Bronagh's face and soul ... but then that expression was replaced by one of anxiety and disdain.

"I am sure that, due to the experiences you had and their impact on your mental health and well-being, you will be looked on as trying to save yourself and fulfilling a core need. I am sure He will be happy with that, especially as I am sure you must have prayed about it?" said Finn with great care, understanding and insight.

"Yes," Bronagh replied quickly. "I did pray about it, very much and often. Although I had very troubling experiences, I still believed and trusted in God. I was really objecting to the way that that convent school 'did God' and 'did religion'."

"I completely understand and I sympathise, or empathise ... Thank you for telling me. It means a great deal."

.•.

Philosophers and clergymen are always
discussing why we should be good, as if
anyone doubted that we ought to be.

G. M. Trevelyan, *Clio, a Muse, and Other Essays*

Everything that enlarges the sphere
of human powers, that shows
man he could do what he thought
he could not do, is valuable.

Samuel Johnson, in *Life of
Johnson* by James Boswell

We must make the choices that
enable us to fulfil the deepest
capacities of our real selves.

Thomas Merton, *No Man Is an Island*

Two thirds of help is to give courage.

Irish proverb

"Right, Finn, we've got to go. This alignment from Skellig Michael actually heads right down there" – Bronagh pointed and gestured – "across the open sea all the way over to the southern tip of Cornwall to St Michael's Mount near Penzance, so, although fairly close to the line here, we are nowhere near actually being on it."

"So," Finn wondered, "are there not any other alignments nearer to here than that?"

"Yes, there are, Finn. We can go to one of those – and may have to – but we should really get to one of the hugely significant alignments too … well, you know, just to be there, like."

"Okay, you know best," agreed Finn.

"And anyway, look at the way the weather is changing. Those big dark clouds beyond the horizon are heading this way and herald a lot of rain."

Gulls wheeled, gliding fast over the cliffs, getting powerful lifts from the strong southwesterly airflow as it met the cliff face and was forced to rise.

"You know, Finn," offered Bronagh, "there is a small island just off the coast of Pembrokeshire, southwest Wales, not really that far from here, where thousands of small Manx shearwaters hatch out … being the only place they nest and breed. The hatchlings stand on the edge of a cliff, ready to take their first flight. With that first step and first flight they then end up thousands of miles away … in the south Atlantic! Incredible! Argentina. And then they fly back to Skomer to nest and breed."

"That's staggering! How could anybody do that?"

They walked back along the path to the car, a hybrid that still had petrol in it. The electric charge had run out ages ago, there not being that many charging points in the great rural distances of southern and southwestern Ireland.

First stop was for a hearty meal – a meat pie, veg and gravy … and a pint of proper creamy Irish Guinness.

"Finn, ancient Ireland is a land filled with myths, memories, legends, tales of giants and fairies, butter witches, saints and sacred places. When travelling through Ireland you will come across many places that somehow speak to you of other times and ancient Irish history. Pagan sites in Ireland can be found all over the country, along with sites that may have been featured in Druidic rituals."

"Yes, I am clearly seeing that plenty already."

"Along with the common Celtic people were the Druids."

"Oh no! Not Druids! Those Stonehengey people?"

"Now, now, Finn, they're not all like that! They were the religious leaders of the Celtic peoples and of Irish paganism, but they were also legal professionals, adjudicators, keepers of legends and folklore, as well as medical experts of the times. Since there are no written records, and ancient Celtic traditions were oral, historians have depended upon the Roman culture to give insights into what the ancient Druid culture was.

"It is now commonly believed that Druids may have been around during the earliest periods of human history, with anthropologists suggesting that the cave art in Lascaux, France, could have been part of druidic rituals. Many of the megalithic monuments you can visit in Ireland were quite possibly constructed on the recommendations of the Druids. At that time their knowledge of astrology was used to align the monuments with the Celtic calendar and to mark sacred times of the year."

"Fascinating! Okay, I like it – so where are we heading now?" said Finn, gaining more interest and enthusiasm by the minute.

"We should head to Uisneach. A megalithic researcher, Michael Poynder … I've not met him, but he noted that Knocknarea, Carrowmore, Sliabh Dá Eán, Sheebeg, Loughcrew, Tara and the Hill of Howth are all on a great alignment line crossing the country from west to east. All the alignment lines in Ireland meet at Uisneach, and from this sacred hill, it is said you can see twenty of the thirty-two counties on a clear day, so we should go there for you now, shouldn't we, Finn?"

"Okay, yeah, but what is actually there?"

"It is believed that the word Uisneach pre-dates the Irish language. It is translated as 'place of the hearth', which would likely indicate a sacred ritual space.

"In early written sources dating back to Roman times, the location of Uisneach was called 'Mide', meaning 'the middle'. Originally this was a name for the hill itself, but over the centuries the territory became the medieval kingdom of Mide, which eventually became the counties of Westmeath and Meath.

"The ceremonial and sacred centre of Ireland, Uisneach's roots pre-date recorded history, and its surviving monuments and relics date back to the Neolithic. In the legends and mythology of Ireland, Uisneach is the resting site of the earth goddess Ériu and the sun god Lugh, and as such was regarded as sacred ground. Uisneach was seen as a gate to the mythical fifth province, Mide."

"Blimey! Sounds a bit spooky …"

"Uisneach became the seat of the High Kings in later years, and ancient writings state that the person who claimed the high throne must 'marry' Ériu at a ceremony on Uisneach. This ceremony may have been part of the 'Dail Mór Uisneach', a great assembly and fair held at the beginning of May – Bealtaine – when a great fire was lit on the hill to mark summer's arrival."

"Right!" said a very impressed Finn. "We must definitely go there!"

"I must also tell you about Newgrange later – would love to go there sometime, and at a very particular time," said Bronagh.

"Sounds intriguing," said Finn quietly. He had now had as much information for one day as he could cope with – which was lucky! – and it was nightfall, which was even more lucky for his highly stimulated brain.

He who speaks the truth must
have one foot in the stirrup.

Armenian proverb

Chapter 20

Total Immersion

⤜◈⤛

All things are possible to
one who believes.

St Bernard of Clairvaux, *Letters*

This is a fortunate plan. They have to find their way
back to Dublin anyway; Uisneach can be en route.

Passing through Limerick, which is also en route
to Uisneach, they come across two highly essential
facilities – one, an electric hook-up charging point,
and two, it happens to be right next to a venue
featuring the Kilkennys, an Irish band from Kilkenny
in the heart of southern Ireland that Bronagh is very
familiar with and thinks Finn might enjoy.

As they park up to charge, all of a sudden, without
warning, a set of bright lights, like intense floodlights,
overpowers their vision, and they both exclaim as if
frightened and shocked, "Oh! My! What on earth is that?"

The load grating noise of what seems to be a mechanical
device just glances past the doors of their car. Still in shock,
they realise that it is a close encounter with … a street
cleaning machine. But it seemed more than that, like some
kind of frightening warning to them … but they don't say
anything or reveal that to each other.

Anyway, there is this traditional Irish gig to look
forward to, and they go in.

As they come through the doors, there is the instant impact of warm but stuffy air rich with the alluring fragrance of Guinness, beer, wine and well-cooked roasted fayre. There is the uplifting sound of people chatting with high energy, laughter and expectation. They sense this is a very good place.

There is a low stage set up with the instruments for the band: a fiddle, a guitar, a bodhran, bass, pipes and whistles, a banjo and a mandolin.

They settle into their seats at a table not too far from but not too near the stage and order some Guinness, the customary go-to medium for a traditional event, of course, and some irresistible food. This sells itself via its all-encompassing aroma. The assembled gathering consists of all age groups, from late teens to very mature people.

Loud enthusiastic cheers go up as the band members make their way onto the low stage. Bronagh and Finn are both automatically elevated further into this warm and engaging atmosphere.

The wide-ranging set features "South Australia", "On the Rocky Road to Dublin", "Spanish Lady", "Wild Colonial Boy" and "Fiddler's Green", with the regular, medium-paced, semi-mechanical bass rumble of the bodhran driving a hypnotic, trance-like state. The deep range of rich vocals and harmonies and the free-wheeling fiddle and banjo make it a rousing occasion, with such euphoria that you could feel that you were actually Irish yourself even if you weren't!

What a night.

Even with all the fun and enjoyment, part of Bronagh's mind registers other people around her –

couples with children looking happy, probably settled in a comfortable house somewhere.

•◆•

Back on the road in the morning, with Finn, Bronagh and the car all freshly charged, the fabulous lush green countryside flashed past as they made good progress towards their rendezvous point – Uisneach.

This was now, Bronagh felt, an opportunity to talk to Finn about other features of the Irish countryside while she drove. She settled comfortably and began.

"The peculiar legend of unseen tracks running straight across country aroused the interest of J. D. Evans-Wentz, who, in the early part of the twentieth century, travelled widely among the Celtic areas of Britain and France, collecting fairy stories and other relics of old mythology. In several parts of Ireland he heard about the fairy paths. These paths, sometimes visible as old roads, sometimes preserved only in local memory, were said to be the routes of seasonal processions. On a certain day the fairies passed through the land and anyone who stood in their way might be struck dead or be taken off, never to return. A man whose house happened to be situated on a fairy path must on that day leave his front and back door open, for it was unwise to obstruct the fairy parade. In his book, *The Fairy Faith in Celtic Countries*, Evans-Wentz tells how he asked an Irish seer for an explanation of the fairy paths and was told that they were lines of 'magnetic current'.

"Under the old Molmutine Laws, never repealed, the highways were a sanctuary for the safety of travellers and was assured. They might pass freely through the country, meeting hospitality wherever they rested. In Ireland the custom of entertaining travellers survived perhaps longer than elsewhere. This was encouraged by the feckless generosity of the poor people, who would share whatever they had with whoever asked for it. The old tracks which led straight across the country were sacred ground, imparting to those who travelled them a certain spiritual aura.

"So, there you are, Finn."

"Uhmm, interesting stuff; there's certainly a lot going on out there," mused Finn. "More than one could ever have imagined."

As they approached the Uisneach area, they noticed numerous crows, ravens and choughs on the ground in the fields there.

They were dismayed to find that the centre of the Uisneach feature was actually within a farm and was private ground, even though it is a sacred site with Neolithic, Bronze Age and medieval tombs, standing stones, holy wells and palace ruins. Visits are only available by pre-arranged guided tour. However, they were that close – close enough for now, perhaps.

•◆•

The crow, the slanderous cuckoo, nor
The boding raven, nor though hoar,
Nor chattering pie,
May on our bridle house perch or sing,
Or with them any discord bring,
But from it fly.
William Shakespeare

A sudden very heavy downpour of rain, accompanied by great squalls of gusty wind, buffeted Finn and Bronagh and the parked car. They were the only people around.

Through the open car window, they could hear the regular squawking, coughing and croaking of the annoying birds.

"Contrary to what I was expecting, this seems quite a foreboding place," observed Bronagh, unusually dismally, "and the sign says they only open from one p.m. to three p.m. on Sundays … That's not much available opening time for such a significant place! I wonder why that is?"

"Yes, strange," agreed Finn.

"So we are here, and it's not even Sunday, it's Saturday," reported the dispirited Bronagh.

"It's those crows guarding the place – they don't want us here." Finn laughed.

"Careful what you say in a place like this," warned Bronagh.

Suddenly, as quickly as the heavy rain had come, it went, and a beam of sunshine pierced down on them. It was a great contrast to the dark clouds surrounding the area … it was literally atmospheric!

A country-looking man, dressed in a tweed jacket and cap, slowly approached their car. "Oh no, I think we are going to be asked to move on," said Bronagh.

He tapped on the side window and Bronagh lowered it slightly, not knowing exactly what to expect.

In a broad Irish country accent, the man said, "So, you'd be here to have a look around the Uisneach site, I don't doubt?"

"Oh my!" exclaimed Bronagh, flabbergasted. "We thought you'd be closed, as it's not Sunday."

"Oh, never mind that. Come on in and I'll be showing you around, so I will," came the totally unexpected response from their seemingly new friend.

"Tis the Little People!" said Bronagh quietly but gleefully to Finn before they got out. "They are responding and will help us."

Not believing their luck, they followed the friendly man and spent a wonderful few hours exploring the whole Uisneach site.

They both felt that they were having elated experiences, sensations and feelings whilst they were walking around and touring the features, but they didn't say anything to each other or to the man. It was a mood lift that was as unavoidable as it was unexpected. This gave an answer to Bronagh's earlier question to Finn – would he notice anything in the vicinity of a significant alignment, or indeed, as this place was, the criss-cross centre of many alignments crossing Ireland? What better test!

Chapter 21

Which Road?

❦

Few really believe. Most only believe
that they believe or even make believe.

John Lancaster Spalding,
Thoughts and Theories of Life and Education

Time for the leg back to Dublin, but a stop for coffee, food and chill time was vitally needed by both.

"Finn, may I read you an interesting perception and quote from somebody very famous? You might be surprised!"

"Okay, yeah, sure – go ahead."

"'I am told that there are people who do not care for maps and find it hard to believe. The names, the shapes of the woodlands, the courses of the roads and rivers, the pre-historic footsteps of man still distinctly traceable up hill and down dale, the mills and the ruins, the ponds and the ferries, perhaps the Standing Stones, or the Druids Circle on the heath; here is an inexhaustible fund of interest for any man or woman with eyes to see, or "tuppence worth of imagination to understand with."' There, that was by Robert Louis Stevenson in a note concerning his exceedingly famous book, *Treasure Island*."

"That's fascinating, isn't it? That detailed perception of something so subtle, and all those years ago, and even when maps were not as detailed and accurate as they are today," said Finn.

"The area we didn't get to see this time, but which I would love to see and we will need to see, is the Burren," explained Bronagh, and she reads bits to Finn from Wikipedia about the Burren, western Ireland.

"Pre-history … ah, let me see, there is Poulnabrone portal tomb … Archaeological evidence from cave finds of butchered bones have been radiocarbon dated to 33,000 years ago, showing evidence of hunters during the Ice Age.

"Pollen analysis indicates that in the Mesolithic period of 8000 to 7000 BC, the Burren looked completely different. Ah, people also constructed megalithic sites like the portal tomb known as Poulnabrone dolmen and the court tombs at Teergonean, near Doolin, and Ballyganne − that's near Noughaval. Overall, there are around seventy megalithic tombs in the Burren area − seventy! Finn, would you believe that now? More than half of all of these structures are found in Clare!

"There are also numerous types of prehistoric structure, apart from stone walls. Ah, at the Burren is a late Neolithic/early Bronze Age wedge tomb dated to the period 2500 to 2000 BC. Many examples of these are found on … are you still listening, Finn? Remember these: Roughan Hill near Kilnaboy, including those at Parknabinnia and Creevagh. Others are located at Gleninsheen and Berneens − Rathborney − and Poulaphuca − Carran. Large stone cairns on many hills, such as the Poulawack Cairn, also date from this period … that's about it …

"Oh, and the Burren has a long history of traditional Irish music. It is particularly known for the West Clare style of concertina playing and music festivals in Doolin and Corofin. No, we haven't got time to go to a music festival, Finn, before you ask. The area also has a long history as a source of artistic inspiration and has hosted a number of art galleries. Oh, before you ask, Finn, I do like art galleries."

Finn reflected on it all for a moment.

"My God, Bronagh, you are so literate, as well as very intelligent! All that talk of rocks and stones reminds me of that song the other night." He sings "On the Rocky Road to Dub-ul-lin, one-two three-four five," and Bronagh joins in ... "On the Rocky Road to Dub-ul-lin, one-two three-four five."

Chapter 22

❦

The jovial musical mood changes when all of a sudden, as they approach Mullingar, a town not far from Uisneach on the way to Dublin, Bronagh goes quiet. They stop for that coffee.

Bronagh stays quiet for a while, just staring ahead into nothingness.

She appears white and doesn't react to any of Finn's questions about "… anything to eat, Bronagh?"

She eventually comes round a little but is hardly able to string a sentence together. She utters a few words and short phrases.

"Tuam … Patrick O'Connor … Mary Quinn …"

Finn is quiet now, wondering what that means. "Who are they?" he asks softly.

"I don't know … yet," replies Bronagh. "Patrick goes to see Mary. She becomes very shocked and unhappy, in floods of tears, sobbing at Patrick and shaking him to see reason. Her friend Kate, Kate Murray, cries out, 'Patrick! what are you thinking of? Your life is here! Yes, I know the famine has been tough for all of us … You are promised to Mary! How could you even think of such a cruel thing to do and say? I'll … I'll … go and tell your father! He'll make you see sense … Whatever's gotten into you, Patrick O'Connor? You've gone mad, so you have!'"

Finn, now in deep anguish, enquires, "Well, what's that all about? Where did that come from, Bronagh?"

She continues. "Kate brings Patrick's father into Mary's house. His father is looking full in the face, is stern, angry – fuming, actually – and explodes!

"'Patrick O'Connor, what is the meaning of this? I forbid you to go away. Your future and your promises are here in Tuam. You'll break your mother's heart! Have you thought about that? I bet you haven't … and what about Father Murray? What will he be saying? Do you realise you'll be bringing shame on your family? Have you thought about that, lad? No, I bet you haven't … you're just too selfish and blind to see any of it. All right, I admit it's been tough around here, and for a few years now … but it's been tough for all of us, not just you, Patrick O'Connor! Patrick O'Connor of County Galway. Yes, this is your heritage and a fine one, that your mother and I have given you … All you can think about is money, filthy money and a loose life in the city … You've not thought of all the harm that will bring you, so you haven't … and all the crying and misery you'll bring to Mary and to your mother.'

"Patrick salutes his father but without a word, looking him full in the face; his father is open-mouthed and shocked. As Patrick turns, he gives Mary a final hug and his father says, 'You're not listening to a word I'm saying … I don't like it … you'll come to no good. What do you know about that big world out there? Outside of Galway? Nothing! It's shameful, lad, shameful, I tell you.' And he puts his head in his hands.

"Patrick goes immediately to his mother's house, followed by his father, who is still shouting after him. He bursts into the house, which is sparkling clean, tidy and perfumed with fresh flowers. He gives his mum a big hug, which they hold for quite a while, while he explains to her what he is doing. Because of this big hug and the close proximity of her mouth to his ear, she talks quietly to say that it is, in her view, a great shame … but she understands that he has got to do what he has got to do. She will be thinking of him all the while and will be praying for him every Sunday in church, and also every day anyway.

"'Not to worry, we will look after ourselves, so we will … You carry on and make the most of your life … but do write every week, think of us and come back and see us, so you must. Now be off with you!'

"Patrick turns away to leave but turns back to blow a kiss to his dear mother, who waves and blows a kiss in return too.

"The family dog barks at him profusely as he walks across the yard and down the garden path.

"He turns, goes down on one knee and gives the dog a cuddle. The dog instantly stops barking and understands that Patrick has got to do something very important.

"Patrick's first stop is the pub, where he enjoys a pint of the local brew. He is joined by his best mate, Thomas Kelly. Thomas is carrying a long face and looks into his pint on the table before him.

"'Patrick, so you think you can handle yourself out there?' says Thomas, looking on.

"'Thomas, for the love of God, I know what I'm doing, so I do.'

"'Well, that's all right, then,' replies the unconvinced Thomas, still looking into his pint. 'And you've convinced Mary and your mother that you're going to be okay and that you'll come back?'

"'Thomas, I don't need this – and especially not from you!'

"'Sorry, Patrick, but you know what I mean. It had to be said, so it did.'

"'Sure … I know … thank you for your concern, though.'

"'Okay then, so it's off to Dublin. Then where will you go?' says Thomas.

"'Oh … to get a ship to Liverpool, I expect, like everybody else.'

"'A ship, dear Patrick? And where would you be getting the money for that from?' enquires a surprised Thomas.

"'Ooohh, I dunno – somethin' will turn up for sure now,' says the optimistic Patrick … but of course he would have to be, or at least seemingly, even if he didn't really feel that way deep down.

"'Well, if it's any help, young man, I have to be driving the cart over to Athlone tomorrow morning, so I do, to deliver some goods for me dad. Yer welcome to hop on for a ride if you want … there would be no fare, like!' They both smile and have a good laugh, which breaks the gloom, sadness and grief.

"The great adventure has started, so it has.

"Patrick sets off on foot. This is probably the most appropriate and comfortable start for him. But Thomas does stop by and offer him a ride. He will have a chance to look around at his homeland and to reflect whilst bumbling along on the hard horse-drawn cart. He sees all the places he knows so well, places he played as a young boy and the memories of hospitality with friends inside some of the houses they pass. This is harder on Patrick than he thought it was going to be. Thomas says, 'I know you're suffering, Patrick, I would be too … but you'll be all right once we are away from here. Once you get to Athlone, you'll be fine.' They look at each other knowingly and smile.

"'Patrick, you know what you must do?'

"'Not a clue,' says Patrick.

"'We must stop for a wee while and you must find a stout blackthorn branch in the hedge and carry it wid'ya. As you know, that will keep the ghosts and goblins away – you know, like your grandpa would have said. Use your pocket knife,' says Thomas very reassuringly.

"They stop and the task is done; Patrick will now be protected from bad fortune.

"They part company in Athlone, wish each other luck and exchange the best of chum farewells.

"To cheer himself up and for the long road ahead and all the walking he will have to do, Patrick goes into a shoe shop to find himself a good quality pair of new shoes … and he knows he will have to spend what little money he has on those or he will be getting nowhere.

"A pair of well-fitting brown leather brogues is the perfect choice for the occasion. One proud owner wears them out of the shop! He looks for the road to Mullingar and sets off on foot, feeling proud, confident and uplifted in his new shoes.

"Just the tonic.

"One thing Patrick didn't realise until he had gone some little way was that brogues are a good solid pair of leather shoes; you do at least get your money's worth. This particular pair also had metal heel and toe sole protectors nailed firmly in ... which meant that on firm roads and pavements, people could hear him coming! It made quite a clip-clop. Animals could also hear him coming and scurried away.

"He was also fortunate, though, in being offered a few lifts at various stages by kind farmers and tradesmen with horses and carts also on the same parts of his journey.

"And thus he arrived in Mullingar to spend the night and rest his weary legs."

Suddenly, Finn realises something and thinks to himself – not wanting to interrupt the flow – *It seems as if Bronagh is getting "flashbacks" of the route and life of emigration ... after the famine! How does that work? How can that happen? This has never happened before.*

There are two points: one, it happened when we were near Mullingar, and two, it happened after we visited the special place of Uisneach, which is recent and could be significant.

Guess I'll just have to run this by Bronagh when she has come down and see what she makes of it.

Bronagh continues.

"Patrick started out early the next morning, light and airy. Umm, light and airy? After a night of resting weary limbs? Sounds like he had been in somewhere early for a breakfast of Irish whiskey!

"This would help Patrick at the moment in a number of ways ... he has to stop the melancholy; it's so easy for him to drift back into thoughts of home. He has to keep a focused, clear mind for what he is doing, where he is going and why.

"On the other hand, a drop of the pure does relax the body, remove some inhibitions and increase the chances of fanciful and authentic speech … perhaps.

"This did make for above average good communications with the locals, the tongue of Patrick feeling fairly free and vocal to one and all by virtue of his recent early morning consumption. In particular there was the additional benefit for Patrick that his eyes were also more lubricated and could clearly see an extra number of girls and women – whether they existed or not. He also noted that they did look particularly attractive in these parts.

"He was delighted that they smiled at him quite freely. *This must be because I am a noticeably handsome chap, the likes of which they haven't seen around here lately,* he gloats to himself.

"However, it became apparent that they were not indeed at all on the same wavelength. When he looked away and then looked back, he noticed that they were no longer smiling at him but laughing … but at what? Patrick looked around a little and could see nothing that merited anyone to laugh at anything … Curious.

"Patrick then felt a little self-conscious, which was most unlike him, especially when he had had a few. He thought to himself, *What's wrong with them? Haven't they seen a handsome guy in regular country green tweed trousers, a red tunic and a dark-coloured flat cap before? They must all be wanting me to be their man but are shy or afraid to approach me to get started … ah well.*

"Then one of them asked, 'Fair sir, and where would you be coming from? Do you work? Or are you looking for work?'

"Patrick was not amused at this seemingly pointed line of questioning. It seemed to him that they were doubting his very honest integrity, thus making him feel unduly belittled. Patrick decided that he was now tired of this encounter and should be on his way in his fine brogues again.

"Arriving in Dublin, although only part of the whole journey, was quite a relief for the inexperienced Patrick. The unexpected and a drop of fear were now intensifying. The first part of the city offered him Smithfield and the Cobblestone for a pint of Dublin's finest, together with some of the finest original Irish music in the land. One song was new to the ears and instruments of the performers and listeners – 'On the Rocky Road to Dublin'; it spread like wildfire throughout Ireland."

Finn can't believe it. "What is going on? Here it is again!"

Yes, Bronagh continues …

"This was the start of his views of this fine city. He strolled south through Smithfield, heading for the Liffey. The streets were becoming smaller, with darker side streets and alleyways. The promenades along the banks of the Liffey were busy – in fact, crowded and bustling.

"Patrick noticed that these bustling crowds were different from what he was expecting, especially in this fine city. As some of the whiskey wore off and a bit of a sense of reality started to kick in, he noted that he was seeing very thin, wasted-looking people around him but also mixed in with some of the smarter, healthy people he had expected to see there.

"He was becoming more shocked as time went on to see how many gaunt, thin and weakened-looking people there were everywhere.

"It now dawned on him that what he was seeing was a result of the Famine.

"These thousands of people had all flocked to Dublin in search of relief from their plight. Where were they all going? Patrick then realised that he was on the same quest as these very unfortunate people, but he also felt grateful that he himself was actually in pretty good and strong health.

"At this point he noticed that indeed he did feel stronger. But then a sickening thought went through his mind and he looked behind. The bundle of possessions he had been carrying on his stick ... was no longer there!

"That was why he felt stronger, because the load and stick felt lighter.

"Patrick immediately called out to all surrounding people to look for his bundle or, oh no, who might have stolen it, if that was the case. The reaction he got to this was – well, let's not beat about the bush, abusive; yes, that's what it was, abusive. Apparently, so they told him, he was not from around these parts on account of his Connaught accent (which he didn't realise he had) and should go look for it himself. The mood, camaraderie and atmosphere of this location had changed for him; it was totally different from that which he was used to back home. Was this a sign of things to come?

"Patrick was on a huge mission of his own, though, and he was not going to let this one piece of misfortune get him down, so he continued along the Liffey banks past Sackville Street to the docks and the ships.

"Having found the quay, bustling with tall sailing ships moored or just about to set sail on the high tide and fresh westerly wind, Patrick thought he should make enquiries as to where some of these ships were bound.

"That was easy enough to find out. However, most of these ships no longer had their gangplanks set down on the quay. Panic began to ensue in Patrick's eager mind. Were they all about to leave without him? Was he going to be left behind?

"'Ahoy there!' shouted Patrick to the captain on the deck of the last remaining ship with its gangplank still in place. 'I want to go to Liverpool – can you take me? I will pay a fair price,' he wagered.

"The gruff, well-appointed and hearty captain immediately replied, but with a considerable roar of his salty, seasoned voice. 'Get thee hence – begone. There be no room for ye or any other blighter on board!'

"This was not what Patrick wanted to hear at a time like this. The captain then turned away to carry on giving his orders to the crew for setting sail.

"Patrick saw his moment. He nipped up the gangplank quickly but quietly with no fuss, and he wasn't seen by anyone. He was aboard … this was a great relief.

"But then things turned, well, tense – sour, even. Patrick realised he would need to keep out of sight and hide somewhere. The captain had raised the gangplank, had given the order to 'let go' and was setting sail and forging a course down the Liffey estuary for the Irish Sea and eventually for Liverpool.

"The most tense of moments then came for Patrick. He was spotted … and hauled before the gruff, yes, but now very angry captain. This was not good. Patrick had envisaged a comfortable and pleasant sail, one befitting a Connaught gentleman and in friendly surroundings.

"As it has turned out, things could not be more different.

"Accommodation was indeed found for Patrick, or 'Paddy' as he now became known – down in the hold with the livestock. In fact, pigs were his new cabin-mates. He had to effectively dance around them and the rigging some of the time … you could say he was doing 'hearty jigs', and all of them up to their knees in bilge or hold water.

"By the time the ship was passing Holyhead, 'Paddy' had experienced a goodly number of continuous days in this filth and stench and in a swaying, rolling ship. He was now also experiencing bouts of sea sickness. He was thinking to himself, whilst leaning on his dear old trusty friend that was still with him, his shillelagh, that, given the choice between this and death, the latter might now be his preferred option … or, on the other hand, he might wish to go back and be on the rocky road to Dublin again. My, how things change, and how different things can turn out from what you expect. 'Oh, Paddy, m'boy,' he could hear his father saying to him.

"With a fair wind, Liverpool did soon enough arrive, and to Paddy's relief, slightly sooner than he had expected.

"He did eventually manage to climb up out of the hold, and, in a state of unkempt uncleanliness and odour that even he couldn't believe, he was standing on the deck. He let the fresh air blow into his lungs. He looked around at the Liverpool docklands area. It was magnificent, busy and vast – masts and rigging as far as the eye could see in each direction. A relief indeed.

"He managed to clamber off the ship without drawing too much attention.

"The same could not be said once he was standing safely on land, on the dockside.

"The certain new features that Patrick had acquired whilst in transit from Dublin to Liverpool – namely the new colouring on his once fine clothing, the state of his once clean skin and hair and the new odours he was unavoidably wearing – did draw the attention of certain types that frequented the dockside areas along the Liverpool waterfront.

"These were the boys of Liverpool, and they were always on the lookout for any opportunity to make some money, thieve, steal or generally make some fun and have a laugh. This was not difficult for them when presented with the state that Patrick found himself in. Extensive derision found its way to his ears. The more it came, the more it built and the greater the fun the boys were having.

"Patrick did not currently share their sense of humour. He felt that he should at least let them know his own personal point of view on this delicate matter.

"However, surprisingly to Patrick, this only fuelled the hysterical crowd to more baiting. Their taunts featured, I guess you would say, the obvious – the stench of pig filth, the fact that Patrick was covered in it from head to toe, and Patrick's lack of their sense of humour.

"There was a distinct possibility that this was not going to end well, by virtue, of course, that Patrick was now in a considerably enraged state. His only friend was his trusty shillelagh.

"The boys chose to move on to an additional topic that amused them equally. The fact that Patrick was clearly Irish, they felt, compounded their opportunity to have more laughs, although unfortunately at Patrick's expense.

"'Hurrah me soul!' said Patrick. He let his shillelagh wield a course of its own through the air in the direction of some of his abusers.

"The boys of Liverpool responded in kind but with any stick, bar or bottle they could lay their hands on. These were clearly not favourable terms from Patrick's point of view.

"But suddenly, at that point, some Galway boys were on the docks too, led by ... it was Thomas, his friend Thomas from Tuam! They could clearly see Patrick was a- hobbling. With a loud 'Hurray!', they joined in the affray.

"With these reinforcements, they quickly cleared the way ... for the rocky road to Dublin.

"One-two three-four five, hunt the hare and turn her down the rocky road, and all the way to Dublin, whack-fol-lol-le-rah!"

Finn, now totally flabbergasted, said, "Wow, Bronagh! What a fabulous singing voice you have. You certainly picked up that song!"

Bronagh now looked totally exhausted.

"Bronagh, do you know what just happened to you? Any idea?"

"Finn, what do you mean? I just had a sip of coffee," said Bronagh.

"You have no idea? All the other people in the café joined in with your singing!" said the amazed Finn.

"*My* singing? Singing what?" said the equally amazed Bronagh.

"You know, the rocky road to Dublin – one-two three-four five," Finn informed her.

"Well, we were singing it in the car a little earlier … if that's what you mean …" replied the curious Bronagh.

"Okay, we can talk about it all again sometime," said Finn in an understanding manner. "Anyway, it was a cracking story; they all loved it – they applauded when you finished!"

"What are you on, Finn?" enquired Bronagh, clearly totally oblivious to the recent dramatic performance she had put on for everyone.

Chapter 23

❦

After an interlude, she was off again. "You know, Finn, something else I have realised is about St Patrick – you know who I'm talking about there?"

"Yes," said Finn. "The patron saint of Ireland."

"Quite so," said Bronagh. "I also have to put St Patrick into correct and true perspective. It's important we get this right, because everything else is based on this, so it is. Christian worship had reached pagan Ireland around 400 AD. It is often misstated that St Patrick brought the faith to Ireland, but it was already present on the island before Patrick arrived.

"He was a Roman citizen of Britain, known as Patricius, who was captured by pirates at the age of sixteen and sold into slavery in Ireland. He escaped back to Britain, became ordained as a bishop and returned to the land of his captivity as a missionary in 432 or 433 AD.

"The facts are, Finn, that Patrick was British, and a lot of people would be surprised about that, so they would. His birthplace doesn't mean Patrick was a Brit, however – at least not technically. During his lifetime the British Isles were occupied by the Romans, a group that included Patrick's parents and thus the saint himself.

"I must also, though, refer to St Columba. He lived between 521 and 597 AD, born probably in Donegal, Ireland, of royal descent. He studied at Moville under St Finnian, and I think that that's where your name comes from, Finn."

"What? I've never known of any Irish connection in me!"

"Then in Leinster at the monastery of Clonard. In early Christian Ireland, the druidic tradition collapsed due to the spread of the new Christian faith. The study of Latin learning and Christian theology in monasteries flourished. He was ordained before he was twenty-five and spent the next fifteen years preaching and setting up foundations at Derry, Durrow and Kells. St Columba was an Irish abbot and missionary evangelist credited with spreading Christianity in what is today Scotland at the start of the Hiberno-Scottish mission. He founded the important abbey on Iona, which became a dominant religious and political institution in the region for centuries."

"Ah, yes, I've heard of the Iona Community."

"He is the patron saint of Derry. He was highly regarded by both the Gaels of Dál Riata and the Picts and is remembered today as a Catholic saint and one of the Twelve Apostles of Ireland.

"Possibly because of a family feud which resulted in the death of three thousand, and for which he considered himself partly responsible, he left Ireland at age forty- two and landed on the island of Iona off the coast of Scotland. There he built the monastery which was to become world famous. With Sts Canice and Comgall, he spread the gospel to the Picts; he also developed a monastic rule which many followed until the introduction of St Benedict's.

"There are also many stories of miracles which he performed during his work to convert the Picts. The most famous was his encounter with an unidentified animal that some have equated with the Loch Ness Monster in 565 AD. It is said that he banished a ferocious 'water beast' to the depths of the River Ness after it had killed a Pict and then tried to attack one of Columba's disciples!

"St Columba also directly associated with angels whilst on Iona by, during some evenings, going up into the mountains.

"He died on Iona.

"So Kells became very significant, giving rise to the beautiful and famous Book of Kells … and Iona became a historic, famous and artistically significant location in the Middle Ages, the Iona Community."

"Wow, Bronagh, that is a great picture for me of the Celtic era and its evolution … got it!" reflected Finn.

"The final link is with St Aidan. He went on a mission from Iona and set up an abbey on Holy Island, Lindisfarne, in northeast England. It was the last refuge in a barbarian era … St Aidan was purposing Celtic Christianity southward, after the Romans, who had adopted Christianity in England from the year 300 and then left. Roman ways had been perpetuated again and had spread north. The Council of Whitby was an attempt to put a stop to that in 663 to 664. The vote went against St Aidan and the Celtic version of Christianity – England would not adopt it and preferred the European version.

"Much later, on the 8th of June, 793, Vikings in longships from modern-day Norway plundered St Cuthbert's monastery on Lindisfarne, capturing and killing monks. So, you see, things have gone pretty much full circle and back to England again.

"I'm tired now, Finn." And Bronagh dozed off for a nap, a long nap … she needed it.

When she woke again, Finn wanted to figure out exactly why she had been talking about St Columba: why was it important to her? So he asked her.

"We know St Columba and his monks went on a mission to spread Christianity northward into Scotland. They luckily made that base on Iona, the little Scottish western isle. So, you see, they were trying to keep things going, so they were, which is more than you can say for a lot of them."

"So was that a success, then? That's hardly the whole of Scotland, is it?"

"Oh no, they built a strong base camp there and then kept things going by sending a representative round the north coast to Holy Island."

"Well, that's still not the whole of England, Bronagh."

"Okay, Finn, they were doing their best, weren't they? They then tried to work it down through from there."

"So then what? "

"Okay, okay, so it didn't work out; there were obstacles."

"And then what?"

"So, it had been down to St Augustine, the missionary, yes, and sent from Rome by the Pope. He landed at the same place as the Romans had landed in 54 AD, at Richborough Port, near Sandwich in Kent. Augustine arrived in 597 AD. He was the one to establish Christianity again."

"This seems a bit like full circle and going nowhere fast."

"Well, this time he did try to resurrect Christianity and did good."

"Thank goodness for that. So now you are happy?"

"With that result, yes, but that doesn't change how much it chopped and changed or my impression of what happened with the Catholics in Ireland later on, though."

The reality which smashes every
ideologue and his system is human
nature, incessantly striving towards
a personal achievement in a world
which is essentially free and personal.

Joyce Cary, *Art and Reality*

By law of Nature, no man can admire,
for no man can understand, that of
which he has no echo in himself.

Francis Thompson, *Works*, Vol. 3

I have examined myself thoroughly
and come to the conclusion that
I don't need to change much.

Sigmund Freud, *The Letters of Sigmund Freud*

A person needs at intervals to separate
himself from family and companions
and go to new places. He must go
without his familiars in order to be
open to influences to change.

Katherine Butler Hathaway, *Journeys
and Letters of the Little Locksmith*

The ordinary man is involved in action,
the hero acts. An immense difference.

Henry Miller, *The Books of My Life*

Chapter 24

Presuming One's Way of Life

❧☙

Bronagh was reading widely but also thinking more broadly too – to herself, that is; she still didn't have that much confidence to openly discuss her thinking with anyone.

However, after a glass or two of beer …

"You know, Finn, it troubles me greatly that the Catholic teaching at convent school was all about exactly that – Catholicism! But that only crept into Ireland *after* it had crept into everywhere else in Europe. And it was the Romans who approved it for England around about 300 AD, so that was all down to Constantine. He's got a lot to answer for! They had been in England for 250 years before that. What had they been doing all that time? Sitting on their backsides playing tiddlywinks? And then after that, they up and left! What kind of religious authority is that? Pray to God alive."

"You're hilarious, Bronagh! So it's all falling apart again. If they left, how is it going to move forward? How is it going to get to Ireland?"

"Ohhh, don't tell me you haven't heard of St Patrick, Finn! He is the patron saint— oh, I remember, yes, you have. Anyway, he eventually came to Ireland and got it going for us, and that lasted a good while but not forever.

"The trouble is, Finn, and I tell you this now, nobody's got any staying power. You see, they never told us all of that, about how transient it had been, only 'pray like this, pray like that, learn this, learn that'. And has their staying power changed? Well, I haven't seen much evidence of it, so I don't think so. So there you are.

"You know, Finn, at one point I did consider taking my own life. My parents didn't help me in my struggles with convent school life – they were on their side. The whole world was against me, and where was God – the one this worship and chanting was all about?"

Finn gave her a big embrace and hug. They both dwelt there for some time in silence.

Chapter 25

❦

Southern England, 55 BC.

Looking more closely at those Romans … what benefits? Roads?

Looking out to sea on this fine summer's day. A light southerly breeze; gulls swirling around at great height. Some occasionally dive down into the water and rise up again with small mouthfuls of baitfish.

Probably worth throwing out a few nets for some mackerel. Nothing better than a freshly cooked mackerel with a bit of seasoning and herbs, a drop of vinegar … and some freshly baked bread … oh, what a day ahead!

What's that I discern on the horizon? Some of our neighbours out for a sail? Or picking up loads of mackerel?

As they get closer, I notice the boats are actually quite full of people.

How strange. Is this some new kind of enterprise that the local council have come up with – boat trips around the bay?

They get closer, and I can clearly see now that the people are wearing armour. They have shields, and also spears and swords. Must be a local training exercise.

The thing is, I do not recognise any of these people or their gear.

Perhaps, then, this is a "special expeditionary exercise" by some distant neighbours?

They ram their boats into the shingle of the beach. One chap disembarks and walks over to me.

"Good afternoon, old chap," says he. "My name's Julius Caesar. I've just dropped by to see if you'd like to discuss a conceptual ambition I had in mind."

"Oh, that's awfully kind of you, very thoughtful … what exactly did you have in mind?" I enquire.

"Well, we have a few people who could help introduce you to some of our ways of doing things. For example, we pay people in the salt business, and I see you've a lot of potential for that around here!" He laughs loudly at his own joke; I politely laugh along too.

"We are good at building very straight roads and we have some further improvements in mind, and we probably have some other technologies that might interest you too. Well, what d'you say?"

"Oh, sounds very interesting … can I think about it?"

"We'd like a decision today. Come on, man! Why spoil a great day?"

"I'll have to discuss it with the others in the village and local town."

"Okay, we'll come with you and we can all discuss it together."

I'm thinking, *Not sure if this is a good idea* … the rest is, as they say, history.

Chapter 26

Those Visitors

⟨✤⟩

Bronagh took an increasing interest in affairs outside of Ireland. After all, the history available was of the British Isles and of Europe, as well as the Holy Land.

You can see that Bronagh was trying to combine, where possible, her new readings from the mobile library with the background material she had learnt at the convent school.

From that social visit by Julius in 55 BC there transpired the adoption of many Roman practices and innovations across virtually the whole of Great Britain, bar a few skirmishes here and there on the way.

Anyway, by 43 AD their persuasion of England was complete – well, by 122 AD at least; Hadrian, the new visitor, said "enough is enough" and built a wall across the northern demarcation boundary.

These Roman settlers now had to figure out what they were doing here, what they were going to do and where they were going to do it.

You can see their simple, logical plan immediately: "Why waste energy travelling around when you can travel in straight lines – the shortest distance between two points?"

So that was exactly what they set out to do.

Those Romans who had landed from the English Channel in the Axe Estuary in east Devon settled at

Seaton. They set out (and why not?) in an approximate northeasterly direction and built a road to do this regularly, going through Axminster, Tytherleigh, South Chard and Windwhistle.

Well actually, they had been in the southeast of England for a while. This new and magnificent road, the Fosse Way, served two purposes – one, its embankments created a boundary against the unwieldy English residents northwest of the line, and two, the sturdy conversion of any existing tracks to create a battalion-bearing transit service between Axmouth – a protected sea port in the estuary in those days – and Lincoln, on the North Sea coast.

Roman life in the English countryside, with its wide range of topological features and local historic and religious sites, soon built up an interconnected network of Roman roads right across England and parts of Wales, which peter out the further north you go.

The Roman Road runs straight and bare
As the pail parting-line in hair
Across the heath. And thoughtful men
Contrast its days of Now and Then,
And delve, and measure, and compare;
Visioning on the vacant air
Helmed legionaries, who proudly rear
The Eagle, as they pace again
The Roman Road.
Thomas Hardy, 1840–1928

This turned out to be a long-term benefit for British residents and also to international travellers.

Total credit should not be given to the Romans, however. The Ancient Britons had previously been using the shortest or most sensible practical route from one place to another, both over shorter distances and longer distances. Let's face it, it's common sense. The Ancient Britons had figured it out by several methods – by line of sight in good weather and using markers or waypoints en route, by practical experience to get around both boggy ground and rocky, steep ground, and also probably by astronomical methods at various times of year. Neolithic man, Celts and geomancers would all have made a contribution … amounting to prehistoric engineering and Neolithic wisdom, perhaps.

Thus the Ancient Britons' routes were established and well trodden by a number of people and animals for various purposes.

But … was this little-known to them or well-known to them? The appearance of our modern Ordnance Survey map system is that of their efficient network.

The Romans, therefore, used many of these originally devised routes anyway, but they went on to use the increased straightness principle of theirs to a great extent, which is why so much of the Roman road network is still in use even today.

Chapter 27

The Mystery of This
One Particular Alignment

∽◈∾

Another dawn, another day for Bronagh.

Oh dear, oh, okay – so, it's shower, floss and brush teeth, load the washing machine – oh! What to wear? Get dressed while I listen to morning television, dry hair and embellish accordingly, makeup, healthy seeds-fruit-nuts-muesli mix prepared in bowl, topped with Greek yogurt, oh! and oh! – now for the intensely stimulating and uplifting procedure of selecting the ground coffee of the day, spooning it into the cafetiere, sniffing and breathing in deeply the aroma of that perfection of a simple pleasure. Do not scald it, let it brew long enough, select an aesthetically pleasing coffee cup that will complement how I feel, think of how I am going to grab the day by the scruff of the neck, and pour that nectar of screaming purity and the definition of achievement into the perfect cup. I have already achieved complete satisfaction before the day has even formally begun ... and breathe!

What next? Oh! I can't just look at it and admire my work of art – I have to actually drink it! That first mouthful circulating, waiting for my taste buds to send the message of my coffee-making exam results to the brain; the anticipation is electrifying. The results arrive; I read them, pure bliss! I am in heaven again.

But here it comes – wasn't expecting it so soon. Screaming into focus from the back to the forefront of my mind comes the reminder of ... the Quest!

It is saying to me, "What am I going to do today to put my life on the right track?" This is in very sharp focus. I cannot argue with it.

Let's look at the facts of the case. There is background material here that is going to form the basis of Bronagh's life. These are the sorts of things she has to contend with in her quest.

The sites that make up this particular alignment were created at different times over thousands of years of history. (And I just know I am going to have to discuss this with Bronagh, although I suspect she probably knows about it already.)

What has become evident in Bronagh's learning and thinking is the emergence of patterns and even the significance of straight lines.

"The alignment of the eight locations in question is as follows...

- St Michael's Mount, Cornwall, which has always been there. Neolithic man was based there, but there was the addition of a consecrated monastery from the eighth to the eleventh century.
- The Hurlers, stone circles in Cornwall.
- Brent Tor, Dartmoor, Devon.
- Burrowbridge Mump, Somerset.
- Glastonbury Tor, Somerset.
- Silbury Hill, Wiltshire.
- Avebury stone circles, an enormous site in Wiltshire.

- The church at Ogbourne St George and the Inn with the Well, Wiltshire.
- The Icknield Way through to East Anglia.

These and other fascinating locations all fall on a straight line on the national Ordnance Survey system, extending approximately 370 miles.

This particular alignment, and many others too, were noticed, observed and checked by none other than Sir Norman Lockyer, an Astronomer Royal. The Norman Lockyer Observatory on Sidmouth Hill, East Devon, is named after him.

Lockyer also noticed another remarkable alignment – that of Stonehenge, Old Sarum (a set of prehistoric earthwork rings and cathedral) and Salisbury Cathedral.

When observed on a map of England, these sites appear to fall on a straight line across the map, known as St Michael's line, from Cornwall to Wiltshire and beyond to East Anglia.

A question arises. These consecrated sites, some on naturally occurring geographical phenomena and features, were all established at very different times and over thousands of years. Could any living human at those times ever have known that these locations lie on a straight line across the whole of southern England? One automatically doubts it.

Why? Well, there are a couple of very basic reasons.

The first world map with anything like an accurate representation of Europe and the Middle East was the Fra Mauro world map.

This map was made between 1457 and 1459 by the Venetian monk Fra Mauro. It is a circular planisphere drawn on parchment and set in a wooden frame about two metres (6 ft 7 in.) in diameter. This original world map was made by Fra Mauro and his assistant Andrea Bianco, a sailor–cartographer, under commission by King Afonso V of Portugal. The map was completed on 24 April 1459 and sent to Portugal, but it did not survive to the present day. Fra Mauro died the next year while he was making a copy of the map for the Seignory of Venice, and the copy was completed by Andrea Bianco.

Only a few medieval maps of Great Britain still exist: the earliest known map of the island of Great Britain – the Gough map – dates from the mid-fourteenth century.

So, we see, if people of the ancient world were to align monuments of any type, there was no chance of them being planned on maps over hundreds of miles, because maps didn't exist then!

There was obviously no detail on those maps to be able to see, show or measure the concept of an alignment – a major stumbling block.

But there could be no drawing of any alignments on maps anyway, because maps didn't exist – an even more serious stumbling block!

But the fact that these alignments can be observed today, after hundreds or thousands of years, still remains. There was no possibility of a concept like this for any of the people at those times and no way they could have practically applied such an idea on a map. The only possibility, therefore, is that they imagined something. Even taking into account the possible extent of their awareness, how could they achieve enough accuracy? And how could the concept be passed on by word of mouth over thousands of years and by people who didn't even speak the same language?

One thing does appear to be a common theme with the locations on an alignment.

All the sites seem to have a focus on social, spiritual and/or religious energies – that is, they are sites of social, work-related, spiritual and religious collectives with an emphasis, perhaps, on recognising a focus of human collective energy for these purposes.

It is perhaps worth considering that people then and now do not have to actually live on these alignments to feel or achieve benefits. All they have to do is recognise the locations where they feel those feelings and benefits and visit them as often as necessary. That would have been the collective purpose too.

The significant points from this are that:

- some features on alignments pre-date both Islam and Christianity,
- some pre-date the Roman and Greek empires,
- some pre-date the Egyptians, the Babylonians, the Hebrews and the Chinese dynasties.

Examples:

- Ur – Abraham, 1800 BC
- Knowlton Rings, the Cursus, and Dyke, Dorset/ Hampshire border, 3000 BC
- Norman church added here, 1000 AD
- Ness of Brodgar, Orkneys, 3000 BC

And these are adrift from Stonehenge by approximately 500 years and from the Pyramids and the Bronze Age, following the Stone Age.

Some alignment locations have been added to, as have the pre-existing tracks, if present, during the course of time. For example, Christian churches have been added, at widely varying times, to Iron Age and Bronze Age burial sites as well as other features. (Although sited at each location, perhaps unbeknown by those who did so in forming an alignment?)

The questions still remain about how and why these locations were situated in this way.

Do we have to call it 'part of our evolution'? Perhaps we do.

Is this due to humanity's innate genetic and spiritual awareness? Or is it due to some other external forces or influences that we are not aware of but that influence our individual and/or collective subconscious?"

Bronagh won't let this lie. She wants to get to the bottom of this – you know what she's like! – and let's be honest, if you are going to base your life plan on any theory, it has got to stack up. It has to be investigated right to the heart and soul of the matter, and this is what she is doing here – and incredibly effectively, I think you'll agree.

We've got to look at what people like Carl Jung think of this sort of thing, and I'll have to discuss this with Bronagh … I've read Joseph L. Henderson's chapter, "Ancient Myths and Modern Man", in the publication *Man and His Symbols* (1964), conceived and edited by the eminent Swiss psychologist and one of the founders of analytical psychology, Carl Jung. He writes: "It has helped to break down the arbitrary distinction between primitive man, to whom symbols seem a natural part of everyday life and modern man, for whom symbols are apparently meaningless and irrelevant."

As Dr Jung points out, the human mind has its own history, and the psyche retains many traces left from previous stages of its development. More than this, the contents of the unconscious exert a formative influence on the psyche. Consciously we may ignore them, but unconsciously we respond to them and to the symbolic forms – including dreams – in which they express themselves.

An individual may feel that their dreams are spontaneous and disconnected. But over a long period of time, one can observe a series of dream images and note that they have a meaningful pattern, and by understanding this, one may eventually acquire a new attitude to life.

Some of the symbols in such dreams derive from what Dr Jung called "the collective unconscious" – that is, that part of the psyche which retains and transmits the common psychological inheritance of humanity. These symbols are so ancient and unfamiliar to us today that we cannot directly understand or assimilate them.

The analogies that exist between ancient myths and the stories that appear in the dreams of people today are neither trivial nor accidental. They exist because our unconscious minds today retain the symbol-making capacity that once found expression in more primitive rituals and beliefs, and that capacity still plays a role of vital psychic importance. In more ways than we realise, we are dependent on the messages that are carried by such symbols, and our attitudes and behaviours are profoundly influenced by them.

So, arising from that, this is an argument that Bronagh will appreciate: when we consider the population of England today, we have cities with populations in the one million to eight million range, for example. The whole United Kingdom has a population of approximately sixty-seven million.

What many philosophers, historians and analysts forget, and hence fail to mention, is that in 2500 BC the population of the whole of England was only around a quarter of a million people. The whole country!

This rose to approximately half a million by 800 BC – still an incredibly small total population by today's standards.

So, with this small size of population, which would probably be widely dispersed, there was a low chance of ever meeting anyone anywhere very often!

This is where it gets even more interesting.

Perhaps, then, there would have to be a good reason to see or meet anyone anywhere.

There were no communication systems as we have today, so trackways and routes and their navigation would have been even more important and significant in the daily lives of the people … for one thing, so as not to waste too much time getting lost! It would all have been a very delicate matter.

So what would they have been guided by?

A chance meeting with anyone anywhere would have been a very significant moment in their daily lives, with extended greetings, conversation and familiarising –and being guarded too, but then sharing information and advice.

This may have resulted in moving further along the track together, extending friendship and help. Directions and waypoints would be given and warnings and local knowledge shared. This would have extended their learning and sharing, giving a sense of community building.

This is valued today, as was seen at the Dublin Castle: Pathways to the Cosmos conference in September 2018.

The particular focus was on the alignment of megalithic tombs in Ireland and Atlantic Europe.

In his foreword, Malcolm Noonan TD, Minister of State for Heritage and Electoral Reform, states, "We will continue in our mission to highlight the value of our heritage of which we are all now custodians and will continue to make those connections that are so important for the vitality and well-being of us all."

Bronagh thinks, *Wow! They were an exceedingly good few cups of coffee!*

"You know, Finn," she says, "I've for years and years now looked at all this material, considered it all and thought about it until I can think no more. It virtually drives me mad!"

Finn immediately responds, "I don't think you're mad. It is a good thing that you've been doing."

"Okay – thanks, Finn. I like that, and I needed that. I think I need … direction – yes, direction. I need to see a kind of plan, like a road map unfolding. I've got to find my place in life."

"Bronagh, if this analogy helps, English springer spaniels, even when they haven't been trained to do this, can go into a wood and flush pheasants to fly in the direction of the owner. They do this by instinct alone, without having been trained. So my question is, how did that get into their instinct?"

"Good one, Finn."

"And it doesn't drive them mad – they just do it, and they love it!"

Chapter 28

A New Paradox?

ᕲᕲ

Time spent at the window is never wasted.

There is always a changing picture out there. Every day the clouds are different, sometimes darker, sometimes lighter, and different shapes, which tell stories in the mind's eye.

So, then, its pure blue sky and sunshine, with the inevitable criss-cross of high-level vapor trails.

Lowering my eyeline a little to below the roof line and to the street view is another forever-changing picture.

There is someone who must be the bespectacled and bearded Mr Chowdery. He ambles along here at the same time every day in his long brown raincoat and colour-of-the-day turban. He will meet up with someone who must be Mr Khan at about … now! And yes, there he is! Right on cue. They meet and greet; they are wonderful! In similar dress, they will continue along the street to a café. They enter. So, the big question – what will they order? And what will they be discussing today?

Mrs Williams and her friend will stop and look in the window of the hairdressers and again at the furniture shop. I think they will spot the new curtain drapes on display there for sure. They are now eclipsed by passing youths, not on bicycles but on phones.

They themselves are brushed aside by a bunch of street dudes.

All of these people are focused on one thing, whether it's money, shopping, fashion, phones or social media. How could any other approach to life break into their capsule, cocoon or bubble of thinking?

People are often on their daily mission at the shops or other dedicated cause. If one of these fails to be achieved, deep anxiety may prevail for the rest of the day, and possibly a sleepless night as well.

Mrs Williams and her friend both know there are chores to do at home, but they must get out for this escape. It is a crucial part of their daily lives. Although there are these chores to do, I wonder if any of those people out there have something on their mind, drifting back to a preoccupying theme of a need for direction, a plan, an exciting reason to change their daily routine or life mission?

If they do, how will they handle it?

Bronagh now thinks, *Has a new paradox now arisen, then?*

Once we become aware of this apparent system of alignments and their potential significance in our lives, do we recognise it? Or do we ignore it?

Do we or should we uphold it? Or do we treat it with much of the usual contempt rampant in 21st-century cultural awareness or unawareness?

Will people – and how many? – actually look very closely at this and realise that there are or may be benefits, actual real benefits, to individuals who recognise them as such, study them further, and indeed follow this, support it and promote it?

Is this possible? If so, how would individuals go about this recognition?

This is an evolutionary awareness, then …

It should be said here and now that this line of thinking is not a religion. It does not replace or claim to replace any religion or its beliefs and practices. It does not position itself above any religion hierarchically, either currently or historically.

Bronagh is so excited by it all! Realising this has empowered her.

There are also those who have read about, and some who try, concepts such as the Secret, the Missing Secret, the Law of Attraction, and Manifesting. The New Age movement has many adherents. I've moved on from that now.

Millions of people worldwide follow their own religious beliefs, rites, practices and individual interpretations. They will always continue to follow their faith, of course. It is their individual freedom, their individual and collective bonding with their gods, their saints and so on, that is so valuable to human existence and the future.

There is a commonality here with the principles of "Creation" and "the Fall". The whole of creation has been affected by the break of relationships with the creator, hence humanity is continually trying to make amends with the creator in its own particular way.

A very important point here is that just because something pre-dates Christianity, the Bible, any other material or any other faith or set of beliefs, that does not mean the earlier things are wrong. They were just the way they were for our evolution and understanding at that time. It would not, of course, be fair for us in the modern world to judge people in the past by our present-day standards and understanding. They were just doing the best he could for themselves, their offspring and their species. They wwere doing the best they can to survive, and often under very harsh conditions.

It may well have been the frequency and extent of these harsh conditions that drove the people of various civilisations to extensive spiritual heights. They sought salvation and relief from their harsh life conditions.

We eventually see, over time, evidence of civilisations thinking alike and conspiring together for solace.

The universe is a very large place. There is a lot going on in it, some things good, some things bad. How do we each tune in to the universe and what is going on? We have the freedom to try to tune in or not to tune in.

If we do choose to try to tune in, should we tune in to everything in the universe or only some of it? And which bits? Which bits will be good for us? Which bits won't be?

Thus we all have our beliefs, which will automatically set our limits, which will protect us from bad things or too much bad ... we hope.

I know Bronagh had lots of problems dealing with this sort of thing. She was not sure about much of this and felt vulnerable. She was young. Her problem was that she couldn't figure out how to find help, advice or direction from a reliable source or an adult well known to her.

Chapter 29

Seeking a Path,
Seeking a Direction

One of the things Bronagh likes about her flat, particularly because it is in London, is that she only has to look out of one of the windows in any direction to see, rising above the thousands of rooftops, a pinboard-like distribution of church spires, mosques, temples and synagogues rising majestically above the limits of the architectural average.

These wondrous views never fail to remind her of the mix of faiths that is present in every city in England. With each of these views it is reinforced that these beliefs exist side by side. Not only do these faiths live side by side with each other, but so do the thousands of their adherents. It is an amazing experience to just sit and reflect on this for a moment … or even two.

Bronagh finds that this experience draws her mind to wander over the detailed history of how each of these iconic buildings came into being and wonder what drew the people to focus their communities there.

The following is the sort of thinking and the sort of material that Bronagh has valued most in putting everything in order and making good sense of it.

God is omnipresent and omnipotent. So, was there God in 3000, 4000, 5000 BC?

Was primitive man aware of Him? (God was aware of primitive man!)

Hmm, that's interesting. So, if we follow this line of thinking for a moment, as Bronagh will have done, it appears that primitive man had a drive to find and observe a spiritual life. It appears this is an innate human feature.

He may have felt the presence of God, and God's communications, at specific ceremonies or in certain places, exactly as we do today.

These places could well have been some of the locations along the alignments. This would account for the "energy" and "spiritual" aspects of the feelings reported by people at some of these sites –both by non-believers in God and by believers.

That is interesting!

During the thousands of BC years, the primal spiritual aspects of human lives would be directed to unknown deities or gods – but as far as God was concerned, God was still God and hence it was Him.

Bronagh suggested that I should look at this, the Call of Abraham.

God said to Abram,
"Leave your country, your family
and your father's house, for the
land I will show you."
So, Abram went as God told him …
Abram was seventy-five years old when
he left Haran. Abram took his wife
Sarah, his nephew Lot, all the possessions
they had amassed and the people they

had acquired in Haran. They set off for
the land of Canaan, and arrived there.

Abram passed through the land as far as
Shechem's holy place, the Oak of Moreh.

Genesis 12:1, c. 1900 BC

The name "Oak" or "Terebinth of Moreh" may also
be "the teacher's" or "the Diviner's Oak". It must have
been a "holy" tree and the place an old Canaanite
sanctuary. Although it is difficult to understand
Abraham's motives for visiting this place, there is
no reason to suggest that he recognised the sacred
character of the place and wilfully adapted himself to
it. The reference to the Oak of Moreh merely serves to
indicate the place where Abraham camped and built his
own altar.

It is difficult to understand Abraham's motives ... or
is it difficult to understand?

There is here the first distinct possibility – yes,
possibility – that Abraham had "sensed" and "tuned in"
to the old Canaanite sanctuary. Hence he would have
recognised the sacred character of the place.

Wow, Bronagh! Is that the earliest bit of alignment
tracking? And without a map!

Perhaps it's not the only instance ...

There's also Abraham's apparition at Mamre, where
he encountered three angels.

God appeared to Abraham at the Oak
of Mamre while he was sitting by
the entrance of the tent during the
hottest part of the day. He looked

up and there he saw three men
standing near him ... he ran to meet
them, and bowed to the ground.

Genesis 18:1–15

The Oak of Mamre (in Greek, η Δρυς της Μαμβρή, or hēDrys tēs Mambré), or Oak of Sibta at Khirbet es-Sibte or Ain Sibta, in Hebron in the West Bank is a site venerated by some as the "Oak of Abraham". It is distinct from the more ancient site of Mamre. It owes its name to an ancient tree, which seems to be dead but has a young sprig growing next to it, and stands in the grounds of the modern Russian Orthodox Monastery of the Holy Trinity.

The old tree fell in 2019, but there are plans to preserve its trunk and sustain the growth of the young shoot.

The site is located two kilometres southwest of Mamre (Hebrew: מַמְרֵא), historically near Hebron and now inside the city. Also called the Oak of Abraham, it is an ancient oak tree (*Quercus coccifera*) which, in one tradition, is said to mark the place where Abraham entertained the three angels or where Abraham pitched his tent.

Abraham was clearly "tuned in"; he knew where to sense, and thus where to find, God.

Interesting too is the fact that in both cases it was a very specific tree that was the notifying local feature.

How curious is that? How does that work?

So it now seems we have the significance of nature ... and putting things into context ...

"In the beginning ..." – one of the most famous quotes in the world.

Man has no right to anything on Earth and has never done so until God ordained that man would be the guardian of the plants and animals on the Earth (Genesis 1:26–31).

We only exist on Earth and in the solar system and in space and the universe due to one thing – the seasons.

Without the cycle of the seasons, there would be no natural seed growth cycles for plants for our food, nor the insect cycles to pollinate our crops for productivity and harvest. Both of these things are also forms of life.

Early humans learnt to appreciate this and eventually celebrated it with ceremonies and rituals as only we knew how and at certain key focal places.

One of these is most likely to be, according to archaeologists and historians, the famous Stonehenge. Studies of the structure and positioning of the various key stones in the Stonehenge design show that there is recognition of and alignment to key points on the horizon of sunrises and sunsets at the unchanging annual events of the seasons.

This seems to indicate that the people of the time gave thanks for the seasons, the effects of the seasons on the growth of crops, and harvests – their lifeline supply of food. And why not? Is this not something of very high value? And to celebrate it like mad – of course. So would I.

How bold a recognition of the gift of life given to humanity.

The Earth was put here by God for us to live on, and the wheels were put in motion by the rotation of the Earth and by the seasons.

After all, this is life, is it not?

It is testament to humanity that we did manage to appreciate life in this way; we are not stupid; we know which side our bread is buttered.

It is recognised that God communicated with us first through nature – we saw that it was good, and "God had also seen that it was good", and we responded in kind.

Second, via the Old Testament and the Dead Sea Scrolls.

Third, via the life of Jesus Christ.

Fourth, via the Bible, when written and distributed.

Fifth, and perhaps most vitally for us all now, we learned to recognise and live by the signs of the Holy Spirit.

A key thing here is the Holy Spirit in all its forms and translations in all religions – and I must repeat, all religions where it is relevant.

"May your God go with you," said the late Dave Allen, comedian.

The programme *The Universe* identifies the extent of the time-immemorial universe, the existence of dark matter – that is, prior to the Big Bang – the originating stars and solar systems over the next thirteen billion years, and the ability for the Earth to be formed.

During that time God clearly still had a job to do – "Then there was light."

So, after thousands of years, all of these signs and symbols are still laid out everywhere for us to discover. This is what Bronagh has learnt, and this is a part of what her quest is all about, it seems.

"Finn, there is something that baffles me. I have never heard anyone talk about this, and I don't know why. It doesn't make sense. What do you think?

"Newton – the major scientist – Mary Anning, Einstein, Fleming and one hundred plus of these amazing and famous scientists who made major studies, major discoveries and innovations, all contributed to the nation's wealth and to the way of life we have today."

"And your point is?" asks Finn with a quizzical expression.

"All the textbooks, encyclopaedias and documentaries about any of these people never ever mention one simple fact about them all."

"This is gripping!" says Finn with an expectant smile. "And what is that?"

"It is never mentioned that they all had an extremely strong faith. They were all Christians. They were all very active in Bible study, church-going and clerical writing. Why has it never been mentioned or made public or written in books?"

"Um, you're right, Bronagh. That is very curious. Does it suggest that the books or the writers and the historians were not believers themselves and could not appreciate the significance of what you've pointed out?"

"But the bigger picture here is that all of these major scientists and their pursuits were a consequence of God. God gave them the skills and abilities to do their work the way they did and to make discoveries, and they themselves appreciated and valued that."

"That is thought-provoking, Bronagh."

•◆•

Seeking a path or direction today ...

Awakening and putting on a soft, warm dressing gown, Bronagh puts her fingers into the curtains, opens them a little and looks out from her London flat.

The rain has stopped. The view through the window pane is a kaleidoscope of the normal rooftop interlocking boxes, stretching off into the distance as far as the eye can see, interspersed with the inverted images of the same views through the drops of water on the glass. It is inspirational as well as artistic. One could sit and study it all day, or until the drops dry up or run off.

These drops of water act like lenses and focus the broad view into a fish-eye lens panorama – inverted, but does this matter? It forges the viewpoint of the mind to look at and consider the broad view, the broad concept of things, but also the narrow, specific take on life – the individual lives being lived beneath each of the rooftops out there.

Humankind over the many years has sought to benefit itself and to evolve.

During the twentieth century, a range of expressions appeared in business and management life such as "positive mental attitude", "goal setting" and "scoping". Each of these can, of course, also be applied to individuals in their private, personal and social lives.

Many people already do these things, and many have been adopting them for a long while in their lives, automatically, without even thinking of them in these specific named terms.

There are many philosophies, practices and techniques concerning how to conduct one's life to lead to successes and to achieve goals. Naturally, each of these needs a plan for an individual to follow over time, and patience is required.

The emphasis of all of these approaches is inevitably on the thought process and on time and patience. Coaches and advisors may assist with some of this,. but it often takes the form of self-help. So far, so good.

The results of previous practitioners are clearly essential for others to follow along these routes. The achievement of good results helps people build and maintain momentum on the "path to success".

However, things have changed a lot between the twentieth century and the twenty-first century and particularly into the 2020s. The source of most concepts and information is predominantly a smartphone, laptop or tablet.

Some people still use physical or online bookshops, but all probably start off via word of mouth from a friend, colleague or family member.

So, where do people typically do these processes and practices? At home, the office, a coffee shop, a couch or a bedroom, most probably. All sounds easy enough, then – but time and patience are needed, along with the ability to take advice.

Could anything else help the process? Some would say it's necessary to mentally and physically prepare, and some would add … pray about it.

Praying is believed to be an act of communication with God or with a saint, spirit or deity, depending on the particular religion or spiritual attunement of the practitioner. This is equally applicable, of course, to Christianity, Judaism or almost any other religion.

It also applies, perhaps, to the way someone pursuing the Law of Attraction would work – in this case calling out to "the universe" rather than to any god specifically.

Bronagh has told me that she tried most of these techniques before arriving at her own conclusions, methods, and most importantly her own results that matter to her.

She also identified that it might matter where, physically, you do these things.

Hey, I am so pleased with myself for thinking of this.

"Bronagh, I've been thinking about what you were saying about, you know, finding my, your or our place. Actually, I don't know whether you have thought this too, but 'place' could be a job, a role, a fit in the community or a family, couldn't it? Not just a physical location kind of place, if you know what I mean."

"That's very true, Finn, and I have thought like that too. Perhaps that's the answer to my need about finding a direction, a plan or map unfolding before me," said Bronagh, with much greater clarity now in her mind.

Bronagh thinks, then, as a result of having read these well-researched materials over many years, *I am now very clear, and I am sold on the route I want to go down in life to find my path and my place. I take all this on board, and it is clear to me. I like it very much … I now just have to live by it.*

But I will still read on and think around everything I come across.

"I would like a special place for us to live, Finn. You know, a place that is special to us that we can call home. It would be in, perhaps, a village. I think villages are special and cosy – that's important to me. There would be a primary school, a shop or two, a pub and a post office. Countryside would be all around us."

"I like the sound of that too. I love the lush, vibrant bright green of the fresh growth in springtime –

oh! There is nothing like it! I need the countryside, Bronagh. I like the flowers in meadows, country lanes and bridleways."

Bronagh joins in the rejoicing. "Yes – farm life and farmland all around us. Our children will love the animals – baby lambs to feed from the bottle and calves."

Chapter 30

Personal Experience, Research and Observation Counts

❦

Now, I must remember, I can't stress strongly enough to Bronagh how important it is to keep her eyes peeled and her senses tuned in to feel her way through the maze that lies ahead out there.

I cannot, of course, tell her everything in sufficient detail. As we know through our own experiences, we often learn best by making our own mistakes and being left to make those mistakes. We then learn from our mistakes and draw our own conclusions.

But I can hardly contain myself. I must tell Bronagh about a book I bought as a student. I hope that, later on, she tells you all about it. It is linked to things that happened when I eventually opened it. I must also tell her this …

I was looking, post-Covid lockdowns, for a fresh local church to attend. After checking out a few over a period of a few months for a "best fit" and for contentment, as well as happiness with the style of sermons and the message and the warmth of social interactions, one was found.

This fresh place I visited in January 2023. It was a small, parochial, low-key church in a newish building, with about twenty in the congregation. The style was "no frills" and straightforward.

Later that day I noticed a number of significant communications spontaneously happening with family members and friends. These were greater than anything before and were worthy of holding up for celebration – a really major day!

Other spin-offs from that visit occurred, such as special interest groups and lunches.

It was clearly a special location. I cherished it and noted it … and made return visits.

So, obviously I had to ask myself the question, how could this happen so specifically and so significantly? And why?

And then it dawned on me. I noticed this location happened to be sited on an alignment, spanning about twenty miles locally but a lot farther when extended.

The alignment included sites such as two churches, an abbey, a card shop, my first ever house, the church in South Boarhunt at the centre of this book, and two sets of historic motte and bailey earthwork remains – as well as this newly found church, Hill Park Baptist Church. Phew!

There are also further extensive continuations of this alignment approximately 100 miles or more eastward and also around 200 miles westward – an amazing discovery.

It is interesting that the times of the formation or creation of each of the features along this alignment span around 2,000 years.

This has been a modern experience for me, probably indicating that the alignment system is still in place and is still active and effective today. This is sensational stuff, but it has been hardly been noticed by anyone else at all.

Another visit was made to St Columba's Church on this alignment, and from my recent experiences, I expected, if the pattern was followed, something significant might happen again. Coincidentally, the visiting reverend on that day was also on her first visit to St Columba's.

The first hymn, coincidentally, had lyrics in line with the storyline of "On the Rocky Road to Dublin". I could hardly believe it.

The reverend, in her first sermon at this church, made reference to "A special place or event that has helped me in my faith journey … holy ground. I can always go back there and visit on any day to be reminded of how it was. God was there, and I never realised it. Unexpected places, unexpected people."

This suggests that interesting developments in one's personal life can be anticipated at any time. This amounts to another call for hope, surprises and miracles.

Yes, I must tell Bronagh about this. She will thank me for it – for sharing. I know she will be on the case immediately!

…"Expect a miracle"…

PART 2

⋞◑◑⋟

The backgrounds and the mysteries
of places and of people …

Their lives and adventures continue to unfold.

Chapter 31

Level Heading

Where to go next? And why? Our travellers are still fairly fresh, but a bit of chill time at a hotel with a pool and gym is called for.

"I sense something is brewing, Finn … don't know what or where …"

"Bronagh, I don't know about you, but I did have an amazing sensation back at Uisneach," revealed Finn.

"Just to be perfectly clear and honest with you … do you accept that I regard the combined and joint Celtic areas – you know, when they were originally Celt occupied – as being especially northwestern France – and especially Brittany – Cornwall, Devon, Somerset, Dorset, Wiltshire, the Lake District, all of Ireland, Wales, and the west side and northern isles of Scotland?" enquires Bronagh.

"Okay, I hear what you say," said Finn. "So that is where most of the evidence is, right?"

"Exactly right, dear Finn," said Bronagh with a pleasant smile.

"We will really have to go to some of the locations on the St Michael's alignment and see what it's all about, don't you think?"

They head west to the southwest – Wiltshire, Somerset, Devon and Cornwall.

Initially they go via the M4 and then the M5 south. It is a relaxing and panoramic drive, passing many significant prehistoric sites, such as Avebury.

Swinging south, with views across to Wales, the Severn Bridge and the Bristol docks, they enter the flat countryside of north Somerset, with the prominent Mendips, Polden Hills and Quantocks also coming into sight. Glastonbury Tor is away on their left.

They arrive at Brent Knoll, another unusual geological outcrop looking like a dormant volcano. Luckily there is a motorway service area just by it. A stop is required to rescue them from driver fatigue and cramp. After coffee and a sticky bun, they decide to swap drivers for the next leg.

Just ahead of this service area are the Somerset Levels.

"When I was at school in a west Dorset small town, I remember my teacher talking about the Somerset Levels," says Finn. Bronagh looks it up on Google and discovers a book by the Prehistoric Society and a Somerset Levels project from 1980.

"The Somerset Levels are an area unique in the British Isles. The region consists of low-lying peat moors interrupted by numerous islands of sand and rock, and it is bordered by the Mendip and Quantock Hills. This uneven landscape was occupied and intensively exploited by prehistoric man for over four thousand years, up to the time of the Roman Conquest.

"The area is unique for archaeology too because it still contains a vast array of evidence about the past, buried deep within the peats. Most of this evidence consists of wood, but there are other objects as well, of pottery, stone, flint and bronze. These provide a graphic picture of man's activities in the Levels and of early man in his landscape.

"We go back to a time several thousand years ago when the area consisted of a vast inlet of the sea with many small islands of sand and rock providing refuge for hunters and gatherers who occasionally visited the area. They possessed dugouts and rafts which allowed them to move across the watery landscape between the hills and islands, and they pursued a shadowy existence until the arrival of the first farmers six thousand years ago.

"These farmers, newly arrived in Britain with their knowledge of cereal cultivation and the domestication of animals such as sheep and cattle, settled the barely touched lands and began to clear the dense forests in many areas, selecting the best land for crops and pastures. Because agriculture does not yield an 'instant' food supply, they often chose areas such as the Somerset Levels where they could work the land and also hunt, fish and gather wild foods from the hills and marshlands. Thus they could provide food and shelter for their families.

"Great reed swamps began to form around 4500 BC, at first with brackish waters, then with fresh water which encouraged the growth of the Phragmites reed, standing up to ten feet tall. Subsequently, the growth of the peat beds and the development of a fen woodland over much of the area marked a drying of the landscape and created better conditions for farmers and herdsman. Many platforms and tracks across the irregular and uneven landscape mark their presence and their need to move between farmsteads, fields and wild lands."

Finn suddenly blurts out, "'Many platforms and tracks' ... While you were reading that, Bronagh, I got this image of a guy in that era, here, called Edmund. Edmund saw a boggy patch ahead of him on the straightest path he envisaged for transporting his weighty wares to the festival gathering. He had to be there ... Everybody had to be there."

"There was the discovery in 1970 of the oldest wooden structure yet found in the peat. Mr Ray Sweet, a peat cutter known for his sharp eyes, was engaged in winter work clearing ditches and he found low down in a ditch several solid worked timbers and nearby, a flint arrowhead. He recognised the importance of these finds and ensured that they were reported to archaeologists. Preliminary work suggested that the timbers might come from a trackway, and the following summer the first stretch was excavated of what has since proved to be the earliest and perhaps the most important of the trackways in the Levels. It has been called the Sweet Track after its discoverer.

"The trackway was built across soft swamp-like ground where reeds and edges grew and there was often standing water. The aim of the builders was to provide a firm plank walkway raised above the water, and to do this they first laid long poles on the ground, end to end along the proposed route. These poles were held in place by pegs, short pieces of wood sharpened at one end and driven obliquely into the ground like tent pegs; the pegs were set in pairs on either side of the poles, and together these elements formed a firm sub-structure.

"Next, peat and vegetation were heaped up over the poles to give extra support to the planks that were then put in place, wedged between the groups of peg tops and lying parallel to the basal poles. Finally, the ends of the planks were stabilised with slender vertical pegs driven through holes cut near the ends of the planks; these extended down into the peat, sometimes reaching the underlying clay.

"Excavation at various points along the Sweet Track has shown that it was built along the line of an earlier structure, sometimes making use of its wood and sometimes diverging from it by a metre or more. The earlier track, now known as the Post Track, consisted of hefty planks placed on the marsh surface and with stout posts driven vertically into the ground alongside at intervals of about three metres.

"The generally excellent state of preservation has made it possible to apply a wide range of studies to the wood from the Post and Sweet Tracks, and most of our knowledge of early Neolithic woodworking in Britain comes from these impressive structures. The people who built them six thousand years ago were undoubtedly excellent woodworkers. As we have seen, they seem to have deliberately chosen certain tree species for certain functions, and they showed sound judgement in the way they exploited the properties of different woods. Oak splits readily and so was used for planks, and the trees were carefully selected to give strong, straight timbers without knots and side branches.

"In the details of the woodworking, the skills of the craftsmen can also be seen, whether shaping the end of a board to fit round some other piece or sharpening a peg so that it would drive easily through the surface vegetation down into the peat below.

"All this work was done with stone axes, stone knives and wooden wedges and mallets; Neolithic farmers had neither metal axes nor saws."

"So that is how Edmund would have got to Glastonbury with his load, then. How convenient but ingenious to have created those trackways in that manner and in those days ... incredible. Of course, he might have had to use a dug-out boat or a raft as well," ponders Finn.

"Yes – incredible that they actually thought to use those methods back then. Isn't it amazing how humans are able to use their brains and minds to come up with solutions to almost anything? I am in awe of us all!"

Bronagh smiles, and that makes Finn laugh.

She continues, "From 3500 BC onwards, other forms of trackway support were devised. One consisted of panels or woven hurdles; a forty-metre section was discovered at Walton Heath near here ... they can now be seen in Taunton Museum.

"Another construction was discovered between Westcay and Burtle Islands near here in 1835; it was built in 2500 BC. It was named the Abbot's Way and was two and a half kilometres long!

"The amounts required to build then were thirty thousand alder planks or split logs and about fifteen thousand pegs and stakes of alder, hazel and ash."

"Wow! So this is amazing evidence that ancient trackways did indeed exist, even through or over normally impassable terrain. This means that when we see tracks, footpaths and Roman roads on Ordnance Survey maps, shown as dotted lines ... there could be more continuations of trackways than the maps actually show," mulls Bronagh.

"Yeah, that's right," says Finn. "Good thinking … and … and … they could also form part of alignments too!"

"Yes, they could; part of a physical transit between alignment locations … how fascinating!" concludes Bronagh. "Hey, Finn, as we are right nearby now, why don't we start off at Glastonbury Tor instead of Burrowbridge?"

"Yes, okay," replies Finn. "And then we can also see the path that Edmund followed – how exciting!"

"You know, if people could hear us chatting, they would think that we use each other's names a lot, don't you think?"

"Yes, but we do it to show respect for each other – confirming that we are not taking each other for granted. Isn't that right?"

"Yes, it is, and it also shows that we are drawing each other's attention – we are listening to each other properly. Just like it's important to put your phone down and not be on it during a conversation – and right from the start too! That's why we do it."

They hug and share a kiss.

Their next stop is to be Glastonbury Tor in Somerset, a much more significant location on the St Michael's Alignment. It is strikingly prominent on the landscape from a considerable distance as they approach the vicinity of Glastonbury. It is a massive cone on an otherwise flat panorama and has been unmistakable as such for thousands of years. The Tor has an altitude of 518 feet, rising above the Avalon Marshes of the Somerset Levels.

Glastonbury is one of the most famous and popular places in the British Isles that visitors and tourists from abroad head to. Glastonbury town and area has a following all of its own. This is all apart from and nothing to do with the Glastonbury Festival.

Hence there are always a lot of people visiting all of these places at any one time.

After parking at the National Trust car park, Finn and Bronagh walk up the rough path that spirals its way up the conical hill or tor.

Skylarks that seemingly hide in the grass tussocks on the slopes of the hill suddenly dart up, often so quickly that they are out of sight ... but you know they are there due to their amazing fast trilling song. Try to look for them again and you don't see them, but you still know they are there. You have to spend time scanning the sky with your eyes focused at different distances. Then you get a surprise – you actually spot one! It's a challenging game they play with us.

There is St Michael's Tower standing alone at the top. Finn and Bronagh spend time looking across the countryside in all directions; there is much to see in every direction ... it is breath-taking.

They can even see across the Somerset Levels to the sea, the Bristol Channel, and even across to the mountains of Wales.

"Over there are the Polden Hills and the flat peat area to the side of them where Edmund would have walked across on his trackways, Finn," says Bronagh excitedly.

An American voice enquires, "Oh, who is Edmund? Is he a friend of yours? I'd love to meet him. That is such a beautiful area to live in."

"Oh, he's a friend of mine I used to know. Don't see him very often now, though," responds Finn with tongue in cheek.

"Oh, that's such a shame. I hate losing touch with friends. Hey, what are your names? I'm Martha, from Pennsylvania, USA … pleased to meet you!" says Martha warmly and with a wide smile; they introduce each other and shake hands. Talking as they go, they slowly walk around the top of the Tor together. This warm accord continues as they descend the pathway back to the car park.

"Hey, guys, why don't I take your numbers so we can keep in touch?" says Martha.

"Of course – great idea," responds Bronagh, and they exchange numbers and then move on to their separate ways.

Finn and Bronagh proceed further southwest into Somerset to Burrowbridge Mump. This is an isolated conical hill that has been there for thousands of years, rising just seventy feet above the flat, marshy land of the Somerset Levels, similar to but much smaller than the more well-known Glastonbury Tor only ten miles to the northeast. This hill is also topped by a ruined or incomplete church, as on Glastonbury Tor; they share the same name, St Michael's Church, though they are of different ages. The building on Burrowbridge Mump dates from 1793, replacing an earlier medieval church, although it was never finished; there is no roof, but the remaining parts – the tower, walls and arched windows – are still substantial. The flatness of the surrounding land ensures that the views from the top of the mound are extensive, despite its relatively low eminence. The site, again, is managed by the National Trust.

Finn and Bronagh admire the views from the top, getting a feel for the place and tuning in to its history. What events might have taken place here? They imagine the people of the times and their circumstances. They also notice some sudden bouts of wind gusting from various directions. This seems most extraordinary, as it is an otherwise calm day.

High up, way up above them but unseen, this air turbulence is being caused by the frantic and vicious fighting of swirling demon monsters in flight, turning with energetic swishes of their long, flailing tails to change direction mid-flight. These demons are active against the best interests of Finn and Bronagh and, it seems, against their welfare. It's as if they are trying to ward them off from something, stop them in their tracks or even physically attack them.

These demons are being fought off by a team of airborne angels, who also have to perform flailing flights to force the demons away and hence to win the battle.

Chapter 32

The Unseen

მადლობა

The problem is that there are people who are just bent on destruction, force and power, with no awareness of quality of life or of better ways of life or of how to achieve these things.

Many are unaware of the subtleties of forming lasting relationships with other people and of the delicacies involved in maintaining and nurturing them. So many people just keep resorting to being competitive, to winning and crushing others at nearly every opportunity. They resort to making themselves heard, winning the argument, beating the other person down. They will talk behind people's backs to undermine them socially if they appear to be gaining some credibility or becoming more knowledgeable or stronger … and if that person is uncomfortable and feels undermined and weakened, they will persevere until they feel back on top and are winning again themselves.

Do any of these people ever consider whether the people they are talking to or challenging might have a condition such as autistic spectrum disorder or narcissistic personality disorder … or any other condition? Probably not …

Equally possible sometimes, of course, just to make things more complicated, the challenging person may also have one of those conditions.

The people who are suffering, who have one of the disorders, may have asked themselves the question, *What if you never turned up for your own life?* – a very probing and thought-provoking question.

And it may be followed by the thought, *Maybe I can learn to live ...*

The Devil, Satan and other dark forces take advantage of and work on those situations as well as with those people, whether they are aware of it or not.

But God still works in His ways ... His teams of angels are still working. And yes indeed, they have had to be working for quite some time now.

Back in 1933 through to 1939, someone or something had noticed the sociopathic, psychopathic, egotistical and eccentric mentalities of one Adolf Hitler (who was not very accomplished at hiding his thinking) in Germany and had decided to latch on to him ... with or without his knowledge.

This was Satan in action ... in the charismatic form of a gargantuan dragon of typical mythical proportions, featuring a pterodactyl-like head and wings with claws and a long open beak with thousands of needle-like teeth; not the prettiest of sights.

Satan had helped spearhead the Third Reich's actions in Poland, hence officially triggering World War II. He had continued to bolster Hitler's plan to push the British Army back to the sea, encircle them and annihilate them on the beaches of Dunkirk.

Little did Hitler know, and neither did Satan read, what was initiated by King George VI. Neither had foreseen the planning, preparation and announcements of the National Day of Prayer.

This national outpouring of prayer was noticed and led to a requisitioning of the highest order – the official commissioning of Archangel Michael to head into action once more against his old foe, whom he had already beaten down a number of times before. This time the loudest and strongest of flurries, passes and warnings by Michael were sufficient. Satan flew off and slithered back into his cavern hideaway, the entrance to which was in the southern Alps, near Cannes.

The new-found peaceful conditions over the English Channel allowed for the successful evacuation of the maximum possible number of British soldiers from the Dunkirk beaches by flotillas of vulnerable small boats that headed bravely out from English shores.

One may be surprised when considering the established conventional image of any form of angel. The historic image is of graceful white robes draped on a slim human-type figure with golden locks, huge but elegant white-feathered wings, a golden glow and choral music. There are several types of angels, with images distinctly different from the conventional images … but this does not detract from the fact that they are all highly effective in their purpose and actions and, as always, totally reliable.

Also, in the new name of spiritual warfare, their tactics have had to become smarter, employing ploys and different disguises where necessary.

Archangel Michael had been holed up, ready for action, out of sight, disguised as a slithering, slimy black streamlined body dripping thick treacly black oil from old cavities underground in the Texas area of the southern Rockies, United States of America.

Michael had already flown a few much earlier passes over Nuremberg, Germany, to witness for himself what was developing there. He had been most concerned by what he had seen and more still with what he had sensed. He had reported back accordingly.

High, high above the Earth and unbeknown to most, the Battle of Britain had been observed as a battle of wits, a battle of warplanes and a battle of men, but with great losses, sacrifice and carnage on both sides ... and with a large amount of pain and grief. It was a great waste, there was no getting away from it, but in humanity's planning and defence, it had to be done.

Again, this battle had been initiated by the Third Reich's Luftwaffe, behind which, of course, was Hitler.

A greater brain, with a persuasive skillset and increasingly large amounts of assets at his disposal, Winston Churchill, had deduced, with his Ministry of Defence teams, with the War Room and with his international friends and allies, that a well-planned and coordinated counteroffensive was in order.

High, high above the Earth, this was noted.

A team of cherubim was detailed to leave their headquarters in caverns below the Norwegian fjords. They had been discreetly waiting for a call to action from this well-disguised and unlikely sleeper location. They travel in the dead of night so as not to be seen – at least by the enemy in the spiritual world.

In their humanoid form, cherubim have an unusual combination of features, displaying any combination of several different faces on the same body, selected from humanity, with long fair or dark hair and angelic faces.

They may also look like an ox – strong face with long mane and horns – eagle, lion or cherub. They have four wings, stiff legs with calves' feet and either two or four graceful hands, all complete with marvellous white or slightly coloured robes.

They act for good and are involved in the judgement of actions and in guarding things or situations, possibly even weapons.

In this next instance they were called to take up their station high, high above Southwick House in Hampshire, the planning headquarters with the map room for D-Day. They only revealed their presence as doves, fluttering or sitting in the trees above Eisenhower's operational working caravan.

The planning and preparations and the all-important deception of the enemy were going exceedingly well. Everything, and masses of it, was in the right place at the right time. What could possibly go wrong? The weather, a storm …?

However, with exceptional people in the Southwick House map room and with the latest Meteorological Office data, reporting and interpretation, it was quite in order for the best decision to be made by the top brass and their teams about the D-Day landings. The go-ahead was given.

Meanwhile, high, high above the Earth, and unbeknown but actioned from below ground, in a seemingly empty cavernous void, in darkness, with the occasional fast fluttering of winglets, airborne creatures could be heard circulating. The occasional drip of water into pools and onto rocks broke the silence … the calm before the storm? The music of Claude Challe of

Buddha Bar and "Weather Storm" by Craig Armstrong accompanies this scene.

Teams of seraphim slithered as fiery serpents – well, they would become so on rising above the deep waters within the Great Glen, Caledonia – and left their secret hideaway entrance portal in the deepest depths of the large loch, on either side of Foyers, at the exit from their cavern – old bauxite mines, their own little place.

However, things had not always been this easy for the seraphim. Originally, they were to be found under Schiehallion, a mountain – in Gaelic Sidh Chaillean, or the Summit of the Caledonians, which is the centre of Scotland. The mountain is hard quartzite stone formed by the pressure of the ice in the Ice Age.

On its southern side is a network of caves in a band of softer limestone that runs along Glean Mor. The caves were the home of those supernatural beings. One cave, Uamh Tom a Mhor-fhir (Cave of the Great Man), was the entrance to the underworld.

However, this became known. The seraphim had enough important and delicate work cut out for them by the reckless antics of people and their egos. They could not afford to be plagued by voyeurs in the mountains, following them on exit and re-entry. Their alternative option was to slither under cover of darkness each time up Glen Rannoch and onto the vast, boggy peat moors and swampy pools of the bleak and desolate Rannoch Moor, then onward to their targets.

After struggling in this way for a period of time, they found it easier to dive into the loch of Great Glen and into fresh hidden caves.

He only can behold
with unaffrighted eyes
The horrors of the deep
And terrors of the skies.

Thomas Campion, 1567–1620.

Seraphim proclaim God's holiness to one another. Their mission was clear, from their general purpose in the form of fiery serpents sent by God to show judgement where needed.

Again travelling under cover of darkness, flames on standby, they were to arrive at the allotted hour over the beaches of Normandy to give spiritual support, and hence ultimately also material support, to the landing Allied Forces. There was much German resistance to overcome.

The landing Allied Forces were also joined by …

… high, high above and unbeknown …

… the spiritual entities called "Living Creatures". These are a force for good. They have travelled from hideouts in underground sulphur mines in western Canada.

They have six wings and resemble a strong man, an eagle or a lion – in this instance probably a team of all of them. Their function is to deliver judgements for God on Earth.

Their purpose here is intense. They are fired up for action … they have caked-up condensed yellow sulphur on their beaks and whiskers on either side of their jaws, dripping with fuming red and black molten sulphur, with pungent poisonous gases venting out.

Their quest was spiritually, and thus materially, against all German resistance beyond the beachheads created by the Allied Forces and inland.

There was headway to make, but, in time, they all prevailed together.

There were losses, yes, but it was known by all in advance that there would inevitably be casualties. This was war.

Tis madness to resist or blame
The force of angry Heaven's flame;
And if we would speak true,
Much to the man is due.

Andrew Marvell, 1621–1678

Chapter 33

The Innocent Moor No More

⁂

After a refreshment stop in Taunton, Bronagh and Finn drive on down the M5 through to Devon, past Exeter and, via Okehampton, north of Dartmoor and then south to Brentor.

You can hear the sparrows shuffling and tweeting in the car park. But, only slightly distant, there are two more ethereal cries, one of the curlew and the other the almost babyish high-pitched crying of a buzzard – in fact, two, circling upward on a rising thermal.

Now, if you ever wanted a bleak, intimidating natural backdrop for a film, this is it.

Dartmoor is regarded as a rugged and bleak enough open moorland in itself – desolate, mostly treeless, but with rock and boulder outcrops to negotiate when walking through or around bracken, bogs and mires. It is no wonder Dartmoor Jail was built virtually in the heart of Dartmoor at Princetown: who in their right mind would want to escape from there? And with the Hound of the Baskervilles out there somewhere … much safer to stay inside, surely.

They stand, gazing up in awe at the top of the tor.

"What a most unusual place to build a church, especially in those days," observes Finn.

"Yes. Staggering, isn't it? What incredible efforts to haul the materials up there. Shall we go up?"

"Yeah, okay."

It is a short climb up the side of the tor to the sombre setting of the church. After a clanky turn of the massive handle ring, the heavy front door is pushed open. They wander in. It feels cool but sheltered in there.

"This has an air of being a bit of a creepy place, Finn, don't you think?"

It is lit only by the scant light penetrating the small number of stained glass windows, although they are beautiful in themselves.

Although it's a well-timed and opportune visit to the shelter afforded by the church, the musty smell of the enclosed atmosphere is getting to them. "Shall we leave?"

"Yes, it's about time now," says Finn. They turn to leave through the main door.

A shock electrifies their bodies. There, in front of the exit, is a skeletal figure in a black coat with tails, a black top hat and a pale grey complexion. His dark, sunken eyes confer an eerie countenance.

"I'd better tell you what you've missed while we've been away," he says to the now petrified pair in a slow, thin, deep voice.

"Ah, okay ... y-y-yes, please do." Finn's voice is strained and his face now totally ashen. His eyes are almost popping out; both he and Bronagh are frozen to the spot.

The figure speaks again ...

"The giants were all dead and the witches had fled to Wales, driven there by the friends of Bowerman, but one evil genius still remained. The Devil roamed the moor, looking for victims and terrifying the

countryside. Churches and wayside crosses were places
of safety, but the inhabitants of Dartmoor knew that
the Devil only needed a slight mistake and he would
pounce and carry off his victim.

"Don't you two become his victims, mind!

"One day a rich merchant ship was sighted making
her way up the Channel coast, bringing spices and
silks from the East. The Devil had been a long time
without any victims, thanks to the vigilance and care
of the moor people, so he at once decided to wreck the
ship and destroy its merchandise. That night he created
a terrible storm. The rain and wind extinguished
the warning beacons on the coast and on the top of
Brennon or Beacon Tor, which we now call Brentor,
right here. The night was pitch dark except when lit by
terrible flashes of lightning. The wind roared, driving
the ship towards the rocky coast, and the thunder roared
threateningly. All night the captain of the *Virtue* – for
that was the name of the ship – battled to keep her
afloat and away from the dreadful jagged rocks, while
Hugh the Merchant stayed below decks praying.

"The Devil flew high above the ship, where he was
in complete control, laughing and shrieking with glee
as the ship drove towards the rocks and certain death
for the crew. Towards morning, Old Hugh came up
on deck only to be informed that no mortal power
could save them now. On hearing this, Old Hugh at
once knelt down on the heaving deck and prayed to
his patron saint, St Michael. He vowed that if the ship
was saved, he would build and dedicate a church to
St Michael on the highest point of land he first sighted.
Almost at once the wind slackened and changed

direction, taking the ship away from the shore. The Devil, enraged, summoned up all his power but was no match for St Michael.

"As soon as Hugh set foot ashore, he pledged to fulfil his vow by building a church on Brentor, which was the first and highest point of land sighted after the storm. It was a formidable task, as anyone will know, like you who have visited Brentor. The grateful merchant toiled away unsparingly, giving freely of both money and energy, until he had assembled all the required materials on top of the steep tor. Hugh breathed a sigh of relief, feeling that his task would soon be completed.

"That very night, however, the Devil happened to pass over, and realising at once what was happening, he felt very angry indeed and scattered the building materials round the foot of the tor, chuckling all the while in devilish glee. Hugh was shocked to see what had happened when he arrived the following morning, but, being daunted by nothing, as strong as his pledge was, he started all over again, carrying the stones back up to the top. Each night the Devil scattered the materials and each morning Old Hugh carried them back up to the top of the tor. After some weeks, St Michael, realising what was happening and knowing that Old Hugh would need help before he could fulfil his vow, decided to intervene.

"When the Devil arrived the next night, he found St Michael waiting for him. On seeing his old enemy, the good saint seized a huge granite boulder and hurled it at the Devil, who had turned to run away. The rock caught him on the heel and sent him off, roaring with rage and pain.

"Because of his injury, the Devil kept out of the way, allowing Old Hugh to complete his task, and the church was finally dedicated.

"The church at Brentor is the smallest on the Moor because poor Hugh, in his long tussle with the Devil, had wasted a lot of his money; however, it still stands to this day, a tribute to St Michael and to the determination of Old Hugh the Merchant who built it."

"Thank you for that," says Bronagh as she pulls Finn by the arm and drags him past the figure and out of the door. They can't believe what they have just experienced. Curiosity causes them to quietly slip the door open and peek back in. They can see nothing – no sign of the figure.

After a rushed descent down the wet and slippery rocky pathway, and after a few tumbles, they gather their wits and look back up at the church.

"Wow!" says Finn. "What a story or legend ... and scary. And how ironic coming from a guy like that!"

"That certainly brings this place to life very vividly, and instantly gives you a feel for the place and makes your hair stand on end. Who was that guy? What happened up there?"

"Mine too. Dunno," says Finn. "You know, I get the feeling that such things could actually be going on for real now too," he adds fearfully.

"You could be right, Finn, but I'll look after you." Bronagh cuddles him.

Chapter 34

It's a Beautiful Country

❦

Brentor is on the St Michael's Alignment, and the quest is for Finn and Bronagh to get to the southwestern end of the alignment at St Michael's Mount, in Mount's Bay, near Penzance in Cornwall. So off they go.

The main route would take them over Bodmin Moor, but for a change of scene they decide to take a route that skirts by Bodmin Moor … from Launceston heading down to Liskeard.

"What a fascinating country this is, Bronagh."

"I entirely agree. It is wonderful and beautiful. I would never have dreamt that we would have seen and discovered what we have – not in a million years," agrees Bronagh. "You know, Finn, I thought we would be experiencing some big positive energy flows by now, so I did. It just seems like that whenever we try and move on to bigger things and more significant places on the alignment, we just keep getting knocked back by negative feelings and energies, so it does."

Finn mulls this over for a while and then acknowledges her. "Bronagh, I agree – I have noticed it does seem like that at times. But I would say have confidence … have faith and keep faith … don't doubt yourself or your views or the plan."

"Wise words, Finn! By the love of God, where did you get that from? I am impressed!"

"Ah, something someone just told me once," reflects Finn. "It's nice enough roads on this route. I quite like Cornwall; it's very unspoilt … looks quiet."

All of a sudden, a vehicle in the opposite direction to them swerves at high speed around a bend, heading towards them, halfway over their side of the road. Bronagh has to make a sudden turn of the steering wheel one way and then quickly back the other way so as to avoid a collision and then avoid going into the hedge.

"Phew!" says Finn. "That was too close for comfort. Are you okay?"

Bronagh, shaking and as white as a sheet from fright, says, "Can we stop, please?" She is panting from shock.

"Sure. There's a small roadside café just up ahead," says Finn.

So they stop there, calm down a bit and try to recover. A hot drink and something sweet always helps in these situations. They take about an hour, and naturally Finn offers to take over the driving, which Bronagh accepts.

All is fine; along they go. Bronagh has largely recovered her nerves and all is well with the world. A chill music CD helps as well … some deep therapy and relaxation … much-needed relief.

The car starts to make some "hard work" noises and it appears to slow somewhat, not going as fast or as easily as it should, even on fairly level stretches of road.

"Is this happening because you've taken over the driving, Finn?" enquires Bronagh cheekily. It worsens.

A check of the map shows that they are able to head to Bodmin, but there is quite some way to go still.

By a stroke of good fortune, perhaps, they pull in at a car park on the right at Minions. It is the car park for a place called the Cheesewring and coincidently for the Hurlers stone circles ... these being on the St Michael's Alignment!

"That's making a bit of a racket, mate," says their parking neighbour.

"Yeah, but no idea what it is," says Finn.

"You know, Finn, I don't think we are going to make it to St Michael's Mount on this trip. It just seems too much hassle ... nothing but trouble and problems. I'm just not feeling it now."

"Don't worry, Bronagh, I'm feeling exactly the same. Let's pack this trip in and come back some other time, okay?"

"Oh, thanks, Finn – sure." And they cuddle reassuringly.

Choirs of angels are aligned in banks and arrays, all singing in harmony .... the sound of which, it could be imagined, is like the King's College choir at a choral rendition on a special occasion at Westminster Abbey. This is an experience that lifts all human spirits to great heights of emotional upwelling and sends a tear down the cheek, leaving long-lasting feelings and memories of warmth in the heart and soul. It is at such moments that a king at his coronation takes oaths of allegiance and faith in God, showing all that he is serving the people under his oath to and before God.

And afterwards, in the humdrum monotony of everyday life, it is all too easy to forget about that –

to forget that the king, the prime minister and all of us, over thousands of years in Great Britain, have been driven and expected to respond from our souls to the direction of God.

With the car now fixed, they make the return drive up through the West Country to London. It is a peaceful and reflective time for them – a good opportunity to think and to chat.

After much mulling it all over and thinking about the ins and outs of everything and considering the what ifs, Finn eventually spills the beans. "You know, Bronagh, it's as if all of this time, at various times, angels or something have been looking over me and us, maybe, and intervening ... in some way."

"I know what you mean, Finn, otherwise how could all this have happened the way it has? Would it all have happened ... the way it has? Yes, it seemed like it. Were they really there?" Bronagh postulates, "If you believe in God or if you don't believe in God, the Holy Spirit, part of the Holy Trinity of the Godhead, consisting of God, Jesus Christ and the Holy Spirit, can still act for you and on you.

"This acting for you and on you can be in several different ways.

"It could be encouraging you to do or think something.

"It could be discouraging you to do or think something.

"It could be drawing something to your attention.

"It could be preventing you from noticing something.

"It could be encouraging someone else to act in your interests.

"It could be discouraging someone else to act against you.

"Also, each of these ways could be a response to a prayer you have prayed to God at some time or that someone else has prayed for you, or it could be an independent action by the Holy Spirit. God and the Holy Spirit may have decided to act for you anyway, simply because He likes you and He feels like it. But God can also do this even if you feel that you are on unfavourable terms with God."

"I quite like God, then," says Finn.

"God may have a plan for you that you don't even know about. Have you ever noticed any 'coincidences', Finn? Always have a good prayer in mind," Bronagh advises. "Angels are part of the 'communicating team' from God, the Holy Spirit and Jesus. Of course, the 'opposition' also have a communicating team too, hence the power battles that sometimes need to ensue."

"Bronagh, don't you feel that we are all – how shall I say? – war zones in our heads? We always seem to have these battles to contend with."

"Part of the driving force behind 'coincidences' could be this," reveals Bronagh. "'I go to prepare a place for you. And if I go and prepare a place for you, I will come again and receive you to Myself; that where I am, there you may be also.' That's from the Bible – John, chapter 14."

Chapter 35

Departed Souls ... Have a View

⚬⊙⊙⚬

"Finn, I know stuff about environmental issues and so on, as do you, yeah?"

"Yeah."

"This is what we know of the state of affairs now, though. We should, in my mind, also listen to people who have gone before us. In other words, how did the environmental state get to where it is today? What do we have from the past, as personal views, to compare with? Here are a few of them.

"'Oh, to be in England, now that spring is here' is the heartfelt cry at the perception of the beauty of the countryside as shoots grow, multiple shades of green leaves open and hedgerow and meadow flowers begin to bloom, at that seasonal time when day length increases the light needed and warmth rises to the necessary level to trigger this miraculous show.

"But what lies beneath?"

"Neal reports that 'The surrounding countryside where I lived in the 1960s was composed of lots of interconnecting fields, gates and hedgerows. Rabbits could be seen around every corner, when you wanted to creep up on them. Many of those fields are still there, but in other parts of the country hedges were grubbed out/taken away, to create very large area fields for crops. This type of farming required massive tractors and pieces of machinery to work it, hence small fields and hedges would have got in the way. Of course, this removed much habitat from the land bank for the likes of rabbits, birds, and flowering plants.'

"I hear you say, 'We want them all back again – we need the natural habitats to allow all we have lost to flourish again!' Well, I can tell you, it ain't gonna happen! Too late – it's all gone. It would be too expensive and energy-consuming to try to do anything like that. The glory days were there, yes … you should have made the most of them and kept more of the field and hedge network intact.

"This loss of hedgerow and meadow flowers has had a damaging effect on the number of bees in the countryside, which are also essential for the pollination of the flowers of a range of food-producing crops, as well potential honey production. A separate issue here is the increased use of pesticides and herbicides in agriculture, which inadvertently appears to have had an effect on the reproduction rates of bees, hence also reducing their numbers.

"Clearly it is essential to reduce and eventually stop the use of those damaging chemicals, both to avert a greater catastrophe and to allow some kind of restoration of bee populations.

"Will that happen? Well, let's see …"

•◆•

"Whilst on the subject of agriculture, a subject that has always been close to my heart as I worked with farm animals, horses, poultry and small animals, and I also had a smallholding with my own animals … I must turn to some of the careless practices that have taken place over many years in farming. I refer to the disposal of slurry and farm effluent. Unfortunately for the fish in rivers, the insect life in the beds of rivers and the water quality itself, slurry and farm effluent had been allowed to drain into rivers directly. Some was also washed into rivers by rain and flood water. More was also spread onto the fields by farmers manure spreading as a grass growth fertiliser. Some stayed in the soil to do its intended job, but much of this also ended up in the rivers being washed in by rain water … the run off.

"There were several effects of these practices. Fish and river insects were often poisoned by the concentrations of the effluent. The gradual decomposition of the effluent once in the river water took dissolved oxygen from the water that is normally used by the fish and river insects to breathe. This kills the fish and river insects.

"The effluent contents, typically of nitrates, phosphates and other minerals, which are nutrients for river weed and plants, causes these to grow in a more prolific way. This extra plant growth can choke up the river, causing a restriction to the natural and normal water flow. The slower water flow rates bring about changes in the habitat conditions for the indigenous fish and insect species. For example, the brown trout needs a continuous medium to fast flow of very clean river water and a suitable supply of insects that live in such waters. If those conditions are no longer met, then the insects will no longer flourish there and the trout will move on … if they can find better, more suitable water; if not, they will not flourish either.

"High levels of excess effluent nutrients can also cause the growth of populations of unhelpful bacteria and algae in the river water and on river beds and on river plants. These algae can be very detrimental and destructive to healthy river life.

"All of these types of effects have been seen in British Isles rivers from the 1960s right up to the present day … resulting in wiping out completely, or reducing populations considerably, of brown trout. Various species of coarse fish, such as grayling, barbel, bream, perch, roach and chub, are similarly affected. Largely, these effects are not easily reversible to restore their earlier ideal state. The heydays have passed once again."

•◆•

"It is also noticeable that when I first drove a car in 1972, in the summer, the windscreen would become covered in impacted squashed flies that had been hit at speed. Insect life and fly life abounded in the countryside and everywhere else … it was perfectly normal and natural. I used to have to clean them off daily. By 2008, there were virtually no impacted flies on the windscreens. (I see that, now I am able to travel forward in time, you still have the same situation … no impacted flies on windscreens.)

"The sad fact is that the agricultural practices referred to earlier regarding bees have been having similar effects on countryside fly life."

"So, Bronagh, my fly fishing experiences would have been a lot more productive had I lived fifty years ago!"

"Yes – shocking, isn't it?"

•◆•

"Well, that's nearly enough from me … my last point is a very sad one. It concerns the calamitous loss in numbers of many small bird species. Surveys, repeatedly carried out every year and over many years, continue to show very dramatic and startling falls in the populations of small birds and smaller migrating birds … now demonstrated over, say, forty or fifty years.

"There are, as you would imagine, a good number of contributors to the list of causes of this bird life loss. One is, as alluded to earlier, loss of habitat and loss of food sources in the British Isles. This also applies to other habitats across Europe where they might normally be expected to be found.

"A key point about the reference to loss of habitat is that it is the loss of nesting sites in those habitats that can have the most profound effects on loss of egg laying and hence new fledglings.

"Another contributor, that is nearly always forgotten and hence rarely referred to, is the practice in some Mediterranean countries, and especially Cyprus, of erecting very tall and very wide-spanning fine mesh netting, held up by poles, all along some of their south-facing coasts. The purpose of these nets, believe it or not – and it does seem incredible – is to trap as many small seasonally migrating birds as possible. This they do; this they achieve.

"What is the purpose? What is the reason for this practice? Well, again, believe it or not, the practice in these places is to take the trapped small birds and cook them as delicacies and dishes for the local humans to eat … and enjoy doing so.

"As I said, believe it or not!

"The consequence of this is pretty obvious … a very dramatic continuing fall in these bird populations for as long as this horrendous practice continues. How can these lost birds be replaced? Well, again, the answer is probably obvious … How can a dwindling small bird population continue its present population level, let alone replace its 'lost' population numbers? In other words, it's an impossibility.

"So the even bigger questions are … What actions are being taken to close down this netting? And what actions are being taken to ban the practice of cooking and eating small birds? And, more importantly, when will these closures and bans be effectively put into place and enforced? I rest my case."

•◆•

Mick used to be a very keen fly fisherman and naturally appreciated the importance of the quality of the environment for fish, insects and all other aquatic life.

He would be appalled to see and hear what is happening today regarding the severe downgrade in the quality of the water in our rivers and streams.

However, it is not only the quality of the water that is of great concern, it is also the lack of water in the rivers and streams compared with the natural flow levels of fifty years ago.

These two issues combined have even more far-reaching consequences than either one separately.

Regarding fish, who can live nowhere else except in the rivers and streams, in the water they rely on for dear life … there are two separate groups of fish.

One group that live in rivers and streams – for example, barbel, chub, perch, roach, bream, dace, pike and grayling – are known as coarse fish.

The other group is the migratory fish; that is, salmon and sea trout. These are spawned and hence born in the headwaters of particular river catchments. They spend a couple of years in those headwaters growing up by feeding on insects, flies, water snails, worms, etc. They then swim down the river, through the estuary and into the open sea. Here they will spend the bulk of their adult life, feeding on such things as sand eels, shrimp and small fish. They grow fairly rapidly on this rich diet and sometimes to a considerable size. After a few years, they swim back to their original river estuary, up the river to the headwaters where they were born. Their purpose then is to mate, spawn and hence produce millions of fish eggs, of which only a small proportion will hatch, survive and grow into new fish. In normal conditions, this process is enough to perpetuate a healthy population level.

Change any of the above parameters – the water conditions in the rivers or the estuary, the flow rates, the water temperature, the food availability – and the salmon and sea trout will encounter unnecessary problems and issues in their life cycle.

Add also the effects of the netting of salmon and sea trout in estuaries and in the sea over many decades in the past, and the negative consequences are obviously even greater.

As a consequence of this set of current parameters, the Atlantic salmon, of English, Welsh, Scottish and Irish fame, is regarded as being on the "At Risk" list – meaning that it's potentially heading for extinction.

The natural question arises again – will action be taken to help prevent the salmon's extinction?

Or not?

The brown trout is in a similar situation to these last two species, but it lives in appropriate rivers in the British Isles and does not migrate to the sea and back.

So, on to the main causes of this water quality degradation over such a long period of time, of which there are two.

One is the amount of water taken out of the springs, bore holes and rivers that are the sources.

Why is the water taken out? To provide water to all the taps and hoses of the millions of new homes that have been built over the decades.

The other is the amount of sewage and effluent that is being placed in the rivers and estuaries by the water companies.

Will any of these things change? "Didn't see it in my lifetime!" says Mick. "It only got worse and worse over the years."

Footnote to Mick's account: "And it still is exceedingly bad and getting worse still."

"Bronagh, this all makes me grieve for the quality of life and the opportunities that our children one day won't be able to have when compared to our childhood lives, let alone those of Neal and Mick."

"I know, Finn. This is stirring me up. I've got to fight it somehow."

•◆•

There is, running through the spine of Europe, a broad mountain range known as the Alps.

It is very famous – for its beauty, its grandeur, its seasonal changes and, above all, its high-altitude snow cover and winter sports. This has been the case for hundreds of years. Every winter, people have expected to go to the Alps for a skiing holiday. This has been regarded almost as a "human rite".

Equally, every summer, millions of holidays are taken for walking in the mountains, visiting tranquil and green picturesque valleys, small towns and villages, and driving the mountain passes. And people take train journeys through inaccessible high and deep-sided ravines, all tree lined, up to the highest tree line. Rugged mountains and cliff faces are an automatic part of every panoramic viewpoint.

Atop much of this scenery are glaciers – "rivers of ice", as they are often called.

Most of these tend to be a permanent feature all year round. They have been made permanent by layers of regular winter snowfalls being compacted one on top of the other for hundreds if not thousands of years.

For all the locals who have lived in these valleys over the years, this has been their natural and expected backdrop in perpetuity. They have never known anything else.

However, again, all is not as it seems or, perhaps, as we would like it to continue to be.

We have another application of the affliction of global warming and climate change.

These twins have been causing higher temperatures at higher altitudes too. This is exactly where the glaciers have been for thousands of years.

As the glaciers are made of compacted snow and ice, they cannot stay in that form at the new higher temperatures, so they spend more of their time melting during the year than building up again. This causes the glaciers' lower faces to melt and shrink back up the valleys.

Hence the glaciers, often tens of kilometres long, are shortening every year. What is the prognosis? Continuing at this rate, some glaciers may disappear completely very soon, some later on.

The snow coverings, whether for skiing or for scenic beauty, are also vulnerable to more rapid melting, thus shortening the sports season or making skiing and snowboarding impossible in the most vulnerable resorts, and again, this may affect others later on.

•◆•

The air quality in the Alps is generally very high. The more highly populated lower lands of Europe, as well as North America and the Far East, are not so fortunate. Large towns and cities create and harbour traffic fumes and heating emissions. These accumulate to such concentrations that the poor air quality gives rise to higher rates of asthma amongst the human population, affecting all age groups and increasing death rates as a result of the polluted air.

Surely this cannot be what modern living was designed to be … can it?

•◆•

Grandparents and great-grandparents will remember a number of summer holidays by the sea in their youth.

They will have photographs in black and white, holiday pictures at the seaside … deck chairs, pebble or sandy beaches, blue sky and sunshine, buckets and spades and ice creams. Some photos will show the cliff behind the beach; some will show the view out over the sea and the beach from the cliff top. All looking great.

However, the grandchildren and great-grandchildren will know what those places look like today. They will be very familiar with the current detail. Their parents will also be familiar and will verify those details.

"Grandad, that place doesn't look like that anymore. The beach huts have gone. That ice cream van can't park there anymore. That house at the top of the cliff in that picture isn't there anymore. In that picture, it's all pebbles now; the sand has been washed away. The sign in that picture which says 'Beware Dangerous Cliffs, Falling Rocks' isn't there anymore either. I wish I could have gone to those places when they looked like that, Grandad. Grandad, so much has changed. There's just a concrete, stone and rock protection thing there now."

There is not a lot that Grandad can say about this without a tear coming to his eye.

He knows that the sea level has been rising, causing more and faster coastal erosion.

•◆•

The whole world has been proud of the dreamy image of the never-ending jungle, swamps, lush greenery and wildlife species of the Amazonian rainforests. Their extent is virtually the northern third of the South

American continent and a huge portion of Brazil. It has been a self-perpetuating set of ecosystems and habitats for thousands of years. The natural beauty of all of the parts of Amazonia is beyond belief … it is spiritually stimulating, calming and satisfying, bringing about a feeling of peace and perpetuity. We feel we can always rely on the Amazonian rainforests – and rely on them we do, for producing a large proportion of the atmospheric oxygen that animals and plants breathe the world over. They are also a naturally created medium-term storage facility that has taken millions of tonnes of carbon dioxide out of the global atmosphere by the wonderful process of photosynthesis in all of its green plants and trees.

However, all is not well. Swathes of the forests have been cut down, in some cases for the resale value of the timber, in others for the value of the fresh workable land for growing crops for human consumption or for farming cattle or other herds.

The consequences of these mad actions speak for themselves to us now and for future generations. Another consequence of great concern is that global weather and climate patterns are also being affected.

Generations of indigenous Amazonian peoples also have tragic stories to tell about all of this.

•◆•

There are people around you today and elsewhere who lived in a world where newspapers were read by most people daily. Most people did not have a black and white television. Some had a thing called a telephone in their home; the rest had to walk up or down the road to the nearest telephone box to make a phone call. Mobile phones did not exist, computers did not exist, the internet did not exist, PC games did not exist, social media did not exist … but people were happy. They had less intense cares, and they had good quality mental health. Liking that.

•◆•

Another of the Earth's most reliable features for thousands of years has been the polar ice caps. Although these change seasonally in area, thickness, mass and shape, maximising in the winter and minimising in the summer, they are always there, providing a guaranteed anchor for the climate and also for Arctic and Antarctic wildlife. This would seem to be a reasonable and straightforward enough process. Of course it is.

What could possibly change? What could go wrong?

Well, surprisingly, shockingly and overwhelmingly … quite a lot, actually. No, I know, we didn't want to hear that.

What don't we want to hear?

That …

The melting rates of the polar ice caps have been increasing nearly all year round.

They have been melting faster in the early spring, in the longer, hotter weather of the summer and in the later autumn and winter.

The ice caps are melting more below, underneath the floating ice, as the sea water they are in contact with is warmer than it used to be.

Add to that the greater deposits of dust and soot particles from the atmosphere landing on the surface of the ice. These darken the colour of the normally gleaming white ice and snow.

The darker colour absorbs more heat from the sun than is normal; this speeds up the melting process still further.

The Arctic ice cap now gets smaller and smaller every year when comparing the measurements of its area in September year to year. Why does this matter?

One consequence is that there is less ice reflecting the sun's heat back into space, so the Earth warms even more quickly.

Another consequence is that the reduced area of ice provides less living area for Arctic mammals. They become stressed, and their ability to hunt and feed is reduced.

Another consequence is that the melted water from the ice cap is all fresh water – in other words, with no salt in it. Why does this matter? Because fresh water is less dense than salty sea water.

This melted ice water is also warmer than the cold sea water that it is entering. Why does this matter? Because warmer water is less dense than colder water.

Why does this matter? Because less dense fresh water, which is also warmer than the surrounding water, floats on top of the colder and more dense salty sea water.

Why does this matter? Okay, bear with me; we are getting there. Because there is a worldwide circulation of ocean waters, believe it or not. Part of this circulation is a lukewarm water current travelling north in the northern Atlantic, which cools in the Greenland and Arctic regions, turns south again and sinks, because it has now become colder and hence more dense. It flows under the north Atlantic as a cold deep-water current. This is good and normal? Yes, it is, but the ice cap meltwater is warm fresh water, and so floats even better.

Why does this matter? Nearly there ... because as it flows, floating south on the surface of the north Atlantic, it meets the North Atlantic Drift or Gulf Stream, floats above it, and thus sinks the end of the Gulf Stream. This has always travelled northeasterly on the surface, and thus it provides the British Isles, Scandinavia and northern Europe with a milder climate than would otherwise be the case at those latitudes.

Okay ... so why does this matter? Because if this does become established as a new regular flow pattern, it could curtail the normal flow of the warming – influence the North Atlantic Drift towards Europe ... and so? This would mean there would be a high risk of the British Isles, Scandinavia and Europe having a much colder climate, possibly all year round, than they have historically been used to.

And does this matter? Yes, it does, because agriculture and crops would be affected, travel would be affected, heating bills would be much greater and ... well, the residents wouldn't like it that way. It would probably be an irreversible change to our way of life, which would also have economic impacts ... and we don't need any more of those either.

How this pans out in practice will be even more complicated by the effects of the El Niño and La Niña phenomena. These are already known to have impacts right around the globe, not just in the eastern Pacific where they originate.

Ultimately, it is the drive of the jet streams and the polar vortices that will continue to initiate patterns of weather extremes.

"Okay, I catch your drift" ... if you'll pardon the pun.

This is, of course, a truly colossal impact.

Clearly this now makes it even more urgent to reduce carbon dioxide emissions in particular ... according to all sources, it is very, very urgent indeed.

For this to be comfortably achieved, there will need to be the maximum possible introduction of renewable energy sources for generating electricity and charging EVs.

Will that be all? Sorry, no – afraid not. Why? Because a background source of reliable and continuous electricity will also be required, to provide electricity when the wind doesn't blow and the sun doesn't shine.

Okay, so how can this be achieved? By urgently and rapidly building enough small nuclear reactors to provide electricity locally and building a few large nuclear reactors to provide network-wide electricity that the grid can rely on whatever the weather.

Luckily, Britain and the European Commission now treat nuclear energy generation as a qualifying method towards their net zero targets. Thank goodness for that; we might now be getting somewhere.

Okay, got it.

.◆.

"So, Finn, there is a hell of a lot to do to get this environment put right – so important for wherever we want to live."

"And to stop it getting even worse."

"And we've still got to find our place."

Finn and Bronagh simultaneously think to themselves, without saying anything to one another: *Using one's senses, feelings, emotions, observations, perceptions, spiritual directions and confirmations ... one has to feel, find and triangulate onto one's own location where you feel comfortable, happy and content ... and at that place, you feel a sense of warmth and energy working for you ... nothing against you. This is a place where you can always come to get that experience repeatedly – to be strengthened in every aspect of your life.*

After looking at maps to check places and experiences, and getting reports from other people, the long-term historical concept of these places forming an alignment inescapably appears.

Just as for alignments, any network formations are always worth investigating too ... by anyone, everyone, everywhere ... always.

"Finn, did you notice that in Ireland, when we were approaching Uisneach, we saw an increasing number of crows and jackdaws? Did that seem strange to you?"

"Yes, it did. I thought it unusual and a bit ominous – worrying, to be honest, for some reason."

"And then after that, we had a good time; actually, we had that unexpected guided tour surprise. Thinking about it, the crows and jackdaws preceded our visit there. When we were actually on that Irish major alignment centre ourselves, everything was okay."

"A good point – isn't that interesting! And then there was what happened while we were driving, shortly after leaving Uisneach ..."

After a pause, Bronagh, puzzled, asks, "What was that, Finn? I don't remember that. What happened?"

"Oh, ah, nothing really," says Finn hesitantly, anxious because he doesn't fully understand what happened to Bronagh at that point himself. How could he possibly remind Bronagh about it – something that she was not even aware of herself – and then try to explain it? Impossible; don't even start. Bronagh could have pushed him further on this point, but for some reason she didn't feel inspired to do so.

"And then there was that dreadful time we had trying to drive down through Devon and Cornwall! What was that all about? There was the forlorn-looking, misty Dartmoor and the near miss on the road and the breakdown … oh my Lordy days!"

"Yes … so is that a bit like what happened in Ireland? A kind of forewarning, only worse that time?"

PART 3

⁓ೱⓞⓞ⁓

People … places …
Revelations and connections …

The big plots, plans and
adventures into the unknown.

Chapter 36

⟡

Finn and Bronagh have made a wide network of friends during their UK-wide travels and experiences.

The new friend they met at Glastonbury Tor is American. An all-American wilderness adventurer and sporty type is Martha.

Martha has visited England a few times and loves the country and its culture and its history, which was how they happened to meet her at Glastonbury Tor. Neither Finn nor Bronagh had been to the USA, so they were interested to hear anything and everything that Martha had to say about her country. In particular, Martha talked of a characterful friend of hers from back home out west. Ezra had one life in towns and a city, and he worked many years in offices among their sales culture. He eventually had enough and moved himself lock, stock and barrel out into the hills, finding himself a little shack with views down a green valley to the snow-capped mountains beyond. This was tranquil, healthy and spiritually uplifting for Ezra. He tilled the soil at the back of the shack to grow all his own vegetables and salads plus a little fruit. This was exercise enough for his five feet ten inches and wide frame. His big rugged coat and beard, so bushy you could hardly see his face, were washed occasionally. Ezra's shack had an outside toilet but no flush; it did have a roof and windows … oh, and a door, but one with no lock. He also had a log fire indoors and a barbecue-cum-smoker outside. This was indeed Shangri-La. "Good job!" Ezra would frequently say when he was pleased about anything.

Martha met Ezra when she walked down from a mountain adventure into his valley and came across the shack.

It was a winter, so Martha did not know that the valley was normally green. She did not know that Ezra lived there, and she did not know where she was. After trudging all day through the deep snow and trying to get down off the mountain, and feeling painfully cold in her fingers, toes, ears and nose, Martha stumbled across the shack. She mustered enough energy to raise her arm and clench her fist to knock on the front door. Three knocks resonated sufficiently, and Martha didn't feel a thing. The latch clicked and the door creaked open. Martha could immediately feel on her face heat radiating from inside the shack.

"Nice to see visitors; we don't get many in these parts, especially at this time of year. Where you headed?"

Martha, clearly freezing, covered in snow and confused, replied, "Well, actually I know where I'd like to be headed, but I don't know where I am at the moment."

"Hey, you, come on in. I'll brew some hot coffee. That'll warm you up ... Would you like something to eat?" said Ezra welcomingly.

"That's most kind of you. I'd love that and need it right now," said Martha gladly.

"You're welcome."

Inside the shack was a log fire with a griddle and a pan of water by the side. Ezra moved the pan over the fire, set up two large mugs on the rustic log table and prepared the coffee. He put some muffins onto toasting forks.

Martha cast her eyes around the cosy shack and noticed the log-crafted furniture, the window shutters and a bed at one end. Curiously, she also spied a laptop on a handcrafted desk; this struck her as not quite fitting the rustic charm.

"How did you find me out here?" enquired Ezra.

"I noticed a wind turbine rotating against the backdrop of pine trees. I thought that must be a sign of life nearby," replied Martha.

"There sure is," responded Ezra, "and proud of it. We have all mod cons up here too!"

"I wasn't expecting to see a laptop up here; how do you run that?" Martha enquired with interest.

"Oh, I've run a cable up from the homesteader just below in the valley. The solar panel gets covered in snow and the wind doesn't always blow," replied Ezra with a chuckle.

"Ah, I see. That makes good sense," said Martha as she took the offered mug of piping hot fresh coffee and held a toasting fork and muffin close to the fire.

"Folks is helpful up here; we run errands and store stuff," said Ezra reassuringly.

"That's nice – and I guess the only way to survive comfortably?"

"Sure is. Hey, what's your name?"

"Martha," she replied. "I'm from Penn state. I'm up here on a winter hiking trip. I love it up here." She smiled, already warmed up some.

"I'm from Santa Monica. Worked for thirty-five years in the hustle; that was enough for me! Been up here near Mammoth for maybe near ten years now – I've lost count. Best place on Earth!" reflected Ezra. "Things have changed … changed a lot," he mused. A weary, dejected look appeared in his eyes and face and body language.

Martha felt concerned at this. "How so?"

Ezra paused, searching for words. "Well, I don't know about you, but I thinks there's a lot of awful things been going on in the US, and elsewhere, mind you, and it don't make me feel too good."

"What sort of things, Ezra?" said Martha.

"All this smoke and fumes down in the city makes me cough. The weather has been changing a lot … you know all about the forest fires, droughts? And all the other tragic situations … you don't need me to go through all of those none."

"Yes, I know, and I agree with you completely, Ezra. It's been bad, yes – it still is bad, and there isn't yet any evidence of anything improving. I sense you see it as probably getting worse too?"

"Yes I do, Martha. Everybody is still doing the same things that they have always done … still burning too much gas and oil, still using too much and wasting electricity, leaving lights on unnecessarily … it just goes on and on," said Ezra, getting more impassioned and intense.

"Not to mention the waste in shopping malls, streetlights, farming practices, plus the pollution of all kinds from waste to discharges into the rivers, lakes and oceans," added Martha. "Not a pretty picture at all."

"I've been thinking about this for some time. I think not enough people realise or even know about all this stuff going on … and nobody's tellin' 'em enough about it and what it's going to lead to," said Ezra.

"I agree with you entirely," replied Martha. "So what's to be done?"

"I've had plenty of time up here now and I've thought … I don't know. I feel I need to put my remaining time to good use. I want to give something back and try and do my bit to help. I don't know if it will be enough, but I might feel guilty if I don't do a damned thing, you know? So I been using my time up here to write a book … a book about all this stuff and tellin' folks what they need to do!" said Ezra, now nearing peak emotions.

"Oh, great. Good on you, Ezra! Is it out yet? Or when is it due out?"

"No, not yet. I can write okay, but I don't know owt about the world of publishing," said Ezra, deflated.

Up spoke Martha.

"Oh, I can help you with that! I have friends in the business back in Philly. I'm sure I can get them to sort publishing for you."

The title of Ezra's book was *How Did We Get Here? How Do We Get Out of Here?*

Martha contacted her Philadelphia friends and talked about the book enthusiastically. The response was the usual muted "Oh no, not another one!" Martha convinced them that this one was different; it could really get to people, provoke them into feeling uncomfortable and motivate them to get proactive.

It took a good while, but eventually they become sold on Martha's conviction and purpose. The publishers took it on and published it in the USA.

Thus scorning all the cares
That fate or fortune brings,
He makes the heaven his book,
His wisdom heavenly things,
Good thoughts his only friends,
His wealth a well-spent age,
The earth his sober inn
And quiet pilgrimage.

Thomas Campion, 1567–1620

Chapter 37

❦

Finn and Bronagh are really intrigued to hear all about this; it is a captivating story.

"So what is the message of the book that is so effective, then, Martha?" enquires Finn.

Martha takes a deep breath. "Okay, guys, you all ready for this? Okay, here I go …

"Everybody is talking about all this, okay? Our friend networks are all talking about these themes. There are environmental differences between every country of the world – none are the same, right? But people in, like, UK, Europe, Latin America and Brazil and the USA and Canada are all talking about their own country's features regarding weather pattern changes, climate change, extremes of temperature, wind and rainfall and so on.

"I mean, at our age, how are we supposed to form a new life plan, right? I mean, with all these things going on, there is no constancy out there anywhere. You know the older folk talk about the way of life that they knew, right? That all sounds so idyllic, right? But we don't have that anymore, okay … neither do they … It must be hard for them too … but even harder for us, cos we don't know anything about what future to expect! Sorry, guys, I just get so emotional about this, I can't handle it." She has a few tears on her cheeks.

"Yeah, okay, Martha, we get it, it's okay …" says a reassuring Bronagh. "It's all to do with the carbon dioxide emissions and levels and the other greenhouse gases bringing global warming and climate change, especially over the last thirty, forty years."

"Yes, of course," says Martha, who has now gathered herself, and she continues.

"So, regarding emissions targets, net zero targets, etc., what's the point? Some are trying hard, investing and developing as part of a culture of change, appearing to act for an independent culture and independent state for themselves, with autonomy and control … but of course this is *not* an individual country's issue; this is a globally connected issue, and we, the Earth, are all in this together whether we like it or not … which means that everyone everywhere around the world has to act on this together and all at the same time … and ongoing until the task is complete … and when is that? We don't know … but we will know when we have got somewhere, when it happens."

"No mean task; no small order," says Finn reflectively.

"So, Martha, what are the chances of this coordination coming together? And when?" enquires Bronagh.

"Actions have to be started and maintained … by governments, and by companies and organisations, *and* by all individual people in their daily actions, choices and mentality," answers Martha.

"How can this come about?" enquires Finn.

"By government advertising, company advertising, TV programmes to educate and to motivate … but by using the right language! By introducing action plans and incentive schemes for people to follow in their daily actions, choices and mentality. There should be the setting up of discussion, action and help groups.

This is the only chance there is to have the most liveable world for us and our children to grow up in." Martha is virtually spent – this is emotionally draining stuff.

"Ezra has definitely done a master plan and formed a template," says Finn.

"Yeah. I don't know how this could go down in Russia or in China, but it has to," says Bronagh.

"Oh yes, I have just remembered," continues Martha, "and a lot of the solutions for ridding the water and land of pollutants and ridding the tide of plastics are to be based as far as possible on 'natural process solutions'."

"We like the sound of that!" says Finn. "What is it?"

"For example, Finn, that's beavers! They are 'natural' and they do 'process'. In lots of places in many countries there is too much rainfall run-off – in other words, the rainfall runs off the land before it has a chance to soak into the soil and be used by plants, ecosystems and agriculture. That's a waste we can do without – we need that water. So, beavers gnaw through tree trunks, fell the trees, many of them, and create dams across streams. This is where beavers live, in the ponds and lakes behind the dams that they have created. Clever, aren't they? Don't you just love them! And so the water they have held back in their ponds soaks into the ground and makes a success of the local ecosystems – a solution instead of them suffering and risking dying off. It's a win–win situation, Finn."

"Thank you for that lovely explanation, Martha," says Finn with a glowing smile.

"Even in the USA the challenge will be in baseball and the 'good job!' – driving large gas-guzzling cars regularly over great distances and with big houses …

using high-consumption electrical devices, heating systems and entertainment ... all as 'rites'! 'This is the way we've always done it!' they will say ... forever, ongoing, the dream entitlement for all," adds Martha.

Finn ponders. "Yes, Martha, you are dead right. Things have come a long way from the native sacred sites and the plains full of bison, but at least the rights of the indigenous people have eventually been recognised."

"As have the rights of the First Nations, particularly in British Columbia, Canada," adds Bronagh. "Which reminds me, some of the prehistoric sites in Wiltshire are attributed to the Beaker People, as they found remains of their pottery, or beakers, there. The Beaker People first came from the Ukrainian steppes thousands of years ago!"

"And your point is?" enquires Finn.

"Oh, I was just thinking that that might mean they have some sort of alignment systems there too ... that was all," explains Bronagh.

"And that is a good point." Finn smiles. "And in Russia and in China? Does anyone know much about daily and cultural life there?" he asks. They look at him blankly. "Ahh, okay – I'll take that as a no, then ... More work to do, then!" They all smile.

Bronagh has been listening to it all very carefully and is motivated herself now to add, "Wow! I think this is something that we should get going and activated in England. Okay, I wonder how the book is selling, but it would be good to have it in UK bookshops as well as obviously online. How has it been received in the US, Martha?"

"Going quite well in bookshops, so I hear; the profile isn't yet high enough or wide enough for significant online sales yet," she replies.

Bronagh thinks. "Martha, do you think you could ask your contacts to get the book distributed in UK bookshops? All these things take a lot of time, and we haven't any more time to lose. What do you think?"

"Yes. I agree, time is of the essence, as they say, so yes, Bronagh, I will get onto it straight away," responds Martha positively … and she does act right away.

The book is distributed in UK bookshops as soon as it is available. Bronagh and Finn start to promote the book through their social media channels of Facebook, WhatsApp and Instagram; that is the least they feel they can do right now.

They noticed that while they were attempting to do this, they were getting computer or video glitches, send failures and frozen screens, which was a bit unusual and concerning. Eventually they did hear back from friends, and many actually purchased Ezra's book.

These buyers of the book also passed on their thanks to Bronagh and Finn for drawing their attention to the book; they expressed their concerns, particularly about climate change and water pollution. They all appeared to be very frustrated by the lack of action to correct these issues or prevent the impending consequences.

When discussing their friends' responses with Martha, Bronagh and Finn felt that they now wanted to do more about this initiative arising from Ezra's book. They decided that they should do as much as realistically possible by simply starting chats with friends, exchanging ideas and advice about how to move things along and encouraging their friends to do the same with their other friends.

•◆•

Martha travels between the USA and England several times a year. On her latest trip back to the USA, she travels over to Mammoth to see Ezra again. It is a summer visit this time, with glorious weather. There is more lush grass than usual due to the unusually heavy rain and snow of the last winter. The head of the valley is lime green against the clear blue sky and intensely bright sunshine at this altitude.

A variety of bright flowers are also in great abundance – every swathe of colour you can imagine from white through yellows and oranges to reds and purples. This is a transformed landscape to Martha, and it lifts her spirits a mile.

She knocks on the door, which quickly opens, as her approach has been spotted. Ezra opens his arms for a warm hug, encouraging a similar action from Martha, and they embrace in mutual fondness and appreciative greeting.

"Great to see you again, Martha. Thanks for dropping by; do come in; you're most welcome."

The coffee is brewing again and the toasting forks are out. At these altitudes it is not always hot in the summer if there is a strong northerly wind.

"I see you are getting plenty of free electricity today, Ezra!" observes Martha.

"The more the merrier," replies Ezra.

After chatting about life and the progress of the book sales in the US and in England, they arrive at a more concerning juncture. Ezra reports some facts and observations that have occurred in recent times.

"As if life wasn't tough enough sometimes anyway, there appears to be some resistance out there, both natural and some building resistance."

"What do you mean, Ezra? What resistance?" Martha shows concern.

"There are newspaper and media items where some of the oil companies especially, but also some politicians and some senators, are expressing concerns about the potential effects on the economy if the actions in the book are effected too quickly. They want the oil and gas revenues to continue strongly, and the politicians and senators want the taxes on the profit from those revenues."

"Oh dear. I see. That is awful. How short-sighted of these people! Hmmm, let me think ... but that is actually a good thing."

"How so?"

"Because it means that those oil companies and politicians will have to react to their objections by also demonstrating a positive way forward."

"Good point," says Ezra excitedly. "They will have to prove to the voters that they are listening to concerns and are putting alternative plans into action rapidly enough – with the emphasis on 'rapidly enough'!"

"Yes, okay, but will this take care of itself? I mean, will the EV manufacturers, the wind and solar farms and the hydrogen tech have enough clout yet to adequately respond? I mean with the introduction of alternative solutions in a fast enough response time?"

"Perhaps it might need a bit of fuelling or stoking, Martha. Like any good fire, you have to feed it, tend to it and even blow on it!" says Ezra colourfully.

"Nice one, Ez!" Martha smiles. "So that means through any friends and contacts in newspapers, TV studios and documentary makers, right?"

"Sure thing," replies Ezra.

"Great idea. Let's do it. Good job, Ezra!" says Martha with enthusiasm and a sense of humour. "But ... but ... but what about the money for all of this? Who is paying? And when?"

"Okay," says Ezra, "the website is cheap enough. I will pay for that and the SEO ... and perhaps use this 'Crown funding' thing for funding posters?"

"Okay ... there's a plan, Ezra," responds Martha with a big smile and a high-five.

They now need some fresh air, so they go for a walk, strolling up a gentle gradient along a path that leads towards a mountain pass. From there they get beautiful views of the spring and early summer foliage, some of which drapes over their path. They look across a stream in the valley towards a rugged rocky ridge ... breathtaking.

"Were you ever married, Ezra? And children?" Martha enquires quietly.

There is a pause before Ezra responds. "Yes, Martha, I was married once, for about twenty-five years while down in Santa Monica."

"And then ... separated?" asks Martha.

"Separated ... but by her lung cancer, which led to her death," says Ezra painfully. He stops and casts his eyes down to his feet.

"Oh! I am sorry, Ezra. I'm sorry because I didn't ask that very well and maybe shouldn't have done at all … I'm so sorry to hear that … what can I say?" pleads Martha.

A pause again, and Ezra looks up to the far hills. "Ahh … if only we had moved out of the city earlier … that might have prevented her from suffering cancer at all. It's hard."

"Now I understand why you moved here, Ezra … and why you had to write a book. That's two such good things you have done: your wife would have been – and probably is – so pleased," says Martha, putting her arm around his shoulder for meaning and reassurance.

Returning to the shack, they flesh out the timescales for their actions and the styles of working and presentation for both parts of the plan.

Martha also suggests that the same plan of action outlined for the USA might also be necessary for the UK. They agree, and Martha will speak with Bronagh and Finn about the replica plan for the UK on her next visit with them.

Sure enough, the same reactions from oil companies and politicians occur in the UK. Hence Martha's visit to the UK is very timely to initiate a website and crowdfunding there. Bronagh has funds to cover the website and SEO and offers this. She will also launch a UK crowdfunding project alongside Martha's US version.

Chapter 38

⚜

Of course, it is the crowdfunders who are exceptionally enthusiastic about Ezra's book and who are also active on the forum of the website. The website is drawing in its fair share of active respondents too.

Bronagh is webmaster for the site. As the list of crowdfunders builds up, she starts to notice some interesting and curious things. The donors have to give their actual addresses for money laundering purposes, and it appears that their locations fall into clusters. These clusters form patterns.

Bronagh also joins in with some of the forum discussion threads sometimes. After a while, she notices that some of these patterns appeared to configure with some of the UK alignments. *Curious*, she thinks to herself. *This is exciting!*

Meanwhile, back in the States, Ezra, sitting back, mulling and taking a view from the higher perspectives, kind of in a "Sage on the Hill" role, sees no reason why they shouldn't get the book translated, published and distributed in Russia and China. After all, they do form a crucial part of the whole big plan.

He gets in touch with Martha.

"Wow! All right! Yeah, key players in the game; they need to be in as soon as we can do it," agrees Martha.

She contacts Philly. They agree and put the international wheels in motion for Russia and China.

Bronagh thinks about her recent observations of the clusters and patterns. She thinks, *It's time to get out the Ordnance Survey maps, overlay those with tracing paper and plot some of the crowdfunders' addresses. To make it a fair analysis, I need to select a range of areas.*

She picks an East Devon OS map, another for South Hampshire, another for part of Gloucestershire, another for the South Lake District and one for South Derbyshire. It's a lot of work and there is only so much time in the day.

Meanwhile, back in the States, Philly are on the phone to Ezra. "Hi, Ezra. Following on from the initiative from you, via Martha, we have made approaches to our connections with Russian and Chinese publishing houses. Although their executives were understanding and enthusiastic about your book and its objectives, their regulators – read: the Chinese Communist Party representatives – were not enthusiastic. In fact, they have prohibited its publication. It is now on a banned list."

The line goes quiet. "Ezra, are you there?" Further silence.

Eventually Ezra summons a bit of courage to respond. "Does that mean I will be on a troublemakers' blacklist and treated as an extremist, ending up like … I don't know what?"

"No, Ezra; don't worry so much. No, it doesn't and shouldn't come to that at all! We haven't actually published your book there, and it is not a book about religion or any direct criticism of China, so don't worry, it will be okay," say the Philly publishers reassuringly.

"Oh, okay, then. I hear what you say," responds Ezra. "I know you are all doing your best, anyway, and thank you for the call."

"Our pleasure," winds up Philly.

Martha has heard the news too. She immediately calls Ezra. "Hi, Ezra. How's the weather up there?" she says, hoping to lighten the heavy situation.

"About as dark, misty and unrelenting as the Russia and China situation," responds Ezra, even though it was actually a blue sky and sunny with no clouds.

"Sad news about that, Ezra, but we have plenty of positive work to do and things to be getting on with elsewhere. I am sure Russia and China must be brought into it engagingly sometime soon." Martha tries to cheer Ezra up.

"I hope so, Martha. I do hope so."

Back in London, Bronagh has been looking at some of their forum threads on the website. She has been chatting with a wide range of crowdfunders, thanking them for joining and asking about their experiences of lobbying for or supporting environmental initiatives. Most have tried supporting something at some time but have frequently lost energy or enthusiasm, as little progress could be made or they came up against a brick wall. Most commented too that they could support this cause around Ezra's book and felt energised once again with a vision of becoming effective and achieving broader goals.

This is heartwarming stuff for sure! thought Bronagh. She discussed it with Finn and they both shared it on the phone with Martha and with Ezra, both of whom were moved on hearing this.

Bronagh and Finn felt energised too. They wanted to help support the feedback from the crowdfunders by taking it further, somehow, to another level, to gather pace, momentum and effectiveness. Above all, to achieve some concrete progress and milestones towards the net zero targets in practice and not just in theory, as is typically reported on the news. So, as it currently stood, they were getting good feedback and praise from the crowdfunders and on the forum; that is, from individuals. The press, as always, were, as to be expected, their sceptical selves, neither supporting the net zero cause outright nor completely deriding it, as they knew secretly too that substantial initiatives had to be started and progress achieved somehow in order to meet the targets in time.

Oil companies and industry were also on a sceptical footing, as they had to maximise profits for their shareholders, otherwise the financial systems that support us all might be impacted. They knew too, though, that they had to make more rapid steps than they would like for that reason – to progress positively and quickly towards fulfilling their net zero targets and objectives. The comments on news feeds from news corporations and from oil companies and industry were very antagonistic to the efforts and enthusiasm of the likes of the forum contributors and the message of Ezra's book generally.

The antagonism appeared to be gaining pace and building to such a pitch that the crowdfunders and forum members started to feel stigmatised and thought of as troublemakers, similar to Extinction Rebellion and Greenpeace members.

This was not good. This was not part of the plan at all. A subdued mood now pervaded the group's nucleus of members.

The book publishers were still resilient but were getting more stick than previously – but they were persevering, publishing in whatever countries they could. Actually, the most significant were India, Brazil and Saudi Arabia.

Where the group could be most effective was in their own country, England and the UK – and in rolling out their ideas in the USA, perhaps. You have to start somewhere and concentrate your efforts.

"This has become more difficult than we anticipated, but I am not giving up, are you?" enquired Bronagh of Martha and Finn.

"No, most certainly not!" they replied in unison.

Bronagh reported, "On the forum, some people are saying that they have got together in groups, small interest groups, to chat informally and discuss issues and ways forward … but when they tried to speak to the public or hand out leaflets or do lobbying, they are being 'surveyed' by what seems like undercover police, 'heavy agents' and news reporters."

"What?" exclaimed Finn and Martha. "That's outrageous and so unfair. Where is the free speech, the genuine support for net zero initiatives and government support for these?"

"I'm going to write to my MP," said Martha.

"No, don't do that!" interjected Bronagh.

"Why not, for Earth's sake?" asked Martha.

"Well, Martha, although that's a good idea in itself, I'm also thinking that that would draw more attention to our cause and to our forum members and any of their group. Then the negative impact might be stimulated further in the broader social context, and that might trigger greater and worse reactions … and we can't afford to have that happen," explained Bronagh.

"I see, Bronagh. You're right. So we're stuck in the swamp," said Martha, deflated.

Silence pervaded … but the cogs of their brains were whirring prolifically. After a while, and as Martha was a guest on a visit to Bronagh's flat in London, a can of Budweiser was deemed appropriate for each of them.

"Finn, would you do the honours?"

Bronagh offered what she had concluded from her whirring cogs.

"I think … I think … this might just work … if we are careful about it. The problem is that we are all now known, it seems, and are easy targets. So we will have to hide from them if we want to stay active. By hide, I don't mean literally go into hiding. That would serve nothing and would be impossible to operate within, and worse still, they could claim to have won. Now we must put on cloaks – wear cloaks like a cloaking device … become invisible or undetectable."

Finn and Martha were both stunned, eyes wide open, staring at Bronagh and wondering what was coming next. "And …?" said Martha expectantly.

"And," said Bronagh, "we must form a new identity, a cover identity – a name for only us to know that is a cover identity. The name can be openly used in public and it will have a 'front'."

"So, why does it have to be like that, then? How will that work?"

"Okay, if we carry on as we are, we will have to be too secretive for comfort. We will be making life more difficult for ourselves, and we risk ceasing to function. But if we come under this 'cover umbrella', then *we* will know and all our friends will know that it is us and our cause. Everyone else will think it's a normal estate agent and shops."

"Estate agent?"

"We don't intend to do any shifting of houses or that sort of thing."

"Oh."

"We will have pictures of houses, but they can mostly be 'Sale Agreed', 'Sold', so normal people shouldn't bother us. We can have addresses in several locations around England and the US as necessary."

"Oh," responded Martha eventually, "and what is the name to be? I sense you have probably thought of one already … and, equally importantly, how is this to be funded?"

"We can call it Place Finders Estate Agents."

"Really?" said Finn.

"Really," said Bronagh. "We can afford a little bit of funding from the crowdfunding resources for, say, five, perhaps – small shop fronts in out-of-the-way places that will not draw any unwanted attention. They can have volunteers in them occasionally, just to show that they are open and in use a bit. A back room can be used for forum members to gather, meet, chat, etc. and to feel a morale-boosting bit of identity. A few people coming and going occasionally will also generate a sense of legitimacy for any observers."

"Wow, Bronagh, you have given this some mighty thoughts; well done!" said Finn.

"Good job!" said Martha.

"And that's an ideal cover name," added Finn. "That's a clever fit!"

Chapter 39

❦

From here on they agree that everything must be by word of mouth between them only. They will also have to discreetly make contact with key forum members and crowdfunders to set up the estate agent fronts, again by word of mouth only and with people they know they can trust and rely on.

Martha suggests to Ezra that she could bring Finn and Bronagh to the US to visit him, to introduce them and to develop relationships and the cause. Ezra is very happy at that prospect, and so are Finn and Bronagh. This will be a big thing for both of them, but especially for Finn, who has never left the shores of Europe before. They will take a flight from Heathrow to Philadelphia, where Martha will pick up one of her family's cars, then drive them to the Mammoth area out west.

Martha figures that as they will have to drive there anyway, they might as well use the cross-country trip to give Finn and Bronagh some insight into the US. There are its ways of life to experience, and she plans to take the opportunity to meet with many folk on the way. The return trip will include stopping at her home near Binghamton, Pennsylvania, for a few days and visiting Camp Susquehannock, where she grew up. This is an area of beautiful hills and woodland lakes and rivers … a bit of a tonic for them all. The contrasts on this whole trip could not be greater. In addition, this route will allow them all to get over any remaining jet lag before they go to Mammoth and Ezra's shack.

Rather than go directly to Ezra's shack, which might be a bit of a shock to the system for Finn and Bronagh, Martha arranges for them to meet up with him first at a local bar just out of town, as it is his kind of haunt; he is well known there.

They pull up outside and park on the dirt car park.

"Yes," says Finn, "this does look local and rustic; the kind of place that attracts real characters, I should think."

"Right," says Bronagh. "Like a few others we saw on the way over."

Martha leads the way in. It has low, subdued lighting. There is a jukebox, a small stage for entertainers, a pool table, a regular bar and stools. There are the usual clusters of tables and chairs and, catching the eye of the newcomers, a stuffed bear, stuffed fox and others – an eagle, gopher, large trout and bison.

"Interesting," remarks Finn.

There are small groups of locals gathered here and there, and Martha sees Ezra immediately at the bar. They cheer, greet each other and embrace warmly. Introductions are made. They order a round of beers and settle at a table near the bar.

After a few minutes of introductory chit-chat, a loud voice interrupts their friendly bantering. "So this is what you're up to up there, cosy between the mountains in that little old shack of yours!"

They are all startled, and, looking round, they see three locals at a nearby table standing up and slowly walking over to them.

"Hi, dudes," says Ezra. "Why don't you pull up a chair? Let me introduce—" But he is cut off suddenly as the lead guy continues.

"We can see quite clearly, Ezra. You don't need to make up a story ... inviting these youngsters up to your shack. We wondered what you did up there all day on that internet connection of yers."

"What are you talking about?" says the perturbed Ezra.

"That filthy coat of yours, and that beard is too big for folks to see your face! Good cover, you dirty pervert!" says the man ... who lunges at Ezra with a knife.

Bronagh reacts like greased lightning, jumping up and grabbing the man's arm at the wrist. She rolls her arm outwards and upwards in a big circle. The attacker is flung into the air by this action, which spins his whole body over quickly. There is a gruesome crunching and cracking sound just before his body hits the ground with an almighty thump.

The sounds are those of the ulna and radius of the man's forearm – the arm with which he held the knife – crossing over each other and snapping under the strain. He is no longer able to continue his attack due to the amount of shock and pain he is experiencing, as well as being unable to hold a knife at all now. A second man takes over the attacking role. However, he too meets a similar fate. There are now two large, hefty men on the ground clutching their arms. There is screaming, shouting and a furore. Ezra, Finn and Martha run to the far corner of the bar to seek safety. The third man in the group sees the fate of his two colleagues and runs out of the bar at high speed, leaving his beer and plate of food on his table (most wasteful). The events obviously do not go unnoticed by the local sheriff, who, when off duty, is always seen wearing his Stetson, and with much swagger.

The sheriff, although he has seen all the action, is off duty. This is not a situation that would mix well with his usual swagger. His thoughts have already turned to the paperwork, his relationships with the town folks and with the law, and to an appropriate penalty – one that might also be endorsed by a jury.

The sheriff's assessment of the situation is that although Bronagh held the man by the wrist in the apparent act of a social handshake, it was the man himself who, with his own momentum, generated by himself … had actually broken his own arm.

Penalties? But for whom? The man will have to seek medical attention urgently and also pay for it himself, as he is unlikely to have his own health insurance. The sheriff finally concludes, in his own mind, that the financial cost will be the appropriate penalty for breaching the peace, for insulting townsfolk and for an act of aggression.

Yes, that would be totally appropriate and fitting … and so home now to bed, figures the sheriff.

The sheriff, as always, can be seen chewing on his chewing tobacco and spitting every two or three minutes into the spittoon – "ping!" This is a natural skillset of his as he swaggers around in his stetson, thinking that everybody is looking at him as the tough guy who takes care of all community incidents.

The third man, who so urgently hightails it out of there, does not stop to find out Bronagh's self-defence credentials.

"Where the heck did you learn to do that?" enquires Finn.

"When I was at university I joined the judo and karate clubs, which also taught safe and legal self-defence tricks," replies Bronagh.

"Very handy. I like that a lot!" Ezra smiles and pats her on the back.

The barman says, "Now yous all have a great evening, you hear? See you next week, Ezra."

Chapter 40

～◈◈◈～

News has eventually reached the Mammoth area that there is this guy who has written a book, which is popular and selling well. Even the President likes it! The author was even invited to the White House, and this was obviously extensively televised – a grand publicity coup for them both. The Mammoth locals see this and realise that the author of the book is none other than … yes …Ezra!

The mood at the bar is naturally one of great elation. There are drinks galore lined up on the bar for Ezra … more than he can cope with, so he gives them away to everyone, all and sundry. There is a massive celebration for this new local celebrity.

After the full swing has died down a little, a trio of guys sheepishly approach Ezra.

"Hey, Ezra, saw you on the television news … couldn't mistake you … with that beard and all!" They all chuckle and laugh. "We'd like to say that we are sorry for that bad treatment we gave you the other day. We'd like to apologise. Obviously we can't shake your hand" – there are loud roars of laughter throughout the bar – "what with bein' in this cast an all."

Ezra responds, "Apology accepted … just buy a few copies of the book!" Again rapturous applause and laughter engulfs the bar.

Mention of the word "cast" has reminded Ezra of his plan to take Finn out fishing. "Hey, Finn, how do you

fancy coming out with me to do some fly fishing …
pick up some fat trout? It's a good time right now."

"Wow! That would be absolutely amazing. I'd love
to do that – can't think of anything more perfect!"
responds Finn with obvious delight.

"Well, that's sorted, then. The day after
tomorrow … over to Green River and we'll be on the
mayfly!"

Urgent packing ensues as well as sorting provisions,
tent and equipment.

Their car journey is through rugged, beautiful
mountain terrain, which also means winding roads.
Green River is in a deep valley, a wide river in a series
of riffles, glides, eddies and pools. They park up and
walk down the side of the valley on a narrow path
cutting through chalk and limestone strata – this river
is a type of chalk stream.

The arduous walk is well worth it. Even looking at and
absorbing the beauty of the views and nature gives a deep
sense of peace and tranquillity. It also puts one in awe of the
grandiose size and extent of the wild natural environment
and the delicate balance that the natural world has to live
in. It suddenly, too, raises our responsibilities to the top of
one's conscience … and consciousness.

Ezra and Finn see that the river is at a good level for
fishing, with a steady flow rate. The water looks clear
and fresh, with a slight brownish tinge signifying recent
showers or rain in the hills; this is good, as it means the
water will be fresh and oxygenated and therefore the
fish will be active and not dour.

There is a warm and gentle northwesterly breeze,
which creates a slight ripple on the slower-flowing

pools, and where there are small trees, dappled shadows flutter through the clear water on the bronze and copper river bed stones below.

Outlines of a few substantial-looking trout, like dark streamlined mini torpedoes, are slowly waving their bodies and tails to maintain their position in the flowing water. High above, against the blue sky, circle the clear, graceful shapes of eagles, their wings spread, climbing high on the thermals below small cumulus clouds.

As midday approaches, unmistakable large creamy mayfly, like small light aircraft, enliven the beautifully natural and active scene. They break the surface from below, escaping their water-born life from eggs in the river bed to nymph stage, wriggling up through the water and emerging as adult mayfly at the surface to shake themselves, spread their delicate wings and fly off to find a mate ... before they die within the day.

Oh! A trout has been watching carefully, patiently waiting for his own clear view from below. He swiftly glides effortlessly up towards the glistening mirror of the surface, with a slowly opening mouth, towards the struggling mayfly ... which is nonchalantly engulfed. A set of ripples spreading out on the water's surface is the only evidence of this event.

The trout are used to this; they expect it. Such events recur with increasing frequency as the day moves on.

Ezra is used to this and expects it too. He shows Finn how to assemble his own fly rod kit ... fitting the reel, threading the fly line through the rings, tying on the leader line, and then the intricate knot to tie on the artificial mayfly. The fly is a fishing hook decorated with a woolly brown-and-white-striped body, with feathery hackles to simulate the legs and small bunches of deer hair or white feathers to simulate the wings. It is then moistened with floatant to make it float on the river surface.

The most skilful of all activities now has to be mastered – casting the line and fly out over the river for perhaps ten, twenty or thirty yards, and in such a way that they land delicately on the surface without making a splash.

Ezra demonstrates. Finn watches like a hawk, taking in every action, tweak and nuance. They both watch the artificial mayfly bobbing and floating downstream in the river current. It travels yards for what to them seems like an eternity. Then … they see the head of a trout gradually appearing in the water underneath their fly. Over the next few seconds it becomes clearer and sharper. The anticipation and excitement is incredible … will it take? Or won't it? Then suddenly there is a small splash at the surface. Their fly is no longer visible; it has been engulfed by the open mouth of the trout. Within milliseconds the trout has closed its mouth around the morsel of their fly and turned down in the water. Ezra tightens the line and lifts the rod all in one action. The rod bends and shudders; there is a commotion out in the river and the line is a tight, straight connection between Ezra's rod and the fish. The fish has other ideas and heads downstream under the water.

Ezra lets it make this run so that the line doesn't snap under too much pressure, but he keeps in touch with it as it does so.

There is more commotion in the water and shudders of the rod and line.

Ezra concludes, "I think this is a very decent fish, Finn ..." He is having to use a lot of muscle strength and energy to play this fish.

Finn adds, "Wow! This is so spectacular and exciting!"

Eventually the fish tires more than Ezra and is brought gradually, bit by bit, to the net ... the landing net, which Finn holds out by its long handle into the water and scoops under the fish, lifting it from the water in one action.

Finn places it carefully on the bank behind them and they gaze at this fantastically beautiful creation of nature. It is glistening in the sunlight, big dark black-and-red-spotted patterns over its body on a golden bronze and copper-coloured background. They measure it quickly; it is twenty-four inches long. They unhook it and carefully place it back in the well-oxygenated river water for it to revive and swim away to live the rest of its lifetime.

"Phew and wow!" exclaims Ezra. "That was exhilarating! Now it's your turn, Finn." He smiles at Finn.

Finn sets himself up in exactly the same way as Ezra did, only about ten yards further upstream. He does some practice casts. Ezra gives a bit of coaching, some tips, advice and tweaks, and his casting and distance improve.

Time for Finn to cast into the likely piece of water where trout have been seen rising and there are still mayfly around.

He makes two or three casts and drifts, but nothing happens, so he recasts again.

An almighty splash means there has been a keen taker of Finn's artificial fly.

Ezra calls, "Pause … and lift," which Finn does … and he is into a good fish.

This one heads off downstream. Finn keeps some tension on it but lets it run as advised. Two or three more runs follow, but the trout is then brought back to a landing and netting point. A twenty-inch trout is landed … Finn celebrates and the fish is returned to live the rest of its lifetime.

After catching two more fish each, they decide to call it a day and cook up some food – a decent meal on an impromptu campfire: beans, hash browns, eggs, ham … oh, and some salad on the side and a beer.

"You know, Finn, this is a beautiful and perfect environment here, yes?"

"Sure is," says Finn.

"But what if I tell you that there aren't half as many fish here as there used to be … and there used to be clouds of mayfly flying around and masses of them landed, spent, on the water by the end of the day … and obviously the trout were just swimming around hoovering them up?"

"Ah, I see … so what's been going on, then?"

Ezra sighs. "Well, as I see it, Finn, there are several conspiring issues …

"Firstly, the rainfall patterns and amounts and the snowfall in the mountains have become inconsistent. Secondly, there have been increasing heat extremes – you know, extended lengths of high springtime and summertime heat … and thirdly, there has been a loss of forest areas, i.e. logging, forest fires and not enough replanting, so any rain runs off and away too quickly, hence the delicate systems to maintain insect life and fish life have been lost.

"There are also the impacts of the other thing that destroys forested areas – the forest fires, following the now-regular wide and long-lasting droughts in most parts of the USA and now even Canada. Great swathes of orange smog linger and drift en masse across state and even country borders to distant latitudes."

"Oh dear, sorry to hear that. That's not at all good. I am only realising now, or rather over the last few years, the serious extent and impact of all this stuff. It's just mad, Ezra; I hate it! And let's not forget, we haven't had an El Niño for a few years now. There will be one due very shortly. That will inflame the temperatures, droughts and floods, etc. even more."

"Me too, Finn, me too … So you can see now why, obviously, I had to write the book. I couldn't just sit around and do nothing… I had to do something."

"Yeah, I know …" And they both reflect.

Finn breaks the silence. "And it's the same causes at the heart of everything; I mean here, there, everywhere … the same troubles with rainfall, heat … you name it … the same causes behind them all, and caused everywhere in every country, near enough, around the world. And so the solutions have got to be the same everywhere."

"Exactly. Hey, I think we should get our heads down now and get some sleep."

Oh, there are so many nighttime sounds in this quiet, silent wilderness … crickets and cicadas leg scratching, owls hooting, bats' wings fluttering, moths' wings fluttering. The view of the night sky is faultless out here … the bright stars, faint stars, galaxies, nebulae, planets, the Milky Way … The moon is not up yet, just a faint glow in the western sky from the set sun … and zero light pollution.

Chapter 41

⌒◯⌒

Dawn brings the smell of freshly cooked ham, eggs, beans, hash browns …

… and the smell of fresh coffee. "Here you are, Finn. This is what we always cook out here on these trips. We never get tired of it!" They both smile. "Anyway, after sleeping on it, it's also worth thinking on the positives that are out there. I mean, the generation and delivery of electrical power needs to be consistent. So that clearly means you need two themes going on.

"One, you need generation of 'green', low-carbon power, like solar and wind power. Two, you need generation from a consistent and reliable source like nuclear power stations.

"With one, you will also need sufficient means to store a lot of the electricity generated by the sun as it shines and the wind as it blows. Nighttime and windless days need to be covered by stored electricity or nuclear-sourced power.

"You don't need to have great big giant nuclear power stations … the newer advanced small-scale nuclear units, dotted around more frequently, will do the job more cheaply and easily.

"And for the storage systems, you need vanadium battery units in large banks here and there near the solar and wind sites or the urban usage centres."

"Gotcha!" responds Finn. "So there is an awful lot of construction to do for all of that, as well as for

226

electrical distribution and charging points for electric vehicles."

"Exactly so – oh, and hydrogen needs to be brought into the equation, if you'll pardon the pun!" They both smile.

There is a wave of enthusiasm here comparable to that generated by Holst's *The Planets* suite … the Joybringer, Jupiter … "I vow to thee my country …"

"Ezra, I gotta say that friends back in England all feel the same about the things we have been discussing now. After being brought up at home and school, where the outlook for our future was positive and rosy … I mean, that's what parents and teachers have to do, right?"

"Yes, of course they do, Finn … of course they do."

Finn continues. "So then these young people get jobs, look for incomes to buy and support a home and family, maybe look to move house to a better area, etc, etc., plan ahead for a nice holiday or two. But then they realise that things are not turning out as they expected or were led to believe. There are now regular spells of scorching temperatures that ruin their gardens and the country parks. Parched landscapes lead to fire risks and forest and brush fires … which also risk burning homes and communities. Crop production is disastrously affected. Similarly, new rainfall patterns lead to more flooding incidents but also lead to droughts – which are even worse, of course, if associated with the excess heat patterns. And then they easily project forward that things could become even worse for their children and so on.

"They are not happy bunnies, Ezra, not at all."

"I completely understand, really I do. There is a very big hefty burden being carried by everyone everywhere, and I fear it is going to have to be carried for quite a while too.

"The droughts, sometimes worsened further by an El Niño, cut the productivity of wheat, corn and oilseed crops. Some of these are also used to make ethanol for mixing into vehicle fuel to reduce its carbon footprint. Less corn etc. means potentially less ethanol, which then means less fuel mixing and less carbon reduction.

"Things are not going to change quickly and sure enough not overnight. All the infrastructure we spoke about will take a lot of money and time to build … but, as you know, I do believe it can be done – it is actually within our means. There is also the magic of science and its unexpected discoveries and new inventions or new ways to do things. Look how quickly the vaccines for Covid were developed and then introduced successfully for most. Many say it was a miracle."

"Very true, Ezra. On another tack, what do you make of the Just Stop Oil protesters and Extinction Rebellion?"

"Well, they are all driven by a good purpose and have a strong message. I get the impression they are mainly younger student types and some older people at the end of their tether with frustration at the lack of progress following the rhetoric by 'the great and the good'. Are they having a positive or a negative impact on their cause? I think the jury is still out on that one.

"But I can tell you of one organisation that has had a long-term and positive lasting effect impact, and that is Greenpeace. They've been going for years, are very effective, have a strong impact, and governments and business have found they have to take notice of them, listen and act. They are high profile and are at the forefront of being in tune with the latest messages and geographical locations that need urgent attention and action. I am strongly in favour of them."

"Thanks for that, Ezra. Okay, I will see if I can encourage more people with that message ... thanks very much, mate!" They smile, hug and make their departure back up the river valley, trekking back to the car and then driving along the panoramic mountain route from whence they came.

While the boys have been away, this has given the girls a perfect chance to relax, chat and chill a little.

Chapter 42

❦

"So, you're telling me that Glastonbury Tor, where we met and you were talking about your friend Edmund, is exactly on, geographically and geometrically, a straight line lined up with monuments of different eras?"

"Yes, exactly."

"Well, I don't get it. How can that be so? Seems kinda weird!"

"Yes, it does seem a bit strange and also incredible, but that is the way it is. And, Martha, there are lots of other lines like this across England, and in other countries too. Staggering, isn't it? Finn and I call them 'alignments'."

"Martha, I have a confession to make to you."

"Really? You surprise me, Bronagh. What's that all about? I am intrigued!"

"Do you remember when we met on Glastonbury Tor and you heard us talking about Edmund? Well, obviously you do!"

"Yes, of course I do, stupid!" They laugh and fall about, taking any potential tension away from the moment.

"Well, Edmund was a name we made up for an imaginary character we had been discussing who lived in the Somerset Levels in the Bronze Age, more than two thousand years ago."

"Oh, Bronagh! That's amazing! But I love you for it!" And they laugh and hug each other briefly. "Well, whatever next?" exclaims Martha with a sigh.

"Martha, what do you make of this? I have a friend who lives in Hampshire, in the south of England. When he was in his student days, he bought a book from the university bookshop in Liverpool."

"Okay."

"Now, normally, when you buy a book, you excitedly open it and read it as soon as you get home, right?"

"Right."

"Well, this guy didn't. Now, believe it or not, Martha, and this is a true story ..."

"Okay," Martha settles further and more comfortably into her chair, anticipating a build-up and then something special to this story.

"He took the book from place to place with him whenever he moved house and didn't open it for forty-five years!"

"Oh my God! Wow! That's incredible! I wonder why not? For goodness sake."

"He did eventually open it, but at a significant point in time in his life – when he needed both comfort and inspiration, you know. It was a deeply personal thing, right?"

"Right."

"So he opened it after all that time. The book was *The Imitation of Christ*, by Thomas à Kempis. It was a written as a result of Kempis's life and affiliation with the Brethren of the Common Good, a movement in fourteenth-century Europe."

"Wow! Fourteenth-century!"

"Yes. This book became a very significant and prominent force in the adoption of, establishment and strengthening of Christian beliefs and the movement of Christianity in Europe at that time."

"That's incredible. I wonder why he hadn't opened it before? And carried it around with him all that time?"

"I guess he must have known or suspected that there was something special about the book which was waiting for him, and that he shouldn't open it until it was the right time. You know, a special or key right time for him."

"Yes, I get that."

"So he read it and then used the book avidly. It proved very beneficial and useful for his exact needs at that time."

"That's amazing. So, Bronagh, what's the book all about, then? Why and how was it so important in the fourteenth century? And why now, for your friend?"

"Good point, Martha. The book is written as a dialogue between the reader, whoever that is, and God. It gives structure and guidance to thinking and to communications between the two. It makes the whole job quicker and more effective. It is therefore easier to obtain answers to prayers and to achieve good guidance."

"Oh, I see – that's very interesting," ponders Martha. "Even to non-believers and to those who may be struggling."

"And then, Martha, a couple of months after that, he went on holiday to San Francisco, staying with friends in a spacious house on top of the steep hill there."

"I can picture exactly where that is! Overlooking Alcatraz, Fisherman's Wharf and the Bay bridges."

"A feature of this house was that it has a lounge or living room the size of an aircraft hangar! No, really –

it is about fifteen to twenty feet high, about thirty feet long, and a similar width. Along the whole of one wall is a bookcase, but this bookcase takes up the whole wall, both side to side and top to bottom. There are shelves of books going all the way across and from floor to ceiling. So there are naturally thousands of books there."

Martha is stunned, "How can anyone look at or use all those books or remember where to find a particular one?"

"No idea. Martha, for what I am about to tell you, I think you need to hold on to your seat. I think this is the spookiest thing in the world I have ever come across," says Bronagh, now with a very serious look on her face as she puts her hand on Martha's forearm for reassurance. Martha's Adam's apple visibly moves as she swallows audibly. She goes still and silent, preparing herself for what is coming next.

"After a few days there, my friend thought that he ought, given the privilege of being confronted with such a magnitude of books, have a little browse to see if he could find something that would interest him. This he did. Only after about a couple of minutes, his eyes and interest fell upon one tiny and rather inconspicuous little book. It looked quite old, by its lack of a cover and fairly tatty-looking state. It was only about five inches tall and four inches wide, and with less than one hundred pages.

"He carefully retrieved the book from between its more giant fellows.

"He was captivated by the title, which he read over a couple of times, just in order for it to sink in. The title was … *The Seven Miracles of Gubbio and the Eighth*.

"Open-mouthed and gobsmacked, as we both are now, he gently thumbed through it.

"It dated from around 1930-ish. Firstly, Gubbio is actually a small town in Italy. Secondly, the book is actually about a set of miracles to do with things that happened there.

"But thirdly, and most intriguingly, on the first page of the first chapter were some header quotes. He read the second quote. He had to read it several times to believe what he was seeing.

"The quote was actually a paragraph from *The Imitation of Christ*."

"You mean the same book he had carried around for forty-five years and had only just read a couple of months before?"

"Yes, Martha, that's exactly it!"

"If that's true, that's too incredible for words."

"How about this – it was actually witnessed by three people, and there is photographic evidence."

"I don't know what to say. I am perplexed, overcome and incredulous."

"Me too, when I heard it. I think it's amazing. You know, Martha, I wish I had come across that book myself years ago. The accounts at Gubbio are about a wolf problem they had there, attacking their herds of goats and sheep at night. A bad wolf was tempted, and it was negotiated with to become a better wolf by St Francis of Assisi."

"How amazing. Phew! Shall we have some coffee? I need it after all that!"

"Yes, please – great idea, Martha."

A fresh brew of coffee is made on the stove. Martha spends a bit of time searching, surfing on the internet.

"Bronagh, I've just been looking into this name 'Edmund' of yours. It is actually quite curious."

"How so?"

"It turns out that Edmund is actually the name of King Edmund, who became St Edmund, the patron saint of England! He lived and worked in an abbey at … wait for it … Bury St Edmunds. He was buried at the abbey there, but his bones were relocated with the dissolution of the monasteries by Henry VIII in 1539."

"Thank you for that, Martha, I didn't know that. How curious."

"How about this? Francis of Assisi is the patron saint of Italy, nonetheless. He founded Franciscan monk orders. He was a mystic and a Catholic friar. He was one of the most venerated figures in Christianity! He was canonised by Pope Gregory IX in 1228 AD.

"Oh my goodness, Bronagh! He is the patron saint of … this is incredible … of ecologists!"

"What? You are kidding me!"

"No, I am not, Bronagh – the patron saint of ecologists! There you are; have a look for yourself."

"Oh my God! We have now confirmed a direct link of this with the environmental issues and Ezra's book. How really incredible. Martha, are you able to go back in and tell me more about Edmund, please?"

"Sure.

"Edmund's shrine at the Abbey of St Edmund was once one of the most famous and wealthy pilgrimage sites in England. St Edmund ruled East Anglia from 855 to 869 AD and was most likely crowned on Christmas Day. Renowned as a brave king, he was eventually killed by Danish raiders on November 20th, 869, after refusing to denounce his Christianity.

"A wolf is a central figure of his story, which goes that after being tied to a tree and shot full of arrows, Edmund was then beheaded. The king's body was found but his head was missing.

"His supporters heard a wolf call to them and they found him guarding the king's head, which was then reunited with his body, and body and head fused back together. This was the first of many miracles."

"Martha, wow ... this is stunning! Look how these accounts of Edmund and Francis of Assisi and the wolf and the San Francisco events with the two books are tied together."

"Yes, I know. Incredible, isn't it?"

"Well, after all that, I'd better ask the same question again. Martha, can you please tell us a bit more about Francis of Assisi, then?"

"Sure.

"Francis was travelling with some companions. They happened upon a place in the road where birds filled the trees on either side. Francis told his companions to 'wait for me while I go to preach to my sisters – the birds'. The birds surrounded him, intrigued by the power of his voice, and not one of them flew away. He is often portrayed with a bird, typically in his hand."

"So that firmly establishes the ecology and environment link and also, amazingly, with birds!"

"Yes, but wait for this ...

"Another legend tells that in the city of Gubbio, where Francis lived for some time, was a wolf – terrifying and ferocious, who devoured men as well as animals. Francis went up into the hills, and when he found the wolf, he made the sign of the cross and commanded the wolf to come to him and hurt no one. Then Francis led the wolf into the town and, surrounded by startled citizens, made a pact between them and the wolf. Because the wolf had 'done evil out of hunger', the townsfolk were to feed the wolf regularly. In return, the wolf would no longer prey upon them or their flocks. In this manner Gubbio was freed from the menace of the predator.

"On 29 November 1979, Pope John Paul II declared Francis the patron saint of ecology."

"Unbelievable!"

"Quite! I thought we already had it tied up, but we now have even more affirmations. But wait …

"During the last years of his relatively short life – he died at forty-four – Francis was half blind and seriously ill. Two years before his death, he received the stigmata – the real and painful wounds of Christ in his hands, feet and side. Brother Leo, who had been with Francis at the time, left a clear and simple account of the event – the first definite account of the phenomenon of stigmata. 'Suddenly he saw a vision of a seraph, a six-winged angel on a cross. This angel gave him the gift of the five wounds of Christ.'

"On his deathbed, Francis said over and over again the last addition to his Canticle of the Sun, 'Be praised, O Lord, for our Sister Death.' He sang Psalm 141, and at the end he asked his superior's permission to have his clothes removed when the last hour came in order that he could expire lying naked on the earth, in imitation of his Lord."

"Oh my! Martha, those last few words are the same as saying 'the imitation of Christ'!"

"You're right, it is, Bronagh! The same as the title of your friend's original book."

"Phew! I think I will need to take some time to stew on all of this."

"Me too."

"But, Bronagh, there is something more. Are you ready for this?"

"Yeah, okay then. Go on."

"The abbey of St Edmund is in Bury St Edmunds – which is actually on your St Michael's alignment!"

"Oh no!"

"But wait for it …" Martha freezes as she makes a final observation. "St Edmund's final resting place is unknown."

After some quiet pensive relaxing and just looking out of the window to reflect on these amazing links, Bronagh has thought of something else she has been meaning to share with Martha.

"Martha, there is something I want to say, or rather need to say. I haven't said this to anyone else, but I have a fear in my mind. As you know, Finn and I have had some strange and sometimes scary experiences during some of our travels in Ireland and the West Country."

"You mean when you were approaching certain places like Uisneach and some places on the St Michael's alignment?"

"Yes, exactly those. Well, it's the other line, the St Michael's Line, the one that runs from Skellig Michael off Ireland through St Michael's Mount, through Mont-Saint-Michel in France and down through Italy and Greece, ending at Mount Carmel in Israel."

"And so what are you thinking, Bronagh?"

"All of this activity has been at the northwest end of the line. I don't think all the activity is necessarily going to be based there. I am concerned and sense that something may unfold at the southeast end of the line,"

"You mean in Israel. I see. That is scary, and I see why you are concerned. That could be very serious in lots of ways. I don't even like to think about that, Bronagh."

A crack of thunder bursts in the sky above the shack. The two women scream with shock. A deluge of rain and hailstones deafens them both with its incessant drumming on the shack roof. Drips of water run down the window panes. The expected blinding flashes of lightning appear on cue.

The women remain silent, alarmed by the suddenness of it all.

Meanwhile, high above, unseen, in the spiritual realms and above the eastern Mediterranean Sea, there is a standoff. There are two participants: one is Satan and the other is St Michael. They are avoiding a threatened skirmish by both respectfully standing off from one another, as if they are thinking about and anticipating a dialogue of some kind. That is as far as it goes – for now.

What will become of it? No one knows, for the moment.

St Michael has been taxing his brain and has come up with, "Now is not yet the right time for that dialogue – but it is desperately needed, and soon."

"Yes, agreed."

"On second thoughts, it is now time for us to talk and negotiate. If we don't do it now, it will never happen – so it must happen, and now."

Chapter 43

cᏉᏂᏋᎧᏉ

Back at Ezra's shack, the girls have been getting packed and ready for the drive back to Pennsylvania. But they were ready a while ago, so a little baking has made a tasty filling for the spare time. The tired and exhausted boys open the front door to the shack and are confronted by a warm waft of air laden with the appetising and mouth-watering smell of pastry crust on just-baked fruit pies and meat pies and the yeasty smell of fresh wholemeal bread and finally a sweet tinge to the aroma from blueberry muffins.

"Oh my, where have we landed? Is this heaven?" Ezra applauds.

"Of course it is. Where did you think it was?" Martha smiles.

The addition of fresh-brewed coffee completes the perfect culinary experience, and, of course, all are trying it, slavering over and gorging on the feast. With these sorts of things and the primal baking smells, one cannot stop.

"Shouldn't we be saving much of this for our road trip?" Finn sensibly intervenes.

"Finn, you're such a spoilsport!" says Ezra. "We've just driven back from a great trek and you want to stop me from eating this gourmet food? And what about me, anyway? Am I going on the road trip?" They all laugh. The three stop eating but allow Ezra to continue enjoying the food.

Early next morning they load the car, say goodbye to Ezra and start off down the winding dirt track to eventually join the main road ... and then the long haul, but with driver changeovers, naturally.

Having good food and water on board certainly makes a difference, and it speeds up their journey time across the fabulous expanse of the Rocky Mountains and the USA.

They enjoy overnight stops at Colorado Springs and Kansas City, where they change cars for a more spacious manual and automatic version, and then head for Pittsburgh. There are a lot of Harley Davidson motorcycles around, which makes it colourful, and also large trucks, which are often equally colourful.

As they pass Cincinnati, Martha notices something in her rearview mirror.

A car with slightly darkened windows has been spotted, and this is confirmed by Bronagh. She quickly says, "Keep looking ahead, guys. I don't know who they are, but they are definitely keeping a measured distance behind us." Martha speeds up a little ... their followers speed up a little.

Finn observes, "Looks like they are changing lanes occasionally so as not to make themselves obvious."

This cat-and-mouse activity keeps going for quite a way.

"It does look as if we are under surveillance. Not good ... but why?" wonders Martha. Flying past Pittsburgh, although they had originally planned to stop there, they head for Scranton.

"Okay, I've no idea what this is all about, but I don't like it. Instead of going to Binghamton and then the house by Camp Susquehannock, which might be just what they want and what they expect, I think I should head for some back roads I know in the Catskill Mountains near here. I think there is a good chance I can lose them there."

"Good thinking, Martha; we like it!" the others say.

Moving through the gears instead of on automatic, Martha is able to make fast progress along the winding lower mountain roads. They are still being tailed at a distance. Martha speeds up considerably; there is much tyre noise on the sharper bends and the passengers are forced from side to side. Things are getting bumpy and uncomfortable too. Their tail has to get closer to stay within sight due to the more winding roads. Martha deliberately drives close to the side of the road in order to catch dust and stones with her tyres and throw this debris up into the windscreen of their pursuers. She says, "Hold on, guys, things will get more hairy … just warning! Hold on tight!"

She pulls off the tarmacked road onto a dirt track; billowing clouds of dust and stones now follow them permanently.

Finn says, "Can't see a thing out the back now."

"That's the idea," reports Martha confidently. "And they can't see us."

The car sometimes crashes down onto its suspension over the lumps and bumps in the track. Still at a rate of knots, Martha turns off onto a forest track, accelerating on the smoother, straighter sections before returning to the billowing dust cloud technique again.

Finn muses, "They must want us real bad for something … but what?"

Hiding by doing a handbrake turn down a side track, they wait with the windows down and engine off for a minute or two. There is nothing coming; all is silent out there.

"Martha, I think maybe you have lost them," hopes Bronagh.

"Don't count your chickens," responds Martha as the car creeps slowly back out onto the track. The dust clouds have settled or blown away. Still moving slowly so as not to throw up any more dust, they are all on a tense lookout. All appears to be well.

Suddenly a screaming engine noise is heard and its source appears out of a side track. Martha puts her foot to the floor. Their own engine screams. Stones and dust fly everywhere, and they are off again.

"Don't say 'no rest for the wicked', Finn; we are not wicked!" says Bronagh, which brings much-needed light relief and a giggle from them all in this potentially dangerous situation.

The billowing clouds of dust are recreated and Martha carves out her trail of deception, cunning and guile. Just to make it interesting, the light is now beginning fade; it's the end of the day, but they cannot afford to put their headlights on and give their position away. This does, of course, make for even more exciting driving challenges, not just for Martha but for them all.

"You certainly get your money's worth on a USA trip, don't you?" quips Finn.

A huge logging truck appears over the brow of a hill, horn screaming. Dazzled by its headlights, Martha swerves to avoid it, which takes two wheels into long grass and a ditch before she steers them back on track.

"Shut up, Finn! you nearly got us killed!" retorts Bronagh.

"Me?" queries Finn. "Whatever ..."

From out of nowhere, a pickup truck is driving at speed alongside them. They wind down their windows. There are three young lads looking at them and laughing. "Hey, this is great. You are mad drivers! What a buzz! Do you do this every week?" One of the three seeks information as well as winding them up.

"No, we are being followed – no, chased ... get out of the way! You could get killed!" warns Martha urgently.

"No way! You're kidding, right? Hey, we'll just stop sideways and block the road." And with that, they do it – no warning.

Martha zooms off into the distance.

She continues to set a zigzag and random course through the forested area, but now they need to use headlights.

It seems their helpers' ploy may have worked.

"Hey, guys, are you both okay? Sorry about that. There was nothing else I could do."

"We know," says Bronagh. "You are an incredible driver. Thank God you know the area as well as you do." Silence ensues.

Martha thinks aloud, "You know, we should change our plan and not go to Susquehannock ... we'd be expected there. I think we should go to Philadelphia and get you guys on a Heathrow plane as quickly as possible."

"Okay, Martha, whatever you say ... that does make sense. Let's do it," says Finn. And so they do.

A sense of satisfaction and relief washes over them all after the frantic, scary and draining chase by persons unknown.

Their next followers are a little more known to them ... it's the blue light brigade.

The police are now following their car, sirens wailing, lights flashing, and they flag them down. "Excuse me, ma'am, is this your car?"

"No, sir. It's a hire car."

"Ma'am, would you mind stepping out of the car, and can I see your identification papers, please?"

"Certainly, sir. No problem."

"And who are these guys in the car with you, and can I see their papers, please?"

"Sure, Officer. No problem. They are all in order too."

"Ma'am, I'll be the judge of that, if you don't mind."

"Certainly, Officer."

"So where do you think you're all headed?"

"To the airport, Officer. They are due on a plane to London, and I am just delivering them."

"Are they able to speak for themselves, or are you their mother?"

"Officer, they are able to speak. They are just a bit tense and scared."

"And why would that be, ma'am?"

Bronagh defuses the tension by saying, "Good evening, Officer. Delighted to meet you. We are headed to the airport, so we are. Have you ever been to Ireland? Why, it's a beautiful place, so it is. You must go there some time." She smiles, her eyes flashing at the officer.

"So you are indeed Irish … and your paperwork seems to be in order, and no, I haven't been to Ireland and I hear it is wonderful. And who are *you*? What's *your* name?"

"Finn."

"Finn? What kind of a name is that?" The officer sniggers rudely.

Finn feels furious inside but knows he mustn't say or do anything in retaliation. The officer looks at his passport. "Well, I'll be damned! … Finn … so it is! Right, now then, ma'am, where have you just been driving? What route have you followed to get here?"

Another car pulls up. But it is not a police car. It has slightly darkened windows and is a different colour and make from the car that chased them earlier – it is smarter. Two gentlemen get out, wearing neat, well-cut suits and ties. They walk over to the officer.

"Okay, Officer, we'll be taking this situation over now." They show the officer their ID.

He looks shocked, turns to them all by the car and says, "Thank you for your assistance. You all have a nice day now, you hear?" and he salutes them, walks to his patrol car and drives off.

"Is everything all right here?" enquires one of the gents.

"Ah … we … we're a bit confused. What was all that about? And who are you?" quizzes Martha.

"Okay, ma'am, nothing to worry about. We appreciate you had to do some … shall we call it 'hectic' driving earlier today. We were further behind, and we know you were being followed and, yes, chased. That was mighty fine driving, if I may say so, ma'am!"

"So what was it all about?" Martha patiently tries to enquire further.

"Shall we say, there may be some people out there who are interested in you guys … ahh, for some reasons that we are not in a position to specify to you. So, you all be on your way to the airport and have a nice day." The smart gentlemen hastily make their way to their car and drive off promptly, leaving them all totally bemused.

Finn says, "Did you notice they all had guns?"

After this action-packed, eventful trip, Bronagh and Finn return to the British Isles.

Chapter 44

⌒◎◎⌒

Meanwhile, back in the British Isles, things have been gathering pace, as indeed they have in many other parts of the world. The actions and results of the book and campaigns are gradually working and having noticeable effects.

Bronagh and Finn both add Greenpeace to their campaign heavyweights, realising that they should have done so ages ago.

Conspiracy theories, of course, have been the great media concept since the advent of all the social media platforms, including YouTube videos with the expansion of potential "fake news".

However, there is enough scientific evidence to prove that global emissions into the atmosphere are the cause of the rise in the global atmospheric average temperature. It is also recognised and confirmed by scientists, meteorologists and politicians that this is causing climate change and hence extreme weather conditions. This has led to new records being set for localised temperatures, droughts, floods and storms.

Of course, Bronagh, Finn and Martha have been promoting the book, the crowdfunding project and the forum on social media, so end users still have to sort out the wheat from the chaff and decode what is real and what is fake. They also have to try to keep their campaign and message distinct from those of Just Stop Oil and Extinction Rebellion.

At least, though, they have the Place Finders Estate Agents (PFEA) venues to escape into and chat with one another freely and safely.

After one such delightful meet-up and chat at a PFEA venue, with coffee and walnut cake and tea, Finn and Bronagh check that all is clear and quietly walk through the back alley. They check once again before walking along the street. A short distance away, someone draws alongside them from behind and says, "Excuse me, I hope you don't mind me asking, but are you familiar with that Ezra book? It's great, isn't it?" Finn and Bronagh are both taken aback. They don't know what to say, but they both realise that their cover must have been blown.

"Uh, this is strange … that you should randomly walk up to someone on the street and say that," is Bronagh's quick-thinking reaction.

"Oh, I thought everyone was getting interested in it and talking about it. It's a current theme on social media, isn't it?" The encroaching stranger harasses further.

"Is it? Dunno," says Bronagh, and they walk off hurriedly.

Finn whispers to Bronagh, "Oh sugar! They're onto us all – we've been tracked."

"Yes. I think we'll have to not meet there for a good while now – too risky for everyone and for the cause. But the new question is, who are these people? What do they want or who do they represent?"

As they walk along, they continue to whisper to one another.

"Yeah, I know. We'll have to figure it out," says Finn.

"Umm ... we'll have to box clever. Of course, we can't ask them directly – that would only confirm their suspicions and give away our identities."

"We are a bit stuck, then."

"Got it!" bursts out Bronagh. "We need to play the game, feed them some testing questions or info, pretend we are on *their* side, find out more about them," she says excitedly.

"Oh no! This is beginning to sound like hard work, Bronagh," replies Finn despairingly.

"First of all, though, we'll need to chat with Martha and some others to figure out how to tackle this and what to do, what to say and not say, and have a plan that we can all adhere to."

"Okay. I am now feeling relief. Good thinking, girl!" They smile.

Carefully checking ahead and behind as they go, they remove themselves from the uncomfortable and stressful situation.

They update Martha on their experiences and fears and on a possible strategy.

"I see ... most annoying, but also expected, I guess. It was always gonna happen sometime. That means we will all now have to check our houses and cars for bugs and for trackers – oh, and our bags."

"Oh my, how tedious and more than annoying," frets Finn.

"Yes, it is, Finn, but also necessary. You're in this, and its now big time ... well, getting bigger, it seems," says Bronagh."

"Ah, yeah, guys, I guess that's where are." Martha thinks aloud. "Okay, a plan, then. You're right,

Bronagh – we will all have to play along the same lines together. That means firstly, we will have to make sure they think we are not Just Stop Oil fans, etc., and secondly that we are on the edge of our thinking, teetering, and make them think we are on the verge of trying to decide who to support in this environmental ball game."

"You're exactly right, Martha. That will work!"

So they have to have a good think. What messages are they going to put out? How should they word them? Which channels should they use? And, even more importantly, how are they going to field responses and remain as anonymous as possible?

Finn has a flash of brilliant inspiration. "Bronagh, some of these messages will be on Twitter, some on the phone, and some via talking in person, yeah?"

"Yes, right, Finn."

"Okay, in that case we will also need to record the in-person conversations – be 'wired for sound' – and also record the phone conversations," Finn finishes proudly.

"Wait a minute – have you done this before, Finn?" asks Bronagh suspiciously.

"Yes, course I have! No, just thought of it."

"That's brilliant, Finn. Yes, we now obviously need to do that."

After a bit of deep thinking, she says, "Okay, Finn, here are a few draft message ideas that we can put out wherever. What d'you think?

"We know that solar, wind, hydro, etc. are providing, say, up to fifty per cent of the electricity needed by the grid for all purposes sometimes.

"However, the uptake of EVs is pathetically low at the moment in the grand scheme of things. Loads of people can't charge an EV at their own home anyway, for many different reasons. Thus obviously petrol, diesel and oil will all be needed in vast quantities for many years yet. There's no way oil can be stopped now.

"And another ...

"Taxes and revenues from the oil and gas industries generate a lot of cashflow that is used to pay for health and social care benefits, the NHS, pensions and so on. Where is a replacement cashflow going to come from if oil is suspended?

"And another ...

"Plastics and chemicals have oil and its derivatives as their basic origin. Has anyone given any thought to where alternative base chemicals can be obtained if oil is stopped?"

"Great and convincing material, Bronagh – nice work! Okay, so we will need to do three things urgently – a new phone number for these new calls and messages, set up a new Twitter or X account, maybe Instagram too, and obtain a microphone for wiring for sound."

"Thanks, Finn. Do you think you could handle those things, please?"

"No problem – I'm on it!"

Bronagh now turns to the "teetering on the brink" image to be conveyed, mulling it over in her mind. "Uhmm, this is harder ... Okay, so I think the easiest but also most effective approach would be to send alternative pro and con messages, I mean, as opposed to trying to mix the two all in one message – for example,

'Hey, I'm thinking of going on a Just Stop Oil rally or campaign, you know, just to see what it's like.'

"'I am sick and tired of these traffic delays caused by protesters. Why don't the police take more action and step in early? They're useless!'

"'You don't hear much about Greenpeace these days. What are they up to? Anything? Or nothing?'

"Let me know when you have the gear, Finn. In the meantime, I will run these past Martha."

These first six messages are all issued via a range of media, including all those mentioned, and to a couple of phone numbers of forum members, as well as a note to a suspicious email address. They wait.

Chapter 45

❦

"**W**ow! Hey, Martha, just look at these responses! What have we got here?"

"From the very formal language used in this 'no way stopping oil' response, I'd say this was actually not an individual but a business or corporate entity with interests in the oil industry, wouldn't you?"

"Agreed."

"The next one, regarding replacement tax revenues, well, it's so wishy-washy it must surely be from a political group, again who know their stuff inside out and who have an axe to grind."

"Yeah, right. I thought that too, Bronagh, and there are some American-sounding expressions in there – a bit of a giveaway!"

"And for the alternative chemicals one, this sounds very, very technical indeed. Could only be a chemistry graduate or chemical industry insider."

"Yeah, again, I think you're right, Bronagh."

It is Finn's turn to contribute. "And about the JSO rally idea, with the response saying 'Glad to have you along! Come and join us!' – that's got to be JSO. What a laugh! They are so unsubtle!" They all laugh. "Now, this next one is a different matter altogether. Regarding the reference to the police interventions or not, this is so defensive, so 'avoiding the legal' … perhaps even going the other way so as not to give themselves away."

"Good spot, Finn," says Bronagh. "We'll have to watch out for this sort of stance."

"Now, with this one, it's an update on everything that Greenpeace are currently active on and are organising around the globe."

"Makes you think it's actually Greenpeace, doesn't it?" surmises Martha, and they all laugh.

"Mmm, interesting," ponders Bronagh.

"Sure is," agrees Martha.

"And we will probably need to respond to all of them fairly quickly to keep them interested," adds Finn.

"Strike while the iron is hot," Bronagh concludes.

"I think, from the slightly incorrect English usage in the 'no way stopping oil' one, that this is from an international interest."

"Okay, so who?" queries Martha.

"Well, let's see … it's about oil, it's international, they are agreeing that they don't want oil stopped … I'm thinking it's an international oil company, actually, like … ah, also perhaps based in, say, the Middle East … Arachno? Or Photoenergies?"

"Wow, this is huge if that is the case."

"The replacement taxes one … This is, and increasingly will be, a contentious issue. Where will it have the biggest and most ongoing impact? Well, everywhere, but biggest of all in the complex finances and politics of good old back home … in America. Ah, shucks! That's gotta be the IR or …"

"Or who, Martha?"

"No … never … not the CIA?" states Martha unbelievingly.

"Oh happy days!" Finn sighs and continues, "And this 'alternative chemicals' one must be from a chemicals producer, who are fundamentally … guess who? Oil companies! Well, I don't know – Britopetrol? Motorshell? Photoenergies?"

"Or any of the American ones," adds Martha.

"Okay," says Bronagh, "that leaves us with the police action. Well, it can't be the police, can it? That's obvious; they just wouldn't and couldn't get involved in evidence-based communications here."

"Okay," says Finn, "what about the next level up?"

"You mean MI5?" queries Martha.

"I guess so," ponders Bronagh.

"Boy, what a can of worms! If that's the case," reflects Martha, "all of these do make sense and add up, though, when you think about them."

"Respond, then, we must," says Finn. "I suppose JSO and Greenpeace are both easy enough to play the ball game with," he says pointedly to Martha, and they all laugh and smile. "I can deal with those if you like?"

"Thanks, Finn. That would be great," says Martha appreciatively.

"Now we have two that seem to be in the oily camp and two that seem to be a bit more tricky, kind of delicate to deal with or sensitive, even, in the political business."

Bronagh says, "Yes. We need to work this out carefully … but we need to send them something now, kind of just to stall them but keep their interest and buy us some time."

"Good idea, Brony!" says Martha.

"Oh no, not you as well?" says Bronagh despairingly.

Together they compile a quick, fairly standard holding response to their contacts. For the main follow-ups, Martha will respond to the "oilys", Bronagh to the politicos and Finn to JSO and Greenpeace.

To the "no way stopping oil" contact, Martha responds, "In spite of your discussions, the changeover to EVs needs to be much faster than it is at present. What do you propose to do?"

To the alternative chemicals issue, she responds, "There is a need to be more specific. What are the exact sources, and what is exactly replacing what? Can you be clear, please?"

Bronagh responds to the replacement taxes contact. "What are your exact plans for the amounts of tax? And what will they be levied on? And when does this start?"

To the police action contact, she replies, "Okay, so it sounds as if it's a government decision to do something or not. When will they change this response policy?"

Finn replies to JSO: "Okay, having thought about it, when are the next few rallies? And where will they be, please? Oh, and what are they about, please?"

And to Greenpeace he replies, "Thanks for the full report on the grand work you are doing everywhere … keep it up! We support you!"

This is now a tense moment. Waiting for the cogs to turn. Waiting for the responses from the key players. Will it work? Or have they given the game away by showing too much of their hand?

Well, for a start, Finn is clearly not expecting much of a response from Greenpeace, if at all. He is expecting only the dates and locations of rallies from JSO.

How about the others?

For Martha, from the "no way stopping oil" contact comes, "Why don't you come for an EV test drive and then we can discuss our proposals over lunch?"

"Well, that seems to have worked!" says Martha excitedly.

There is no response from the alternative chemicals contact.

For Bronagh, from the replacement taxes contact comes, "Would be interested to hear your views on these questions and issues. How can we meet?"

She says, "Well, talk about U-turns! That's cheekily turning it around. Not sure about this. Doesn't sound too safe to me … but this is an important contact. How do we progress this one?"

Bronagh gets no response from the police action contact. Finn does get his list of dates and venues from JSO.

Chapter 46

❦

They pick one and just go, as it is low-key, cool and a light relief from the intensity of late.

Bronagh wanders around a little and stands and observes, people-watching.

A voice from behind says in a soft American accent, "So you have finally got to meet us! Well done, Bronagh, for your efforts."

She turns to see a black-suited gentleman in a white shirt and sunglasses, with sharp, neat black hair. He is smiling at her. He continues, "I will continue in conversation to a degree, but in case Finn has you wired for sound and recording, I will not be as frank as I might."

Bronagh wonders what the heck is going on. "Who are you? How do you know my name? And Finn?"

"Let's just say I have my sources. I am an American … in beautiful sunny England. And what might you be doing here, Bronagh?"

"Well actually, if you must know, I'm on a quiet day out … seeing what happens at a Just Stop Oil rally. Is that okay with you?"

"That's perfectly okay, but it's nothing to do with me anyway, is it?"

"I wouldn't be so sure. You make it sound as if it is some concern of yours."

"Oh really? I didn't mean to offend. I must be losing my touch."

"Anyway, thank you." Bronagh turns to walk off.

"Ah, Bronagh, after taking all this time to get to meet you, I haven't quite finished yet. There might be something here of interest to you."

Bronagh stops in her tracks and turns back to look sideways at this curious guy. He puts his hand into an inside jacket pocket and holds it there for a while as he continues.

"There is something here which you might find interesting." He draws her attention to an envelope, partly visible, now protruding slightly from his jacket and hand. He continues, "Have you seen this?" Obviously she hasn't. "Please, do have a read. It's likely only of interest to you, so give it back to me once you have read it in a minute," he urges.

Gingerly, Bronagh accepts the proffered envelope, turns away and opens it. Inside is an A4 sheet of paper, with no ID or contact details on it. It reads, "Do not verbally read out anything on this sheet. This information is personal and confidential to you. Do not visibly react in any way on reading any of this. Do not reveal any of this information or content to Finn or anyone else.

"I need you to gather as much information as you can from your communications with your recent contacts and pass it on to me at our next meeting in London.

"Be at Covent Garden Market next Wednesday at 11.35 a.m. Come alone and tell no one where and when you are going. Do not have your own tail.

"Now pass this envelope and sheet of paper back to me and say, 'Thank you, that's very interesting, but no thanks, I've got one.'"

She turns back to him, says the instructed words and hands the paperwork back to him, which he accepts and puts back into his inside jacket pocket. He says, "Thank you for your time" and turns and leaves.

Bronagh remains there, dumbfounded and stunned. Something like this has never happened to her before. She feels as if she is trapped. She has been told not to say anything about this to anyone. If she did, what would be the consequences ... for herself or for anyone she told anything to?

And ... she has to gather and report information! She thinks, *Oh my God ... it feels as if all the good life and progress has come to an end. This is so shocking. What am I to do? Do I have any options? No, clearly not. I just have to do this. I have to do as I have been told. Oh my God! What will my friends think if and when they find out anything about all this? Oh sugar.*

Naturally, as a consequence of this devastating experience, Bronagh is quieter and more pensive than usual.

Chapter 47

❦

Now, regarding the "no way stopping oil" contact's response – "Why don't you come for an EV test drive?" – this has remained on Martha's mind. She hasn't said anything to Bronagh or Finn about it, but it does strike her as a good way to go kind of "undercover", as it were – to meet face to face with these people in a public place ... oh, and to get a test drive of an EV. What's a girl to do? Nurture a little secret, have a bit of fun ... or not? She thinks to herself, *After all, it's in a good cause.*

Okay, so that wasn't a difficult decision. She decides to have a little space – take some time out.

Martha arranges for the EV test drive. The venue is a typical car showroom, pristine, tidy, sharp and immaculate. She hangs around, looking the place up and down, and checks her phone. So, there is nothing for it but to go up to the desk and announce herself. She is introduced to a neatly dressed young female representative, who welcomes her, shows her around the showroom and checks out what size of car she would like to try.

Martha goes for the smaller end of the range purely on its green credentials and economy. *Well, I am not intending to buy, but the least I can do is sound realistic.*

Even though it is under strange circumstances, Martha actually finds this quite interesting, and it is a useful experience for her; she might actually buy an EV in the UK one day, who knows?

The test drive is like any other test drive, but there is obviously far more explaining of everything by the representative, as it is such a new car, new technology and new experience. At the end, Martha tells the representative that she is very impressed with her thorough explanation of everything and with the car's performance too.

The representative gets out of the front passenger door and a neatly suited gentleman gets in. He says nothing. He looks as if he is of Middle Eastern origin. They stare at each other. Martha is alarmed, worried and feels under threat. She feels even more threatened when she notices another neatly suited gentleman is standing outside the driver's door.

Okay, Martha, de-stress the situation, ask about what you have agreed to … So she simply says, "Okay … is this where we go to lunch?"

"Yes, of course, Martha," the man beside her says in an Arabic accent. "Let me introduce myself. I am Amir Youssef – pleased to make your acquaintance – of the Saudi Arabian oil company Arachno. Please wind down your window."

She does so.

"This is a colleague of mine who is taking us to lunch, as was proposed and agreed, yes?"

"Hello, Martha. Pleased to meet you. Shall we go to lunch?"

This guy has an American accent. Martha is finding this very confusing but realises it is safer to comply for the moment.

They walk, with very little being said, to a nearby restaurant, where she finds a table has been reserved for them.

Martha tries to break the ice. "So, what exactly are we going to discuss over lunch?"

"Well, you did say, did you not, 'What do you propose?'"

"Yes, I do believe I did, but I didn't know it was you guys, and I still don't know exactly who you are or what you are doing here."

"Oh, come on, Martha! You weren't born yesterday. Your thread in your discussion was about the 'just stopping oil' subject, or rather questioning why that wasn't exactly feasible … is that right?" says the American in an attempted jovial sort of way.

"Clearly I side with your view that oil use will continue at current levels for some time to come. Why? It's all simply because there is not the infrastructure in place, and there won't be for some time, as we all know," says Amir.

"That is where you stand, is it not, Martha? Even though you took notice of your conscience by taking the test drive offer," says the American.

Martha ponders for a moment and then says, "Well, yes, sort of … but you've not told me what you propose."

The American sharply intervenes with, "Right, Martha, here is what we propose. We would like you to do these things for us, please.

"Firstly, you must gather all the information, sources, contacts, people involved and so on and report them to me in person on a regular basis. You will not be so pushy and supportive of the EV roll-out being speeded up.

"If I see any evidence of this in your communications – which we are obviously tracking – there will be consequences for you … oh, and possibly others. Do you understand? And is all that clear enough for you or do you want me to explain a little further?"

A scared-to-death Martha doesn't know what to say or think, so she just says, "No."

"So, next Wednesday, twelve noon … shall we say Hyde Park Corner? Yes, we do. That's all agreed, then. See you there … oh, and Martha, a little advice. Don't even think of telling anyone about this or where you are going, and don't have a tail. Of course, we do check on these basics. Have a nice day!"

The bill has been paid earlier, so the two guys leave.

Martha just sits there, stunned. A waiter comes over and asks if she would like anything else.

"A coffee, please." She has no intention of going anywhere else until she has had a chance to recover from this and has gathered her thoughts. No one even knows she is here.

Oh my God, she thinks. *I – or we – are in this big time, and I can't even discuss it!*

Chapter 48

❦

Adifficult week lies ahead. No one knows what has been happening to the other … except that nothing has been happening to Finn, and he is none the wiser about either of the other two.

There is little of the previous bright and chirpy conversation. Of course, they all notice this, but no one can say anything.

Finn, on the other hand, has a clearer conscience than the others and surmises that something is up with the other two. But so it goes; this is life sometimes, they figure.

Stress mounts as both women become more agitated and uncomfortable with everything in daily life as their days approach. They are also both wondering what they are going to say as an excuse for their getaways in London for the day.

Meanwhile, in Langley, Virginia, USA: a CIA office: Directorate of Operations.

"Ed, have you got your finger on the pulse of that 'book club' in London yet?"

"Yes, Boss! We're gonna put a little pressure on and flush out what we can from those kids – I mean flush out information that will be useful to us to see what's going on in the oil camps, ya know what I mean?"

"Okay. The Special Envoy for Environment is pressing for all the fringe progress he can get to speed things up. He's heading up a big organisation with a lotta money now – he will be expecting serious support from us. We might be gettin' some 'fringe benefits', you know what I mean, Ed?"

"Sure thing, Boss. I'm on it."

"Don't let me down now, Ed."

"You can count on me, Boss!"

And in the envoy's office in the USA …

"I hear that this Ezra guy, the one with what I hear they call the 'book club', has already been to see the President. Wish I'd thought of that book idea!"

And in Exobil Oil head office in the USA …

"Hell, these little English kids are creating an unnecessary stink, aren't they? Don't they know it takes a lot of oil, oil sales, and revenue and taxes to run an economy? Don't they learn them that over in little old England? Hey, Irvine, can you get on to Ed over at the DO office? Oh, ha, sorry, no, I mean John at the Counterintelligence Center Analysis Group, please?" *Whoa! Geez, that would have been a real bloomer!*

"Hi, John. Hey, can you do a bit of candle snuffing in London for me, if ya know what I mean? Oh no, don't get me wrong, I don't mean snuff 'em out completely. They're only kids, for Christ's sake."

"I got it, Irvine. Leave it to me."

And in Saudi Arabia, Bahrain and Kuwait at OPEC, where the oil companies' interests are combined …

"These people in London, who are they? Kids! They're only kids! But they are driving me mad. We need to put a stop to this madness. Of course we've got to go on using oil! How can they be so stupid? We've got to do something about them. Yes, I must get on to John at the Counterintelligence Center Analysis Group, the CIA at Langley."

And in Lubyanka Square, Moscow, at the Lubyanka KGB headquarters ...

"Hey, Ygor, even though we have sanctions against us and for the sale of our oil products to the Western economies, we can still continue and actually increase our sales to China and India, who are continuing or increasing their use of oil. Why? Simply because they have to."

"Sure thing, Yevgeny, and our oil to them is cheaper than they can get from the West or the OPEC set prices. So we don't want those interfering little busybodies from that book thing in London influencing the publicity, the masses and the markets. We still want to sell more of our oil – and at the highest prices possible – to our comrade markets."

"So, Ygor, what will you need to do? You will need to make sure that our agents in London get that message across, clearly and loudly, to those little peoples."

And at the CIA office in Langley, Counterintelligence Center Analysis Group: "We're gettin' a lot of call traffic regarding this London cell of wannabes, John. I mean, we got OPEC interests, Britopetrol, Motorshell and Arachno wanting us to control things there a bit already. Seems these kids are gettin' too effective."

"I know, Irvine. It's been on my mind. Had a hunch somethin' was up over there."

"Oh! An' now we got Exobil head office wadin' in – our own big oil company."

"Shucks! We gotta get hold of these kids, get the info off them about all their good and clean environmental tactics, and shut off their green messaging. It's time now."

•◆•

Bronagh finally decides what she is going to tell Finn.

"Finn, my lovely, I've had a call from an Irish friend from the old days who's in London for a few days. She wants to meet up, so I said yes, today suits. That okay with you?"

"Sure thing! Have a good time, then." And she heads into town for her rendezvous.

Martha doesn't have to tell anyone anything, so she just goes.

And she heads into town for her rendezvous.

Chapter 49

⚜

At a private and undisclosed location in Mayfair, London, agents of the Langley DO are discussing and planning their initiative.

"Okay, here's the situation. We stake out – just three of us should be adequate – the Covent Garden Market hall. Earpieces, phones and small arms. Here is the asset – Irish accent, female, named Bronagh."

"Roger that."

···

Bronagh travels in, feeling very nervous and twitchy on the Underground to Covent Garden. She is looking around at everyone there, thinking *Are they the ones out to get me?* This is very taxing and draining on her energy levels and her consciousness. She is soon feeling weary and tired.

Getting off at Covent Garden station, she is still looking around at everyone. It is an unavoidable trait now, instinctive for safeguarding and survival.

She double checks the date on her phone. It is indeed Wednesday. The time is 11.30 a.m.; she is on time. She is aware that her adrenaline levels have soared and that she is as high as a kite.

She slowly makes her way to the market hall. There are a few people milling around the performers' area, some looking over the railings at the al fresco market below. She stands at the corner, leans on the railing and waits … It is 11.35 a.m. Before she notices anything, a voice speaks over her shoulder.

"Good morning, Bronagh. Glad you could make it. My sweet, do you recall that we met, we chatted and we agreed what we were going to do? I respect people who stick to agreements. Is that fair?"

Bronagh doesn't know whether to look or not, but she recognises the voice.

"Well, yes, kind of," comes out her voice, just about.

"Oh, let me make it clear, then … I don't respect people who don't stick to agreements." He pauses, expecting Bronagh to hand over the requested information or at least to tell him the information. She doesn't.

"Bronagh, I don't recall that you have provided me with any information—"

Bronagh breaks away and runs off, very fast, into an open pedestrian area where she can easily be seen by members of the public. They are certainly watching; people have stopped and are following her with their eyes.

The guy has, unexpectedly, not given chase.

She continues up the street a little way, then branches into a side street, hides behind a small wall and stops to catch her breath, panting.

•◆•

In a hotel room in Knightsbridge, London, agents of the Langley Counterintelligence Center Analysis Group and some Saudi members of OPEC, representing Arachno, Bahraini and Kuwaiti oil interests, are deliberating over apprehending their target, Martha.

"Okay, here is where we are. This Martha kid has not provided me with any information as requested. She has not been in touch at all, and we have not seen any traffic on their social media accounts at all during the past week."

"She is not taking you seriously. In my country of Saudi Arabia, we have ways of dealing with people who don't take us seriously."

The Langley agent cuts them off and says, "Just leave it to me. We will handle this. You'll get your part of the information in due course."

"I trust that what you say is true," says the Arab with a glum stare and hard, gleaming eyes.

"You guys, stay here. We will have three operatives in the field, eyes on Hyde Park Corner, earpieces, and small arms on standby."

"Copy."

•➤•

Martha is trying to be very discreet and makes her way slowly to Hyde Park, stopping occasionally and half hiding behind walls and doors along the way. She is trying to look out for any suspicious or likely looking characters, although she has no idea really what they might look like. She is conscious of the need to be there perhaps ten minutes or so early so that she can assess the location and again try to see who is around.

She is clearly aware when she is getting near – she can hear a number of speakers and people shouting on their orange crates or other plinths, telling all of us what is wrong with the world and how to run it. *How ironic*, she thinks.

So her one-person stake-out now begins. She is fifteen minutes early, so she moves around, stopping occasionally to glance surreptitiously about … there is such a mixture of people, including joggers.

What exactly am I looking for? It feels like such a long time.

A voice comes from behind. "Martha, what exactly are you looking for? Can I help you?" It has an American accent which she instinctively recognises. "Martha, do you remember these words – 'Report them to me in person on a regular basis'? What was it about this phrase that you did not understand?"

Martha immediately realises that any attempt at conversation to discuss these, well, academic points would be futile. Without hesitation she hares off out of the park gate as fast as her legs can carry her. She has not had a lot of useful exercise lately, so this feels particularly arduous, but hey ho, it must be done.

She is not aware that the agent or agents are not in pursuit; she keeps going anyway. Diving behind a wall, hidden in an inconspicuous alleyway, she gasps for breath.

To her complete surprise, her phone rings. It is Bronagh.

"If this is a social call, Bronagh, I am not really in a position to stop long to talk. Can I call you back later?"

"Martha, I have got something quite serious to say to you. I am in deep trouble and I need to ask for your help."

"Go on," says Martha, still panting audibly.

"I allowed myself, although without realising it at the time, to be talked into a compromising situation."

"What do you mean?" says Martha with her heart racing, still out of breath.

"Some people seem to have tracked down our communications, and I have been singled out to provide information, tactics and sources about … in other words, I have been trapped and threatened … I feel my safety is in danger … oh, and Finn doesn't know anything about this. God, I feel sick!" There is a pause.

"Bronagh, I hear exactly what you say. I understand … and I must tell you that exactly the same thing has happened to me, believe it or not!"

"Oh my God! Martha, are you all right?" yells Bronagh down the phone.

"Yeah, I'm okay. I have just had to run away from them."

"So have I! Where are you?"

"Near Hyde Park Corner tube."

"Oh my! I am near Covent Garden tube."

"What are we going to do? What a mess this is!"

"Okay, Bronagh, let's take some deep breaths and figure this out. I don't know exactly what a good thing to do would be right now, but we have got to remove risk to ourselves – in other words, stay as safe as possible."

"How?" enquires Bronagh. There is another pause.

"Okay, together we would be stronger, so let's plan to meet up."

"Where?"

"Ahh … near or at Scotland Yard, I guess."

"That makes very good sense, Martha – the best advice I've heard all day!" They laugh nervously.

"Let's do it straight away. I'll keep a lookout for you. Phone to say exactly where you are when near there, okay?"

"Okay," says Bronagh.

Chapter 50

❦

They both slowly and gingerly keep a lookout and make their way out from their temporary cover, Bronagh heading for the tube and Martha deciding to walk to Scotland Yard.

Although they don't know it, there are agents tracking each of them not far behind. The strategy of each set of agents is to put a bit of pressure on the women and scare them into acting for each cell independently. The agents' technique is not to create a stir in public and not to draw the attention of the Metropolitan Police, hence the shadowy tracking.

Back at the Knightsbridge hotel, the Saudi and oil groups are hearing the progress on apprehending Martha and they are not happy.

"What are you doing? Are you crazy? You have let her get away!"

"Calm down, my friend. We are doing a shadow pursuit so as not to draw too much attention."

Back at the Mayfair location, the Langley DO tracking team are fiercely communicating via their earpieces to keep the agents in close enough proximity to Bronagh. Meanwhile, agents of the KGB in London have reported back to the Lubyanka HQ in Moscow about the situation as it unfolds in London.

Yevgeny now sees an opportunity for cornering the situation for himself – well, and the KGB and, well … and for Russia.

"Ygor," he shouts, "this is the moment you've been waiting for! The two girls are there for the taking. They will be ours now," he gloats.

"Yes, Colonel. It is a great opportunity on a plate. Thank you, CIA teams!"

KGB teams in London mobilise in a Range Rover with blacked-out windows. They follow Bronagh, driving slowly behind her for a short distance and then accelerating to draw alongside her by the pavement before she goes down into the tube station. Quickly getting out, they bundle her into the back seat and drive off smoothly. This is all done in such a way that it appears that they know her and are being kind enough to give her a lift.

Simultaneously, another team of KGB agents have also pulled Martha from under the noses of the CIA on Constitution Hill in similar fashion.

There are celebrations back at the Lubyanka building.

At the Mayfair location …

"All units, we have a situation; repeat, we have a situation. The two assets are currently in KGB vehicles, central London, destination unknown."

Langley DO gets on the phone to the Special Envoy for Environment. He is furious at the mess-up. The envoy gets on the phone to the President; he is also furious at the mess-up and orders an inquiry. However, as Martha is an American citizen, the President orders the CIA in London to extract her asap.

Immediately, three CIA vehicles engage. One pulls alongside Martha's KGB vehicle; the others take up position with one behind and one in front. CIA agents wearing dark shades and bullet-proof vests under their suits emerge from the vehicles, carrying handguns fitted with silencers and semi-automatics, all trained on the KGB agents in the Range Rover. The lead CIA agent clearly and loudly states that they should let Martha out of the car without hesitation and drive away.

Realising the futility of their situation, and for an asset of this level, they comply, and Martha is released. She is quickly bundled into one of the CIA vehicles and they all drive off.

She next finds herself at the American Embassy, where she experiences a debrief.

While this is unfolding for Martha, meanwhile, inside the other KGB vehicle …

"Now, my dear, I understand that you have not been very helpful to your previous captors, or should I say suitors, ha ha ha, as we are now your captors." He smiles at Bronagh. "Are we not?" And with that, he touches her leg. "Perhaps now you will be rather more, shall we say, cooperative with us." He smiles at her again.

"So, Bronagh – and that's a very nice name, may I say! – we are going to be driving for a few more minutes yet, to a place that we hope you feel you can call home for a few days." He smiles at her again.

"You gotta be kidding! I am going home today! I am a free person. I have done nothing wrong. Let me out of here!" she shouts and glares at the man. He pauses, not reacting immediately.

"Yes, yes, Bronagh, we can let you out of here anytime, but first you have to do something for us – you know that, don't you, Bronagh?"

"I have no idea what the hell's going on!" she shouts in reply.

"This kind of attitude is beginning to make things a little, how should we say, difficult, perhaps, Bronagh. How do you think you could make things become less difficult, then?"

"I am not about to answer your questions and do your dirty work for you, am I? Let me out of here. I want to just go, now!" There is a longer pause and a silence.

Bronagh has had blacked-out sunshades placed over her eyes and her hands have been handcuffed behind her back, so she has not been able to see where they have been driving.

They eventually pull in to what seems like a low-key hotel site from the estimated time of travel, perhaps on the edge of London.

The car stops. Bronagh is helped out of the car and led along some walkways to a door and a room. She is led in. The door shuts ... and is locked and bolted. A mighty bout of fear and dread flows through Bronagh's whole body. The room smells of damp and mould. Someone pushes her roughly into a chair. The sunshades are removed. Even with her eyes tightly closed, she still experiences pain from the shock of the bright artificial light. She gradually opens her eyes and looks around. Then the cuffs are removed, and she holds her wrists to relieve the chafing.

To her relief there are only two guys in the room, one standing to the side and one sitting with his folded arms resting on the table in front of him. There is no decor on the pale yellow walls and no windows. That is it.

What now? she wonders. She sits with her head down, looking at the floor, not engaging with them.

"Bronagh, it's time for you to do yourself a favour and tell us what you know. It's as simple as that."

"What I know about what?" Cigarette smoke begins to fill the room, making it even more claustrophobic.

"Don't make this tedious for us, Bronagh. We have lives to live too, you know. Don't we, Slav?"

Slav responds, "Yes, we do, but if this is where we have to live, then we might as well start 'living' here, hey, Bronagh?"

She looks at him with a "don't you dare touch me" glare. But he moves closer and stands behind her. She feels extremely awkward in this precarious situation.

"Remember, Bronagh, no one knows where you are, do they? So you don't really exist, do you?" Slav puts his hands on her shoulders and massages them. "Oh yes, she certainly does exist!"

Bronagh turns. "Get your hands off me, you filthy pig!" And she pushes his hands away.

"We could tell people you know about what you've been doing here … what you've been … up to," says the leader.

Bronagh just looks at the floor in front of her.

Going through her mind now is the need to survive, to get out of this in one piece. It's true, nobody knows she is here or where she is. Only she can make a difference now.

She has the opportunity now, by not listening to what they are saying to reduce her morale, to break her down … to think through a SWOT analysis of the situation for herself right now. Strengths – self-defence training and skills and ideas. They don't know she has self-defence skills. Weaknesses – on her own, no weapons, locked in, no backup. Opportunities – these quickly unfold in her mind. Threats – aplenty; they probably have concealed guns on them and knives.

She knows that Slav has a weakness; she should work with that. The leader seems to be an interrogator/torturer type of person. He is older and doesn't look that fit, let alone healthy, judging by his smoking habit.

Just as they are working to a tried and tested plan, Bronagh decides she will have to do the same; that's only fair. She suddenly realises – and there is a strong focus to her mindset now – that it's them or her ... *so it might as well be me!* This point suddenly becomes very motivational for her and gives her fresh courage.

Her brain is now beginning to work overtime, and very vividly.

She figures she will have only one chance at this; she can't afford to blow it by moving too quickly or at the wrong time. So she rehearses her idea over and over in her mind and very swiftly, as there is no time to lose.

It all hinges on getting the two guys in the right place at the right time. It has to be very exact to work at all, let alone succeed.

She prays ... *God forgive me for what I am about to do ... but we know we have got to do it, don't we?*

Whatever the guys have been saying, she has not responded to anything and has just been staring at the floor as if in a hypnotic trance.

The time to act will be when her adrenaline level has risen to a trigger point.

She slowly moves her head to look up at Slav. He is not that good looking, but this is a task, an emergency, so what the hell. She eyes him up, engages in an extended stare, pouts ever so slightly. Slav looks unsure, bemused. She sees his Adam's apple move; he has taken the bait. He moves towards her, closer, and stops, still maintaining eye contact. He stoops, bringing his head down in front of Bronagh's face.

Bronagh now asks the leader, "Can I have a cigarette, please?" even though she doesn't smoke.

He replies, "Sure, my dear," gets up positively and begins to walk towards her.

Meanwhile, Bronagh is now face to face with Slav. He thinks to himself, *My luck is in after all — there is life here!* and he smiles. He is just about to try to kiss her on the lips when the leader shouts, "Get out of the way, Slav! What are you doing?" as he wants to give Bronagh the cigarette and light it for her.

With that, Bronagh suddenly grabs the two ends of Slav's tie and pulls them ferociously tight, causing him to gasp and struggle for breath, unable to talk. At the same time she swings her right leg upward in an incredibly strong, fast and adept motion, catching the leader between his legs and crunching into his crotch with her shin bone. He yelps with agony, clutches his valuables and falls helplessly to the ground, writhing in agony and gasping for air.

She maintains the tension on Slav's tie and also headbutts him. Blood pours from his broken nose and teeth. He also collapses to the floor.

Bronagh rapidly rifles through their pockets, removing two guns, two knives, two wired pieces and two phones from the pair. Time is now on her side. There is no string, rope or plastic ties to tie them up with, so she dashes to the door, still clutching all the gear, unbolts it and tries the handle … it won't open. "Damn it!" she mutters to herself and rushes to the desk, looking for a bunch of keys. Finding them, she grabs them and turns but sees that the leader is beginning to try to sit up. Bronagh runs towards him and kicks him as hard as she can full in the face … another broken nose and dental appointment booked.

She swiftly unlocks the door, has a look around outside, moves out carefully and locks the door behind her. *Where the hell to go now?* she wonders.

Continuously looking from side to side, behind and in front, she sidles along a corridor about the width of a car, seeking her next direction.

She can just see at the end of this corridor, in the open space beyond, a black car with two guys standing next to it, smoking.

"Oh hell!" she declares and saunters back in the direction she came from, past the door of her recent little stay and into an open area with a fence and industrial units beyond.

She looks around for a possible safe escape route and potential freedom. Crawling under the fence would be a reasonable option, as climbing over would be too conspicuous and would make her an easy target. Quickly crossing the open ground, she lies flat against the bottom of the wire fence, trying to keep below the height of the longer grass. All good. Lying still for a while to see if anyone appears, she looks for any weakness in the fence to squeeze herself through.

There is a potential gap about ten metres ahead.

Chapter 51

⋞⊙⊙⋟

With the sun on her face and back, this is a cosy little spot, but she can't lie here all day. There is freedom to be sought. The next move makes her vulnerable to being seen, but in any walk of life, you have to take a risk or two sometimes, or no progress is made at all.

Shuffling along the base of the fence and staying low, she arrives at her new vantage point. Yes, this is do-able … there is a twelve-inch-high parting of the wire netting, which can easily be forced wider – just right for squeezing through.

All appears clear, and she starts to make a worm-like action to wriggle herself through … until a tough strand of wire hooks into her belt.

Damn it! Of all the times! Bronagh is exasperated. This delay and unhooking of the wire causes a slight wobbling of the fence, which is normally perfectly still all day, and she is only halfway through the gap.

An office worker on the upper floor of one of the industrial units notices this movement. She is used to the fence being still all day. She occasionally glances up from her PC screen simply to get relief by looking at a bit of greenery and nature, so this fence movement is alarming to her. She gets up, walks over to the window and looks more closely. She sees a young woman trying to get through a gap in the fence, carrying a gun.

"Oh my God!" she exclaims to her colleagues. "Look at this!"

Unnoticed, but now noticed by Bronagh, the two guys who were standing by the car, having checked the room door and heard the desperate alarm raised by the two severely injured occupants, are holding their guns in front of them and beginning to cross the open ground in pursuit of Bronagh.

The office workers call the police, who encourage them to invoke their internal lockdown protocol and procedures.

Bronagh hurriedly scrambles through the gap and runs past some of the units, eyes everywhere, looking for a hiding place. She tries several vans before she finds an unlocked one. She gets into the back and lies on the floor, hoping.

She can hear some Russian-sounding voices outside at a distance. Her level of fear and dread suddenly rises through the roof; she is not firearms trained, so to engage in any attempt at shooting the guns she is in possession of would be a potentially fatal mistake.

She also hears a number of vehicles speedily arrive and screech to a halt, and not far away, it sounds like.

A number of people are now shuffling and scuffling around outside somewhere. Looking carefully through the front window of the van, she can see that a police firearms squad has turned up. They are creeping stealthily around, wearing the usual body armour, caps, weapons, earpieces and gloves. They take up positions around the car park. The two Russians must also have taken up defensive positions nearby, she assumes.

I mean, why would anyone be after me? Okay, I now have two guns and two knives, but that's no reason to go chasing a young lady around, is it, when she hasn't done anything wrong!

·◆·

In the USA, the Special Envoy is giving evidence to the President's urgently convened inquiry. Even though he has had the Langley CIA DO working alongside him, he doesn't really understand what is going on with what he calls the "book club", i.e. from Ezra's creation via his book. Neither do the CIA, or rather the DO section.

The latest updates from London indicate that his support for the environmental initiatives of the USA is being backed up by the CIA DO – for example, by their approach to Bronagh to get her to provide information to them about the tactics of the oil companies and such groups on social media.

How the Langley CIA Counterintelligence Center Analysis Group has also become involved in this action towards Martha to obtain inside information about the social media activities of Just Stop Oil and the like, and have been so ineffective, is incomprehensible to him … and it remains incomprehensible to the inquiry.

However, just at this point, news comes in that although Martha has been safely and successfully extracted by the CIA from the KGB operation, there is now a serious situation in North London that needs attention.

It is subtly pointed out that as the CIA was involved in the Bronagh surveillance, now the KGB has got involved in it too, the CIA should be the ones to sort it out.

"Okay, let's get going on another extraction, then, guys. Let's do it!" says the Special Envoy.

"Ahh, it's not quite that straightforward, sir," says the CIA lead agent.

"Excuse me, and why not?"

"You see, sir, in the UK, a Metropolitan Police armed response unit is currently facing off against the KGB."

"What in hell's name has been going on? For the love of God, how did that come about?"

"It's a long story, sir, that we haven't quite gotten to the bottom of, but we will have to negotiate with the Met first and replace them with our agents at this now hostile location."

The Special Envoy enquires, "And what about the girl? Where is she in this now? In KGB hands still, I guess?"

"Ahh, no, sir. It's not quite that simple, sir."

"What do you mean? How can that not be simple?"

"You see, she escaped from them, sir."

"Good God, what do we pay you for? Were you not in charge of the apprehension of this girl in the first place? *And* you let her go … she escaped from you guys?"

"It's not quite like that, sir …"

"I've had enough. Don't say any more!"

There is a pause. "Right, I want that first extraction team on this again – nobody else!"

The President says, "Okay, all of you guys, I want a full report on this on my desk before the end of the day. And CIA in particular, I wanna full inside report on your team's activities by that same time."

"Yes, Mr President."
"Yes, Mr President."
"Yes, Mr President, sir."

•—•

Back in London, senior officers at Scotland Yard have been called by ministers of the British government, who have authorised a handover from the armed response unit to the CIA.

In the field, this results in the discreet arrival and deployment of the new CIA assets, exactly replacing the positions held by the armed response unit. The armed response unit is then deployed in the locality to usher the public away from the immediate vicinity and set up road blocks.

Still no one knows the whereabouts of Bronagh.

None of this activity has been on the news channels, so no one knows what has been going on.

The holed-up and now cornered KGB agents have a predicament of their own. They do not have backup. They do have earpieces, so they can talk to each other and communicate about what they are going to do.

They have figured out that Bronagh must be somewhere in the area, otherwise there wouldn't be the police and now CIA interest still.

Their opening ploy is to throw a number of stun grenades, their plan being to cause confusion and make the CIA think there are more of them than there actually are. These are thrown at three-second intervals with the aim of getting the CIA agents to show themselves so they present as targets for a clearer shot. Having identified the CIA locations, they next move on to smoke grenades so that they can shoot in the vicinity of the targets but with smoke cover for themselves.

Bronagh is naturally scared stiff by the incredibly intense noise of the grenades and the rapid gunfire, but she can't see the smoke. She thinks, *I don't know how I got into this mess and I don't know how to get out of it.* She starts to pray.

As the smoke clears slightly, the KGB agents move on to throw a mixture of stun grenades and proper exploding grenades. This causes more confusion but also considerably more danger.

Shrapnel from some of the explosions pierces the bodywork of the van Bronagh is hiding in. It misses her but leaves a few considerable-size holes in the metal.

More gunfire follows, followed by more smoke grenades. Some of the smoke seeps into the van through the shrapnel holes. This causes some agitation to Bronagh's lungs and throat and makes her start coughing. She tries to cover her mouth with her hand and then with a piece of cloth to make it quieter.

Through the Russian earpieces comes a voice. "Hey! I heard something … someone coughing over there." The speaker points towards Bronagh's hiding place.

"It must be the girl."

Sporadic gunfire is maintained in both directions.

"Okay, we need to do some more stuns and then more smoke to provide cover for me to get across and get into that van. You will need to maintain tons of smoke, stun grenades and covering fire. Okay?"

"Okay. We have a plan."

•◆•

Two reports have appeared on the President's desk within the allotted time.

The first outlines the initial background to the case and then the action plan of operations on the day. It highlights the failings of the shadowing techniques, especially on such sensitive and touchy international interest cases, and particularly when the KGB are known to have a number of bases in town with active units.

The second is rather more concerning to the President – very concerning, in fact. Yes, the CIA was operational in both cases.

One CIA branch was working closely with the Special Envoy to obtain information to counteract the oil companies; that is, to attain net zero as soon as possible in line with the Environment Act; this the President strongly endorsed.

The other CIA branch, the Counterintelligence Center Analysis Group, was engaged to work with environmental groups to figure out how the oil companies were plotting against environmentalists on social media – but they were taking payments from the oil companies and their representatives not to do the work – not to report their findings and to turn a blind eye. Hence there was no chance that the CIA would have been working as a cohesive force in those London operations, resulting in this diabolical mess-up. Sure, they were contracted to extract, etc., but that was a presidential directive.

Heads will surely roll over this; charges and court cases will be extensive and harsh without fail.

The rest is yet to be seen.

Chapter 52

⤙◈⤚

The smoke and stun grenades are thrown at short intervals, leading to the impression that there are several KGB agents in their team. The smoke grenades are going off in all different directions and locations, giving them close to invisible status.

The agent tasked with the job, head down, gun to the fore and grenade in hand, runs across the compound to the passenger door of Bronagh's van, opens it and jumps in to lie on the floor and close the door behind him.

Bronagh is startled but stays still, holding her breath for as long as possible, then breathing slowly and quietly. Her new companion keeps his head low but looks back into the van, sees Bronagh's head and says quietly, "Hello."

Although it is nice to hear a "hello" in any accent, she is not really impressed. She doesn't know who it is and stays still and quiet.

"I know your name is Bronagh. I am here to help you. Can you do exactly as I say, please, if you want to get out of here alive."

She is not impressed, doesn't believe he is here to help her, and has no idea of the probability of getting out of this alive.

The CIA have been trying to track and estimate people's movements. They know a KGB agent has entered the van, but they cannot fire any shots at him for fear of hitting Bronagh, as they do not know whereabouts in the van she is. Both the KGB agents know this, but Bronagh doesn't.

She whispers, "It is your job to get me out and away from here safely. I can do nothing."

"I want you to stay still and quiet," he says.

"That's exactly what I have been doing."

"Good. We have an agreement, then," logically assumes the agent.

All goes quiet in the compound, and a light wind wafts the last puffs of smoke away. Who dares make the next move?

While Bronagh is lying quiet, unsuspecting, and at least logically in agreement, the agent sees his opportunity. He slowly and quietly leans his arm back through the gap between the seats and gives Bronagh a sudden jab of tranquilliser in the side of her neck. She is now completely motionless and asleep ... out of it.

Through the Russian earpieces comes his voice. "Okay, Bronagh is now immobilised. Time for you to set off another round of smoke and stun grenades and create your own covering fire. At the time of maximum smoke and stuns, run like stink to the van and dive in through the door, which I will have opened. I will start the engine as I open the door, and as you enter it, we will drive off."

"A piece of cake!" comes the reply.

"Tell me when you are ready to start the grenades and then when you are approaching the van door."

"Okay, got it."

Another pause.

"Okay ... ready to start the smoke and noise in ten ..."

There is a rapid and extensive issue of smoke from various sources around the compound and then a series of deafening stun grenade blasts accompanied by sporadic bursts of gunfire.

The remaining agent legs it towards the van. At the halfway point, he is hit in the leg by gunfire. He calls into his comrades' earpieces, "Aaaagh! I've been hit!"

"Where?"

"In the leg. Open the door in ten."

The sporadic gunfire continues through the smoke. He leaves a trail of blood on the ground as he forces himself, through great pain, to hop across for ten seconds and dive into the van, which screeches off at a rate of knots, leaving the smoky scene behind. The road is blocked by police vehicles, so they steer away across a grassy area and through a fence, dragging some fencing with them draped across the front of the van, onto the open road.

Temporary padding is wrapped around to cover the wound, stemming most of the blood loss.

Meanwhile, police vehicles are in pursuit. A police helicopter is alongside but following the action at a safe distance for them. They turn down side roads and back onto the main road again at every opportunity to make their route as unpredictable as possible.

The police and the CIA and the helicopter all know that Bronagh is on board the van, hence their hands are somewhat tied, but they don't know that she has been immobilised.

A holed van, an immobilised person, another shot through the leg … and so they trundle on.

The wounded man speaks. "What's the plan, Boss?"

"To drive, shoot and blast our way back to Russia! What the hell d'you think it is, huh?" replies the aggrieved driver, now with no idea what to do.

The wounded man is half lying in the passenger footwell, propped up by the seat edge, not really knowing what time of day it is. His head leans back onto the seat, eyes closed, sweating profusely and bobbing with every movement of the van.

The driver does know, though, that his trump card is having Bronagh with them. He feels proud of that. They cannot be attacked or blown up with her on board.

They drive on.

Suddenly, the driver's attention is drawn to some action far ahead. It looks like a police car on the verge on either side of the road, but there's no road block. He figures that they won't shoot at the van due to the risk to Bronagh, so he speeds up to make them a more difficult target.

On passing the police vehicles, he realises, as the steering becomes hard, that they have thrown out stingers to puncture his tyres. It has worked. He has lost control and gradually applies the brakes to bring them safely to a stop. Smoke and the smell of scorched rubber rises in the air around the van.

All is quiet.

There is a shuffling and a murmuring in the rear of the van.

"Where am I? What's going on?" This is Bronagh coming round. The drug has worn off, but she is still drowsy. "I'm thirsty. Can I have some water, please?"

"No," says the Russian voice. "We don't have any."

"Oh, it's you guys … you still here, then?"

"We do appear to be, yes, and we have been looking after you."

"So what happened to me? And where are we?"

"We gave you a little sedative to help you with your cooperation. We are somewhere north of London."

"Oh, no wonder I feel dreadful ... I have a headache, I need water ... Why are we north of London?"

"A good question! Because we had to be here – no other options."

"Okay, well, let me get out of here and get some water." She moves to open the rear door.

"No! Bronagh, *do not* open that door!" shouts the Russian. "You would be met with a hail of bullets. We are surrounded by police and CIA."

It slowly dawns on her. "Ahhh, yes, I see ... I remember now ... So what happens now?"

"We just sit here and wait."

"And wait for what?"

"Will you shut up with these stupid questions!" shouts the Russian.

All goes quiet again.

Chapter 53

⋘◉◈◉⋙

There is now thinking time and recollection time for Bronagh. She notices that the other Russian is virtually unconscious and that there is blood on him and on the van floor on his side. Due to the recent doping, she is not as intense and worried as she might normally have been in a situation like this.

She recalls that she is still in possession of two guns and two knives. She spends some time thinking about that … quite a while, actually.

She forms a plan in her mind and rehearses it over and over. *Shall I say this? Or that? Which would be more effective and productive? Wait a minute, am I really thinking this and thinking of doing this? I guess, yes, I am, and yes, I have to.*

She imagines herself quietly and carefully picking up a gun in each hand and pointing each gun at the Russians in the front. They are sitting looking out of the windscreen and into the rearview mirrors. She imagines putting her fingers on the triggers and saying … saying what? For example, "Put your hands in the air and then flat on top of your heads. You have a loaded gun pointing at each of you – at the centre of your heads, actually, and from close range" … *or should I say that the other way round – I mean, say about the guns first? Yes, that would be safest and best.*

And then she does it! Suddenly, surprising even herself, adrenaline starting to race again … she has said it!

The Russians are stunned. They raise their hands and place them on their heads as directed. Slowly they turn to face her and check that it is for real … they see it is. They both slowly shuffle to the fronts of their seats to give them more distance from Bronagh's weapons.

As their heads touch the windscreen, there is an almighty hail of breaking glass. Holes appear in the Russians' heads, blood pours out and they slump down in motionless heaps.

"Oh my God! What have I done?" screams Bronagh. It appears that she has actually shot them both dead! She puts her hands over her mouth and nose and sits there looking … totally shocked, she can't move or react.

She then falls in a heap on the floor herself, crying her eyes out. She is devastated.

"Oh my God," she screams repeatedly. She has no one to blame but herself. "I never even thought about or intended to kill anyone ever!" she cries.

Police officers tentatively approach the rear of the van in helmets and full body armour. They quickly fling open the rear door. Six guns point at Bronagh. She cowers in a tight ball, crying and screaming.

Officers also enter the front of the van and inspect the two Russians. The all clear is signalled. Paramedics check out the bodies, and ambulances arrive to take them away under armed police escort.

The paramedics check Bronagh over and give her plenty of water to drink, and an ambulance takes her to hospital. The police helicopter is stood down.

Bronagh is medically okay. Female police officers come to her bedside, console her and talk to her briefly through her swirling emotions. They reassure her that she is well, will be okay and will get over this. They try to convince her that she did what she had to do – she did it well and had to in order to survive, to come out of this alive.

Chapter 54

ᴄᴈⓄᴃᴑ

The following day, Bronagh is transferred to Scotland Yard for a debrief.

She is surprised to see that they have a couple of nurses on standby, a solicitor and a psychologist, as well as Special Branch officers. Slowly, bit by bit, they put her in the picture.

When the two Russians moved forward in their seats and their heads touched the windscreen, they were clear shots for police marksmen to take them both out, which they did totally effectively.

Bronagh is in floods of tears yet again and is consoled by the nurses.

She had thought that she had shot the two Russians herself, but no, she had not done so at all. Of course, in the heat of the moment, with all the adrenaline and tension, it was quite in order for Bronagh to think that she had done the deed – the one she had planned so vividly in her head and rehearsed over and over.

The relief is unbelievable.

Now she begins to realise why the nurses are there – to console her – why the solicitor is there – to witness the police admissions about what actually transpired – and why the psychologist is there – to deal with the unwinding of her trauma.

The Special Branch officers repeat that she did nothing wrong; she performed excellently and is in no way to blame for the men's deaths. They thank her for her brave actions and regard her as heroic. They wave, smile and leave.

The solicitor stays a while in case she has any questions; the psychologist stays for similar reasons.

The nurses stay to keep her company.

Bronagh is now quite weak and tired and soon falls asleep.

.•.

The following morning, Bronagh wants to see Finn again. She is now very ready ... she has missed the love of her life terribly.

The hospital call Finn and ask him to come over. They tell him that Bronagh is okay, she is well, she has had "a bit of an accident". She wants to see him and she will be coming out of hospital later today.

So that's all good, then.

Finn is met and briefed by a doctor and a nurse. They say that Bronagh is as well as can be expected. She's had a tough few days following an "accident". The solicitor and psychologist have now left. The doctor takes Finn in to see Bronagh.

It is an emotional meeting. They cuddle and kiss, and the staff leave them alone together for a while.

Special Branch have already told Bronagh not to tell anyone what actually happened, not even Finn. So she doesn't – she can't.

They just spend time together, being quiet and grateful that all is well.

Finn has, deep down, missed Bronagh badly. They have never been apart unexpectedly for this long before. It has had the effect of making him realise how important to him she is and how much a part of him she really is.

They cannot discuss everything in detail now. They are not ready for that sort of thing emotionally after this calamitous set of circumstances and events. Finn knows this without even discussing it, as he knows that Bronagh would have told him all about it as it happened. Bronagh too knows that Finn sees it that way.

They are, surprisingly in some ways, at ease with each other, and their old togetherness is still there. Perhaps, though, because of the depth of their relationship, this is not so surprising.

Martha has been in touch and would like Bronagh to come over and see her at the American Embassy. This is easily done – it was expected anyway – and Finn can sit in reception and wait. They order a taxi.

Neither of them has ever been inside an American Embassy before; it is an amazingly "official" place, naturally, but it also has a relaxed air, calm order having been spawned from meticulous organisation and authority.

A woman from the embassy staff, with official ID and passes, etc., appears with Martha. She and Bronagh hug and smile at each other, which brings them to tears of relief. Martha and Finn share a hug too.

Finn then waits on a lavish, comfortable chaise longue in reception, reading some interesting copies of *National Geographic* magazine. This type of reading material is factual and hence politically acceptable to most visitors to the American Embassy.

The women are led away to a meeting room. Although private, they still have the company of an

American diplomat and the staff member … coffee and croissants are served all round. The diplomat outlines the need for this meeting and the agenda he needs to cover regarding the circumstances they have found themselves in recently, both on that "high-speed" trip to the USA and in the London turmoil.

Needless to say, yes, the CIA was involved in keeping an eye on them in the USA. This he explains to their satisfaction, so they are comfortable with it. They can now more clearly see what has been going on and appreciate the intense dynamics of it all.

More time is spent, however, on the greater complexity of what was going on earlier in the UK. They had not fully appreciated this – but they do now. The looks of shock on their faces say it all. They had not realised what was going on behind the scenes, and internationally as well. Only now do they fully appreciate how much danger they put themselves in.

The main thing to get their heads around is the urgency with which commercial organisations and governments are dealing with these issues. They had no idea how seriously it was being taken.

This has the effect, unexpectedly, of building their egos, but they aren't so much proud of themselves as of what they have been involved in. They are trying to achieve the same goals as Ezra, Finn and others too, of course.

They are now left in private for a chat on their own.

They hug again. Whilst hugging, Martha whispers into Bronagh's ear, covering her mouth with her hand, "Careful what we say. This room will obviously be bugged with all sorts of listening devices. We can't afford to say the wrong thing now, can we?"

They move over to a pair of comfortable chairs and enjoy a spell of relaxing and non-revealing conversation – not that they have a lot to hide now anyway.

They also appreciate the boost in belief in what they have been doing and are working towards. They have found, in the process, respectability.

This is a very satisfying surprise.

The staff member returns; they share their thanks and bid their farewells. Martha heads home and Bronagh joins Finn on his comfy chaise longue for a few minutes ... which is fun ... and then they head home.

Chapter 55

❦

It has been a gruelling time for Bronagh – perhaps the hardest thing anyone could experience in their life. However, she is out of it now – a massive relief, but she will still have to take time to get over it and to heal. How has it affected her? Is she any stronger for it? Or weaker?

That will take time to assess as well.

Bronagh is back, then – a few days longer away than planned, but she is back safe and fairly well.

Things are rather strained, to say the least. She cannot say anything about what she has really experienced. For one thing, it wouldn't make sense and would take too long to explain, and she doesn't feel like it now. She doesn't have the energy.

For another, she has been told by the CIA and the police not to reveal anything about it all to anyone for security reasons, both national and for her personally.

Finn, quite naturally, is bewildered. He could imagine all sorts of things … but doesn't. This is a ploy to conserve his own energy and mental state more than anything else.

•◆•

"This conflict between all of the pro-oil and no-go factions can't continue," mulls Bronagh. "Abu Dhabi may step up to broker the way forward."

Finn ponders this for a moment.

"The Flintstones adapted to the needs of modern life; I bet ya Abu Dhabi do."

The angels and archangels cringe.

Bronagh falls about all over the place, laughing her head off but only slightly injuring herself.

••••

"Finn, I get this feeling – and I've felt it building for some time – that now is the right time … I mean, we must go down to St Michael's Mount … you know, properly – go straight there, no ifs or buts."

"Oh! Right! Okay …" responds Finn.

And so back on the road, the full leg, right down through the whole West Country and the peninsula that, peculiarly, is Cornwall.

The summit of St Michael's Mount features a historic house with a chapel. The chapel itself is not large for such a seemingly prestigious monument. Perhaps that is an apparition or illusion.

Finn and Bronagh arrive at the coastal car park at Mount's Bay. Under cloudy skies, and with gulls culling, the black, white and red oyster catchers with orange legs wade in the shallows and fly in with their characteristic calls. Before them is the causeway across the sands and through the seawater to the Mount.

The distinct, emotionally powerful, triggering odour of seaweed, some of it in a state of decay, wafts around. There is brown kelp and various green and red seaweeds seemingly randomly distributed across the shoreline and attached to a few small rocky outcrops. The mirror-like surfaces of the rock pools dotted about are occasionally rippled by creeping crabs.

A small flock of chirpy, active and inquisitive sparrows have gathered around them on the sea wall. "I don't know what they are expecting!" says Finn.

"Okay, Finn, here we are; do you realise that we are now at the point where the St Michael's alignment from here northeastward up through the country to Stonehenge, Avebury and beyond is crossed by the alignment from Skellig Michael, off the southwest tip of Ireland, to here, and then southeastward down through Mont-Saint-Michel, over on the coast of France, and onward down through Italy to Israel?"

"Wow! That means this must be a very significant place," says Finn, "The chapel on the mount looks very foreboding. There are no lights on inside."

"The chapel must be eerily quiet, as if in the lull before the storm," envisions Bronagh.

"The chapel on the mount looks foreboding. There are no lights on inside. "The chapel must be eerily quiet, as if in a lull before a storm," envisions Bronagh.

The causeway is covered by seawater from high tide down to mid-tide. This means that there is no passage to the Mount except when the tide has dropped enough to leave the causeway exposed to the air, as it is today. The causeway is draining its seawater and subtly drying out. One can walk over to the Mount. Some people drive over.

But the clouds are lowering their bases and thickening … and darkening … more mist is rolling in. Flashes of lightning occasionally light up the clouds in some parts of the sky … but there is no thunder.

"Finn, this is a lovely place; the setting of St Michael's Mount in the bay is so picturesque and uniquely spectacular … but … don't you think … there is something ominous about those clouds?" The temperature drops a little, noticeably. The clouds are slowly darkening further.

There is a mist over the still sea.

"Bronagh, listen," urges Finn. "What do you notice?"

After a pause, "Nothing?" offers Bronagh.

"Exactly. Can you hear gulls or oyster catchers?"

"You're right, Finn. There's nothing."

Even their sociable, friendly group of cuddly sparrows has departed.

The cloud base has now slowly and surreptitiously descended to envelope half of the visible height of St Michael's Mount and the surrounding buildings.

They hold hands tightly. This progresses into a side-by-side cuddle.

The atmosphere is now unnerving.

"I don't feel like walking over there today, Finn, even though we could."

"I'm with you on that, Bronagh … something seems to be afoot."

There are still sporadic flashes of brightness with a red and orange hue in distant pockets of cloud, which highlight the local architecture of those internally illuminated clouds. They are like bulbous, voluminous caverns in the sky … These could not be ordinary lightning flashes.

Chapter 56

Satan, incarnate as the Devil, is heard to chunter, "I supported that heroic pursuer of might and domination, Hitler, but he did not have the depth of resources, organisation and backup and extensive personal strength that we needed for out-and-out victory, domination and world supremacy. He was a big let-down for me. World War I was just as bad. I should have learnt from that one."

The broader spiritual world could hear this and sensed that something was up – something was afoot.

He continues, "This time I think I can successfully support the oil companies, their leaders and their government agencies, as this initiative has a much broader base, more resources and a cohesive strength … and the essential will and determination to succeed comprehensively and eternally."

In all the spiritual realms, all sense this warning – a warning of impending action. It shakes the very bedrock of Earth and civilisation.

Archangel Michael has been holed up ready for action, out of sight, disguised as a slithering, slimy black streamlined body dripping thick treacly black oil from old oil cavities underground in the Texas area of the southern Rockies in the United States of America.

He ponders this threat and prepares his own team.

A team of cherubim is detailed to leave their headquarters in caverns below the Norwegian fjords.

They have been waiting discreetly for a call to action from this well-disguised and unlikely sleeper location. They travel in the dead of night, so as not to be seen – at least by the enemy in the spiritual world.

Teams of seraphim begin to slither, having been alerted similarly in Scotland.

The Living Creature angelic spiritual entities in Canada are warming up on standby.

Satan's other dark forces – demons, evil spirits and Principalities – take advantage of the earlier chuntered warning too.

In the spiritual realms' terms, this is all too similar to the preparations for D-Day, but this is not D-Day.

This is going to take place on the other side of the English Channel. Satan is summoning his forces for a final challenge of Michael. Things have been mounting, or rather drifting, for some time – more than thirty years, in fact. The stage Satan wants to set is in none other than the skies over St Michael's Mount, near Penzance in Cornwall.

Obviously Michael does not want his forces to meet Satan's forces en route to this location. Contingents will set off at allocated times and travel along specified routes. He wants to keep the element of surprise in his favour.

Michael's troops are at organised safe locations, so they will be signalled into action to travel at specific times along their designated routes.

Satan's forces, on the other hand, are all over the place.

Some of the rogue demons or evil spirits from Satan's scattered entourage occasionally come alongside, and even try to intercept, some of the seraphim and cherubim squads mid-flight. However, because the evil forces won't know until the last minute whether they are going to be challenging a man, an ox, a lion or an eagle, they are woefully ill-prepared to complete an attack or interception.

Michael does have a plan of engagement for whatever they find when they arrive at St Michael's Mount. He plays his cards close to his chest, and with good reason. Prior to any engagement, Michael will keep his squads in holding positions some distance from the location. They can be called on instantly and will be "in theatre" at a moment's notice.

Satan's roving individuals or gangs can appear anywhere at any time. Satan doesn't necessarily know if or where trouble will arise, but it always does.

Satan has planned to place at the centre of the action his three chief demons: Gardoon, who has a reddish hue; Hurore, who has a purplish hue; and Gomati, who has an orange hue.

They are arrogant fliers, rarely remaining stationary, even when instructed. By their very nature they do not follow rules or instructions to the fullest detail. They leave trails of colour and swirling eddies of air as they pass through again and again.

These holding patterns prevail for some time, while more detailed plans are forming somewhere backstage.

Suddenly, after a long period of inaction, there is an almighty roar of engulfing, deafening and ethereal proportions, stunning, transfixing and penetrating everything around.

"This is the voice of your universal leader, of universal power and of total authority, Satan, the Devil … I am to be obeyed … I am instructing all my dark powers and evil forces in this looming battle to strike, to engage and to tear apart all forces of good."

Gardoon rallies his troop of demons for action. Hurore gathers his squad for instructions. Gomati leads his combatants in a defiant approach.

Michael listens, watches and waits.

Satan's strategy is for his demonic leaders to patrol actively around, circling in groups, displaying domination of the area. This will inevitably attract angelic groups hoping to drive them out, control the area and restore order.

Satan also knows, however, that he has evil spirits and principalities roaming freely out there, causing havoc anyway. This will confuse the incoming restorers of faith into weakness and giving up.

•◆•

I arise today
Through the strength of
the love of Cherubim,
In obedience of angels,
In the service of archangels,
In hope of resurrection to
meet with reward,
In prayers of patriarchs,
In predictions of prophets,
In preachings of apostles,
In faiths of confessors,
In innocence of Holy virgins,
In deeds of righteous men.
I arise today

Through the strength of heaven:
Light of sun,
Radiance of moon,
Splendour of fire,
Speed of lightning,
Swiftness of wind,
Depth of sea,
Stability of earth,
Firmness of rock.
I arise today
Through God's strength to pilot me:
God's might to uphold me,
God's wisdom to guide me,
God's eye to look before me,
God's ear to hear me,
God's word to speak for me,
God's hand to guard me,
God's way to lie before me,
God's shield to protect me,
God's host to save me
From snares of devils,
From temptations of vices,
From everyone who shall wish me ill,
Afar and anear,
Alone and in a multitude.
I summon today all these powers
between me and those evils,
Against every cruel merciless power
that may oppose my body and soul,
Against incantations of false prophets,
Against black laws of pagandom,
Against false laws of heretics,

Against craft of idolatry,
Against spells of women and
smiths and wizards,
Against every knowledge that
corrupts man's body and soul.

Gaelic poem: "The Deer's Cry" by St Patrick

Whether logic needs its
thread of gossamer
To hold the web of life intact,
Somewhere a voice will say,
"So that's for or against;
the forces conspire."

Colin Krainin

Chapter 57

⌒⊙⊙⌒

At an approximate altitude of 38,000 feet above the southwestern approach to the UK, an aircraft with a full passenger load begins its slow decent to land at Heathrow airport. The pilot notes the turbulent atmospheric conditions over Cornish airspace, reporting sudden gusts in an otherwise more turbulent environment than usual. He notes very large cloud banks in the vicinity, some quite dark or black in places, even though there are no cumulonimbus or thundercloud formations expected in the meteorological forecast for the area. The co-pilot agrees that this is quite unusual.

"This is a conventional aviation fuel–burning plane; let's give it some moral support and fly in formation alongside out of respect," says Gardoon, the red-hued demon. Four other demons form up, two on each side. The co-pilot reports an unusual reddish hue to the clouds at that time, adding that that is also unusual.

Michael signals for a unit of seraphim to disturb the formation and disband it. They fly in in an uncompromising attack formation from above. The seraphim comment that planes using biofuel additions to their aviation fuel would be quite welcome, but this is sheer and utterly flagrant disregard for the conventions agreed at recent COP meetings.

The demonic support formation is thus totally unwarranted, and the seraphim shoot down just in front of the demonic line at high speed, causing further turbulence that disrupts and dismantles the demonic formation. The aircraft passengers think they have hit an air pocket, but they continue to their destination.

Just about to approach a distance of about ten nautical miles due south of the Lizard peninsula, the most southerly tip of Cornwall, a fully laden oil tanker makes its way up the English Channel towards Fawley refinery in Southampton Water on the coast of Hampshire.

The captain can't help noticing, to the north, a huge bank of cloud and a darkening of the skies. It looks like cumulonimbus clouds, but none of those have been forecast. The captain instructs all crew on the bridge to keep a weather eye open.

"Another lovely shipment of viscous black oil to generate fumes and the heavy atmosphere that makes it easier for us to fly and to generate revenue to fund further oil exploration; they certainly need a fitting escort from us," gloated Gomati, the orange-hued leader demon. The escort formed up and settled down at a slow speed all around the enormous but steady vessel. The crew noticed a nice warm subtropical orange glow in the humid air at this point.

Michael signals a flight of seraphim to address this issue. "Obviously Just Stop Oil protesters can't be out here right now. It's the least we can do to make a representation and break up this despicable party." With this, the seraphim drift across close to the surface of the sea unnoticed and wait in anticipation for the surprise that is about to unfold as the ship and its escort approach.

The seraphim collectively shoot vertically up into the air. This causes a vicious flow of mini tornadoes and waterspouts above the surface of the sea. The violent airflows and spray bring visibility down to ten yards. The orange demon group have to take emergency action to regain control of themselves, let alone any sense of an escort formation. They have to dart, jolt and twist to avoid collisions in the spray, both with each other and with the ship. As a consequence, the ship's crew see mini tornadoes, waterspouts and spray with orange streaks of vapour forming and blowing around in the turmoil.

"An extremely unusual phenomenon!" exclaims the captain and reports it to the Met Office personally.

The seraphim are now long gone, but the demonic clan slowly reassembles, and they return to their holding slot with their tails between their legs in embarrassment.

The oil tanker sails on through clear and normal visibility; the crew are left wondering.

When the tide goes out twice a day, groups of organised volunteers, as well as individuals, can be seen walking along the foreshore of Mount's Bay, following the water's edge. They pick up any plastic object that is washed up or still in the water – everything they can find littering the beaches. Bags are filled with the plastic finds as they go along. The full bags are collected and taken to a central point. They are sorted, and as much as possible is sent to recycling centres.

Hurore, the purple-hued demon, spots these volunteers – easy prey. His squad zooms in, following the water's edge at high speed and low, just above the sea.

This in itself creates vortices and spray, which makes life very uncomfortable for the volunteers, who only came out for a quiet, peaceful and relaxing day in the fresh air on the beach … little did they know. After this first pass, the demons circle up and around to make a return pass along the beach, creating repeated discomfort for the volunteer groups, who are now forced to take defensive action and begin to put on their cagoules and raincoats, urgently retrieved from their backpacks. The demon squad regard this as fun; the people are doing exactly what they want, their desired result being that more plastic gets left on the beach and in the water to spoil the quality of life of the sea creatures and also cause more plastics to need to be made. Hey, a few more up and overs and arounds and a few more passes … more vortices and spray; terrific fun.

This so infuriates Michael that he asks the seraphim and cherubim to unite on the case to make a show of force. This is a demonstration of flying skills to display the power that could be unleashed as a result of such behaviour. This is an enjoyable manoeuvre for the combined forces too; they can make repeated sweeps for as long as is necessary to clear the area of vermin. When the Mount's Bay area is clear of demons, the job is done … and it was.

The Goonhilly Downs Antenna 1 radio signal dish received the first live transatlantic television broadcasts from the United States via the Telstar satellite in the middle of 11 July 1962. This was obviously a very significant moment in the communications and technology developments of the UK and worldwide. Goonhilly Downs is at a high point of the Lizard peninsula, and on a clear day it is a vantage point over the whole of Mount's Bay in which St Michael's Mount is situated.

The demons appreciated this technological achievement too and treated it as symbolic of the later communications technology that followed in the UK over the next sixty years.

The three demon leaders instruct the blue-hued evil spirits to take up station on and around the Goonhilly Downs, encircling the antenna site. They can be static on the ground and take up cover behind hedges, bushes and tussocks of long grass so as not to be seen. The evil spirits feel triumphant that they are supporting the cause, symbolically, behind communications technology in general. This technology has led to the degradation of human values through television commercials, adverts, bad television programmes and films, the internet's bad side, and the negative side of social media.

Well, there's history and progress for you. Anyway, Michael, of course, doesn't see it that way. He requests the Living Creatures to respond to this outrage by creeping up over the Lizard cliffs from the beaches, coves and rocks below. By stealth, they can then creep up on the evil spirits and spook the daylights out of them. This could end in hand-to-hand fighting and tussling, but the element of surprise is with the Living Creatures.

The climb takes a good while. The stealthy approach has to be very slow, careful and, above all, quiet. Upon getting within sight of a target evil spirit, the instructions are to stop and not engage until a haunting cry is given ... after which any technique to weaken, destroy or flush the enemy is legitimate.

The coordinated approach and skill of this proves a success.

To celebrate, the Living Creatures take flight and settle at the Eden Project further to the east, just west of Plymouth. Here are the special very large domes that shelter a range of example botanical habitats from around the world, so they can chill, relax and talk amongst themselves.

Another feather in the cap.

Summer is the time of year when the coasts of Devon and Cornwall host a mass of shoals of mackerel, a beautiful dark blue and silver vertically striped fish. Well, that used to be the case, but two things have happened, coinciding at exactly the wrong time. Over the last few decades, the number of mackerel has been depleted by over-fishing by international factory ships, using the mackerel not just for human food but also for animal feed and fertiliser. The other factor is that global warming, due to excessive emissions, has led to climate change and to sea temperatures warning up. Hence the smaller fish and plankton that the mackerel feed on have migrated north and congregate now around Scotland and still further north.

Years ago, the fishing around the coasts of Devon and Cornwall was sustainable, and livelihoods depended and survived well on it. Much has changed, and those livelihoods have now gone.

Evil spirits and Principalities have moved in here to gorge on greed, more greed and decimation. They used to fly through the coastal settlements hounding those fishing villages and driving the fishing industry onto bigger boats for bigger catches to decimate the area.

Well, yes, they succeeded, and they come back here to reminisce every summer.

This time there are a few surprises in store for them. Both Living Creature angels and cherubim are waiting behind the harbour walls and in occasional coastal caves.

At the appropriate moment, there is a surge, a roar and massive turbulence from the angels flying up vertically and intercepting the evil spirits and Principalities from beneath – their blind spot. This is frequently a lethal and effective technique.

The frantic swirls of fighting, with turbulent trails of blue- and brown-hued air, creates a noticeable fog along the coast, but it is also a sign of success – for one of the groups, anyway; in this case the Living Creatures and seraphim.

All along the coasts of Devon and Cornwall, as well on virtually all the coasts of the British Isles, there can be found millions of shellfish, molluscs and crustaceans. Their habitat is the intertidal zone, and, of course, there are millions along the shores of Mount's Bay itself.

For millions of years these sea creatures, living attached to rocks and seaweed, typically, and also to the bases of harbour walls and the supporting piers, have gone about their daily business of living … oh, and of reproducing.

One key thing they do is grow an outer shell. This is very hard, and it provides protection from the elements, harsh wave action and predators. This shell has a very important component that gives it its strength – calcium carbonate.

The shellfish makes this itself, using specially differentiated cells in its body. It draws seawater through its internal tissues. The seawater contains dissolved calcium in the form of calcium ions. It also contains dissolved carbon dioxide. The cells of the shellfish's tissues combine the calcium with the carbon dioxide to form calcium carbonate. It builds this up, layer after layer, to create its hard external shell, which it happily lives within; this is its home, its own little place.

Consequently, some of the carbon dioxide in the biosphere of the Earth has already been taken out of circulation in the atmosphere by these shellfish.

Taking carbon dioxide out of circulation is called *sequestration*. It is a very difficult thing to achieve, but if we could do more of it, it would help to reduce the globally dangerous carbon dioxide levels in the atmosphere, thereby lessening the effect of global warming – an objective definitely worth pursuing.

So therefore … why don't we grow more shellfish? Why don't we farm them? This would have the double benefit of taking more carbon dioxide out of the atmosphere and seawater and converting it to calcium carbonate. Using the calcium carbonate shells for building materials would therefore permanently remove the carbon dioxide from the atmosphere. The other benefit would be that the shellfish meat is a food source, rich in protein. Thus natural sequestration will have been achieved and helped reduce carbon dioxide levels, and we will have produced protein-rich food along the way.

This is strongly objected to, as might be expected, by the demon leaders, Gardoon, Hurore and Gomati. They are pooling their strengths and resources on this one, it is seen as so significant. Their view is that it would be far easier to just let global warming and climate change carry on and take its natural course – I mean, after all, humans did start it.

These demon leaders set about to parade a show of strength around Mount's Bay at an altitude of approximately one hundred feet above the sea. They are joined by all the other demon squads, collectively making quite a throng.

This does, of course, draw the attention of Michael in his hometown. He counters with a combined strength of a team of Living Creatures and seraphim.

The angelic team circles Mount's Bay too, but in a wider circle and in the opposite direction to the demonic squads.

After a few circuits to stabilise and to plan their timing, the angels simply have to steer their flight paths closer and cross the demon squads at right angles at very high speed. This is a highly dangerous tactic, but it is designed to be so. Inevitably there are impacts, collisions and scrapes. Damage is done; broken appendages, parts falling off, tufts of feathers fluttering everywhere, disfigurements … but it has all been worth it, they say. The demons are shaken, highly stressed and in a state of shock. Their orderly formation falls apart. Injured individuals swerve off on unpredictable courses in a dazed state.

This is a great triumph for the angels, even with the extent of their own injuries and damage.

The positive prospects for natural sequestration live on.

Chapter 58

⋘⊚⋙

Over very extensive parts of Cornwall, there has been much mining activity through the centuries.

From the early Bronze Age, around 2150 BC, right up until the mid-twentieth century, the metals tin and copper were highly sought after. This was because people had found many uses for those metals to improve their quality of life. Great value was thus attached to them. Considerable profit and wealth was generated in the process … for some.

But eventually, once the easy pickings, the most profitable extractions from the geology, had been made, there was no more value there – certainly no more profit.

The abandonment of the mines left enormous holes in the ground – dangerous mine shafts dotted all over Cornwall, together with spoil heaps and disused buildings. This was the unintended (or intended?) legacy of a great idea. The evidence is there to be seen … even tourists come to look at it, paying more money in the process.

Generating revenue from processing resources, and additionally from refining them and selling the refined products, has been endemic through the whole Industrial Revolution since 1760. The greed for this revenue has been even more endemic.

One can easily allude to the oil industry too in this context, the refined products being petrol, diesel, aviation fuel, paraffin, tarmac and a vast array of organic chemicals, many of which are used for manufacturing various plastics. This is known as the petrochemical industry.

Once a revolution starts, it is very difficult, if not impossible, to stop before it has run its course. There is also the question of what that course is and what causes it to stop running.

It has been noticed in certain quarters that this particular revolution has been very prolific, with Satan jumping on the bandwagon to propel it to its greatest heights. One could ask ... where would it be without that support?

The symbolic gaudy and incestuous trappings of the oil industry can be seen everywhere – on advertising hoardings and in television commercials, at petrol stations, on petrol tankers and in commercial promotions. This suits Satan's style – it is lavish enough, persuasive enough and compelling enough to entrap the current human mobility trend permanently.

It is now Satan's time, as the Devil, to parade around, touring the coastline and hills of Cornwall, to wonder at the demise of the tin industry and to reflect on how the same can be prevented from happening to the oil industry that he is so proud of.

There are tears in his eyes at the thought of such a tragedy for him, if it were to unfold that way. This has motivated him and strengthened him further so as not to allow such a calamity to happen on his watch.

He is of strong character and has the stamina to maintain his hold over that worldwide industry, so that becomes his devout commitment.

His pterodactyl-like head is raised proudly higher, long beak protruding into the wind.

His pterodactyl-like wings slowly flap around his dragon-like body as he calmly glides, eventually arriving at Mount's Bay and then St Michael's Mount.

Company draws up alongside him as he flies; it is a slithering, oily black character, totally appropriate, of course, for the cause he is supporting. How commendable.

After a short while, the visitor looks Satan in the eyes as they fly side by side together.

Satan shudders … maintains his cool temporarily, and then his rage overflows.

Why the rage? Satan realises that the slithering, oily black character is just a disguise.

It is the covering that has rubbed off the walls of the underground empty oil caverns in Texas. This has rendered the wearer incognito. It is none other than Archangel Michael himself.

Almighty screeching and blood-curdling sounds emanate from the throat and gaping teeth-lined bill of Satan. He lunges to dig the claws of his wings into the body of Michael. Hovering requires sharp downward thrusts of his wings. This generates great bursts of downdraughts that can be felt on the land below.

The Living Creatures fly to Michael's assistance. From their habitat of the old sulphur mines in Canada, they are caked in yellow sulphur. The heat of the turbulence ignites the sulphur, darkening it to red and black, which sometimes burns yellow, sometimes red, sometimes blue. Nonetheless, the burning sulphur produces sulphur dioxide gas, which is very irritating and toxic. These fumes agitate Satan even more. He is irritated and feeling cheated and threatened. He puts great force and energy into flying higher to alleviate these pungent conditions. The rapid swirling of his tail produces greater air turbulence close to the ground. His wings beat with an explosive force and noise, like claps of thunder.

The turbulence at a higher altitude also fans the burning sulphur, producing great flashes of yellow, then red flame, magnifying the dramatic appearance of the cloud formations.

Archangel Michael has not been severely impacted or weakened by the initial charge and continues upward in pursuit of Satan.

Giving great loud growls of annoyance, like thunder, Satan turns to dive long and fast straight down. This conserves his energy for fighting.

He pulls up suddenly as he nears the ground near the Mount, which produces air turbulence, eddies and mini tornadoes in the vicinity.

The Living Creatures have followed him on that downward flight path. They meet him face to face as he turns back up, but they all are close to the ground at this point.

The excessive air flow and forces created by these dramatic manoeuvres have inflamed the burning sulphur to such an extent that it melts in burning lumps and falls onto everything below. Wooden benches, whole trees and the grass in local parks are all set alight. This increases the burning of the sulphur and spreads the pungent and toxic smoke and fumes even more widely.

Bronagh and Finn hurriedly scatter to avoid being hit by falling, burning branches and trees or by burning sulphur. They can only breathe by putting their hands over their mouths or breathing through a piece of fabric or handfuls of grass. Things are desperate; the area becomes an inferno.

Their eyes are watering from the fumes, blurring their vision. It hurts.

The red and yellow glow of the flames lights up the underside of the clouds. The sulphur dioxide fumes add to the conflagration. These dissolve in the moisture droplets in the air and form dilute sulphurous and sulphuric acids. This makes the atmosphere even more toxic, irritating and corrosive in addition to the billowing smoke rising from the burning embers. There are also ash falls, further reducing visibility, with flakes of ash floating around.

The now ashen skin of Satan is cut, corroded and raw. His tired body flails around, sometimes intertwining with the Living Creatures, all of them twisting and turning, trying to gain an advantage. Sometimes one of them dips into the salt water of Mount's Bay. This can temporarily extinguish some flames, but they soon light up again during flight. The salt is rubbed into all of Satan's wounds.

Archangel Michael hovers down to oversee his angels. They are attacking Satan one at a time; it is a continuous agonising and painful experience for him. But Satan is not about to give up, ever, for anything. He has his powerful, massive wingspan to knock attacking angels away, but they keep coming. They are not about to give up either. There is no let-up.

This all adds to the further building of the large cloud formations surrounding them. It is dark throughout, with flaming flashes of red and yellow illuminating every part of the bulbous, tall structures.

Satan tries to make a dash for open water, his flapping wingtips dabbing down on the sea's surface with each wing stroke. He is now too weak to be able to gain any altitude. The angels are in close pursuit.

Satan realises, just before it is too late, that it would be safer for him to return, circling back into the cloud base, where it would be more difficult for them to see him.

He is now in hiding. A little relief, at least. But they know he is there.

Archangel Michael again comes to survey the situation. He knows that Satan knows he has beaten him. He also knows that Satan will not totally give up.

Michael can still keep Satan in this state of suffering, dealing him a dose of his own treatment. That will be even more effective on top of Satan's sweating and sore injuries. There are now no more aggressive screeches or growls heard from Satan, only occasional pathetic whimpers of pain instilled by his weeping and festering wounds.

Michael and his team can maintain this for as long as they like.

A deep, thunderous low-pitched grating and vibrating voice is heard. "Ohhh … Michael, so you win on this day … but don't think that this is the end of it. My work is not yet done," threatens Satan.

"Poor wounded Satan, surely you have learned by now that whatever you support, whatever you do, you can never fully win … at anything. Your power, however great you think it is, is no match for the power vested in us," said Archangel Michael very,

very confidently. "Dwell on those words and thoughts, Satan, for as long as it takes you to realise it."

Satan hears but does not listen, of course, and with that, he musters just enough energy for a final piercing direct attack, shooting out of the cloud with his sharp bill directed straight towards Archangel Michael's chest. The sound of his hard-beating wings gives away his location and intent. This alerts the Living Creatures, who immediately shoot up and form a defensive line in front of their archangel.

Satan realises that he cannot stand another battering and more pain inflicted on his desperate body, so he makes a late swerve right in front of the line. This dislodges and upturns some of the angels. It also creates more air turbulence, which causes ripples on the surface of the sea.

Satan continues in the direction of his swerve, later adjusting his course for home. Archangel Michael and his band of angels leave the scene and return to their respective homes.

Bronagh has cleared her eyes a little and looks around. Then, to her shock and horror, she realises she has lost sight of Finn.

"Finn! Where are you? I can't see you!" She starts crying. She still can't see any real distance but scrambles about around where she is standing. It is no use; still no sight of Finn.

She shouts and yells, "Finn! Finn! Finn! Answer me!" She pauses and waits to give time for Finn to reply … there is nothing, just the sound of the wind.

Bronagh, now in a state of fear, anguish, emotional turmoil and panic, says to herself, *Oh my God! What has just happened? Where is my lovely Finn? The love of my life ... Please don't take him away from me ...*

She sinks to the wet ground in a heap. She sobs. She puts her head in her hands and weeps more and more.

But nothing happens. There is no Finn – no sign and no sound of him.

Is this the end of the world – the end of life for me?

Chapter 59

⋆⊚⊚⋆

Following these tumultuous encounters, where it was evident that all hell had been breaking loose, there was an atmospheric stench of sulphurous air, clouds of moisture droplets, mist and smoke billowing around, creating white-outs and patches of semi-transparency. Was it safe to breathe? There was no choice; you had to.

There were creaking sounds of breaking wood, branches, and twisting or grating and scraping metal … out of this world.

The faint veil of mist faded into a bleak nothingness, but … what was that?

Through those mists … could that be something? Just making something out … something approaching? One can just about make out … is it? Is it Finn? At long last, is it her dear Finn?

Bronagh's heart is all of a flutter. She gets increasingly excited and stands up.

Through the fog and smoke, an outline appears and gets closer … with very slow and deliberate steps … dressed in … loose black clothing … Is it Finn? Or— Oh no! Not the ghost of Finn? No, it is not Finn …

It is …

A Roman Catholic Father. He approaches Bronagh slowly.

"I've been watching you. I know what's been going on … You don't have to take any blame, Bronagh."

In shock!

"How … how do you know my name?"

The Father continues in a slow, soft voice. "We who care about you all know your name; you've been doing a great job. You're a great fighter for the cause, and you are intelligent, very intelligent … You're a great credit."

He comes close to Bronagh and puts his arm around her shoulders. "But Bronagh, you don't live in prehistoric times anymore. You are in modern times. You've almost found your place, and … you can come home as well. The Roman Catholic Church would like to welcome you back in … if you'll have us?"

Bronagh stands there, mouth wide open, face aghast, staring at the figure.

"What's going on? Is this for real?" She just about manages to find words, any words, to respond with something, anything to fill her shock and her numbed and now non-functioning mind.

Fog and whiffs of smoke blow past them in a slow breeze in the dull and clouded remaining light.

"This is unreal," she continues, slowly turning and pacing very slowly, looking down and trying to give herself time to allow her mind to function again. "But where is Finn? Have you seen Finn anywhere? I want Finn, I want my Finn back!" She holds out her arms, but then starts weeping again. She drops her head into her hands and sobs.

Meanwhile, up above, very high above ….

Angels are discussing and explaining between themselves all about Bronagh's family background, her upbringing and her convent school experiences.

The Catholic Father looks at her and says, "Bronagh, look at me. Is he this handsome guy standing behind me?"

In the swirling mist, another figure walks forward … It *is* Finn!

Bronagh can hardly contain herself. She rushes forward and nearly hugs Finn to death.

Emotions, deep, strong feelings, are welling up in Bronagh. She looks as if she is about to stutter and to burst … and then she does.

"Finn, I am bursting with love to give … and I want to give it to you, Finn. Will you accept all the love I have to give? I didn't realise how much you really, really mean to me until I thought you were gone forever just then. Oh, this is just unbelievable, a miracle."

They hug and cuddle for some while.

Eventually, Bronagh breaks away a little. "Finn, I've got to tell you now … I feel terrible, I knew I would … oh my God! … but I've still got to tell you now. Okay, hold hands tightly with me and listen hard, Finn."

She takes a deep breath.

"You know when I had to go away, you know, on those trips into London? Well, actually I had been tempted and pressured, by … you'll never believe it … the CIA!"

"What?" exclaims Finn.

"Yes, I know it sounds ridiculous and impossible, but the CIA, yes. They wanted me to act as a genuine and innocent gatherer of information about the tactics and the sources of information released and exchanged by the Saudi and American oil companies, oh, as well as the European ones … to the environmental action groups, you know, like Just Stop Oil, and, in fact, Finn, that's where they trapped me. Yes, Finn, it did happen;

it is true. No, I know I said it, but I lied – I had to. I was not visiting some old Irish friends! I was also threatened with guns, with knives ... and I hate to tell you, but I have to ... I was almost sexually harassed and blackmailed. But Finn, listen harder ... It didn't happen; nothing actually happened to me in that way. Phew! There – I've said it."

"Bronagh, it's okay. I understand. I love you deeply and dearly. I did sense that you were experiencing some kind of dilemma, and I knew it was pretty intense. I also knew you were having difficulty talking about it and also that you couldn't talk about it, but I knew you would eventually. And I knew it would all work out okay ... I don't know how, but I did."

"Thank you, Finn, thank you ... you are such a great person, and I love you from the bottom of my heart."

Obviously they hug and kiss for quite a while now.

Chapter 60

⌒◯⌒

Finn and Bronagh simultaneously think to themselves, without saying anything to one another, *Using one's senses, feelings, emotions, observations, perceptions, spiritual directions and confirmations … one has to feel, find and triangulate onto one's own location where you feel comfortable, happy and content … and at that place you feel a sense of warmth and energy working for you … nothing against you. This is a place where you can always come to get that experience repeatedly – to be strengthened in every aspect of one's life.*

"I love this exploring, Finn, don't you?"

"Sure do, and I love doing it with you!" Finn replies rapidly. They lean over to share a slow, lingering, meaningful kiss … that continues for quite a while, actually.

It is after looking at maps to check places and experiences and reports from other people that the long-term historical concept of these locations forming an alignment has inescapably appeared.

Just like alignments, any network formations are always worth investigating too … by anyone, everyone, everywhere … always.

They both agree that they now need to assess their whole situation and life plan anew – yes, yet again. Clearly a lot of things have happened, and they need to keep on top of it all. They conclude that, with all their additional wealth of experiences, they should approach the St Michael's Alignment with fresh eyes – revisit it and relax into exploring their feelings more, on top of the analyses and turmoil of the earlier visit.

"Our continuation point, Finn, ...no, let's do that another time. Let's just go to Stonehenge now anyway, and relax."

"Yes, good idea, Bron."

"Hey, you! What's with this 'Bron'? My name is Bronagh!" responds the indignant Bronagh.

"Okay, Bron, keep your hair on!" They smile at each other.

Arriving at Stonehenge, they, like thousands of others before them, cannot help but fall into wonderment at the deep attention that it draws from the eyes and the senses ... its simplicity but complexity, its size, and hence its power, whatever that may be.

The beautifully created shapes of the stones, their precision of placement for such hefty bulks and the atmosphere they create are awe-inspiring. It takes time to stand, stare and wonder ... to take it all in and then to let the imagination flow freely back to those days of its creation and original use. We, automatically, I feel, put ourselves in those original situations in our mind's eye. What were we doing? What did we think and feel? How did we see the future?

As most of us know, Stonehenge is a world-renowned prehistoric site and attracts millions of fascinated observers from around the world. Of course, being the structure that it is, there are many speculations about how it was constructed. Some of these have been physically tested to determine their practicality. Many theories abound as to the purpose and function of Stonehenge and why it is situated where it is. Its relationship to the natural seasonal cycles, agricultural cycles, the moon and solar cycles is strong. Alignments on the horizon are noted, and the holding of festivals there is probable.

Little do Bronagh and Finn realise that there are rallies being held by Extinction Rebellion and Just Stop Oil at Stonehenge in the car park. There are loads of people milling around, and there is a core, central group with banners and placards, as one would expect. It is a very colourful, lively scene, with the sounds of drumming, bugles and trumpets accompanying the chanting.

"Oh my God," says Bronagh. "Look at all this!"

"Unbelievable! Wasn't expecting this today," utters Finn.

"Oh well, let's go and have an explore; you never know what we might find," suggests Bronagh. And off they go, wearing calm T-shirts and cool sunshades, actually looking as if they might blend in rather well.

The general message of the two factions is very clear. But this is the first time Finn and Bronagh have had any kind of encounter with them – not that milling around can really be classed as any kind of proper "encounter", but they regard this as close enough for now. Anyway, all the people gathered appear to be having a lot of fun, enjoying themselves singing, shouting and generally trying to get their message across.

The police are keeping a low profile and only on the fringes.

Another group of people are staffing a quiet, non-protesting stand entitled "Neurodivergents". "That's curious; what's going on there, Finn?" enquires Bronagh. Finn has a little discreet look at some their brochures and fliers, from which he assumes that they represent diverse of groups of people including those with diagnoses such as autism and Asperger's syndrome or somewhere on the ASD spectrum, attention deficit hyperactivity disorder (ADHD), Tourette's syndrome, dyslexia and dyscalculia.

"Wow!" says Finn. "I've come across a lot of those people; many were my friends … in the old days."

"When exactly do you mean, Finn? You're not actually very old!" Bronagh laughs.

"Oh, silly! When I was at school," clarifies Finn.

"Aaahh, I see; you knew them well and closely, I guess."

"I wonder what they are doing here? I mean, why have a stand at all?" muses Finn.

After chatting with them and finding some common interests, some want to find out what Bronagh and Finn are doing and ask, "What other starting points should we explore, Bronagh, for finding alignments?"

"There are the remains of a Roman temple near Warminster and others in the Salisbury area, but also in many other parts of the British Isles.

"On your Ordnance Survey map, look for the usual starting points of churches, abbeys, Roman roads, forts, and artefacts, footpaths, trackways, prehistoric features or absolutely anything else that seems significant to you personally. It is your individual and personal alignment that should be close to your heart, not the alignments or features pertaining to other people's findings. Remember that!" says Bronagh with a smile.

They drive and arrive at another location that is new to them. This is off the main road, and the roads gradually get narrower, and the hedges disappear too, giving way to more open countryside. Drawing nearer very slowly, and slowing all the time, they stop. They sit and look in silence. Something is dawning on them as they do so.

There is a powerful presence which they both sense. It is as if there is a tingle in the air all around them.

They see, in the distance, immense dark brown and dark grey irregular-shaped stone boulders. These are spaced apart by, say, five metres, it seems, but it is difficult to gauge distances exactly here, there being no reference points. The boulders are anything up to perhaps four or five metres tall.

As they get closer to a village, amazingly it appears to be surrounded by several circles of these stone boulders. It is an awesome and inspiring view and experience … they have never come across anything like these sensations ever before. They park up and walk with astonishment to the rows of stones in these very large circles. The whole thing is so immense in proportion and perhaps ominous and overpowering … but, they agree, in a good way.

"How did this get here?" muses Finn.

"I don't know, Finn, but it is one of the most phenomenal things I have ever seen. The circle must be a mile wide!" They continue to wander around the stones and circles in total amazement.

"This is one of those places that has that sense about it and is clearly and evidently strongly determined on the alignment. I've read, Finn, that this location, Avebury in Wiltshire, and all the others on this St Michael's Alignment, are all in a line, or alignment, pointing to the sunrise spot on the horizon on May the 1st every year. How amazing is that?" says Bronagh, clearly staggered.

"So how did that all happen that way?" wonders Finn. "And where did you read that, Bronagh?"

"In Janet and Colin Bord's books *The Secret Country* and *Mysterious Britain* – oh, and the John Michell book *View over Atlantis*."

Chapter 61

❧

Their extensive travels, their viewing of different places, and that key special feeling they get from just being at certain locations has helped Bronagh and Finn tune in to their most favoured places to settle down. Bronagh has been getting broody.

Their sense of "energy spots", feelings about places and just liking a place leads them to the Devizes area of Wiltshire. Nothing to do with this, of course, is the fact that Finn would be able to access trout fishing on the upper Avon river just to the south. The whole area fits their love of rural areas – less traffic and smaller roads, the magnificent nature to be found there … and the tranquillity.

"Oh, wow! Look at this, Finn." Bronagh sounds exceptionally gleeful this time.

Having excitedly looked at the pictures from all angles and hurriedly read the blurb, they make an appointment to visit. As they drive past farmland populated by small herds of dairy cows and beef cattle, visions of a new life build in their minds.

"I have a feeling in my bones about this one too, Bronagh."

"Oh look, there it is!"

They settle for the village of Rowde just to the northwest of Devizes. It ticks all the boxes.

Finn has also been thinking and has arrived at the conclusion that now is the right time.

He pops the question. She says yes!

Widor's Toccata resounds through the main street of the village from the church on their very special day.

Ezra's book and the campaign are now taking care of themselves.

Bronagh and Finn are now able to settle into their "nesting". They have found a small house with a big garden, which is eminently suitable. They have nice neighbours, helpful and sociable.

A year later, they have one child ... two years after that, there is another child.

They are loving this new family life and in this location; it is a dream come true.

Again ... Holst: *The Planets* suite ... the Joybringer, Jupiter, and "I vow to thee my country".

Now with pushchairs on weekend family exercises and outings, they resume their explorations on the alignments. Next up, to the northeast up the St Michael's Alignment is Ogbourne St George church in Wiltshire, in the small village of Ogbourne St George. This is an interesting place because the churchyard neighbours a huge old house which was once apparently an abbey. There are a number of footpaths and trails radiating from here, as it is a popular starting point for walkers and hikers on the Marlborough Downs routes, some of which cross over the top from the Avebury direction.

Walkers like to stop in for refreshment at the Inn with the Well at the other end of the village. It's curious that the well is still there, inside the pub, with a strong glass cover over it that one can stand on and look down into the interior, which is well lit. They park here, have a pint and a ploughman's, and walk up to the churchyard.

"That's weird," says Finn. "I remember seeing those people at a place we visited some time ago."

"And at another of the earlier locations," adds Bronagh.

"But I've just noticed they are all walking around and looking at their phones – I mean looking a lot, all the time."

"And some also have a laptop in their car," observes Bronagh.

Another group, identifiable by their cool sunshades, look like they are wearing ski goggles. They are sitting on the ground and standing in small groups chatting.

A guy notices Bronagh and Finn observing their ski goggles. He interjects. "In case you are wondering, they are wearing the Apple VisionPro AR headsets. You would never know, would you?" He smiles. "Hey! Isn't it great? Have a look at this." The guy is very excited and enthusiastic. On the laptop screen, Bronagh and Finn can see their location, but it has been triangulated by the app or program they are using. There are interconnecting lines, degree-of-confidence data tables, current energy levels and coloured zones around their location and the alignment. They cannot believe it. They don't understand how that they can be seeing this.

"Where did you get this?" enquires Bronagh.

"Oh, it's been produced by some guy; you can download it for free – or it's not a lot of money, anyway."

"What is it called?" Bronagh shows further interest.

"Super-Sensor," replies the guy.

Finn and Bronagh look at each other blankly, both shocked and amazed. They all fall silent until the guy says, "Impressive, isn't it? What are you guys using?"

Bronagh pauses before saying, "Oh, we don't use anything – didn't know you could even 'use something'."

"So how did you find your way here?" The guy is clearly amazed that they are here at all in that case.

"We're just on holiday, wandering around, seeing what we come across." Bronagh attempts to conceal their true methods and quest.

"Of course we are using Auto-GPT as well," says the confident guy, "although some are using Grok AI bot."

"Of course." Bronagh is frantically struggling to keep up. "And so what does that allow you to do?" asks the rapidly learning Bronagh.

"Well, this is far too complex a subject for the average man in the street. This, or these in combination, allows you to work out where you should be, or need to go to, to get your best chances in life and so on – you know, energy from finding your alignment."

"Really?" says a surprised Bronagh, more deeply shocked and mesmerised than ever. She thinks, *These guys are all suddenly so desperate! And with the tech, they are all frantically feeding off one another.*

But Finn quietly intervenes, whispering into her ear, "Bronagh, you see that group of four people over there?"

Bronagh scans around. "Yes, I see a group of four. What about it?"

"What do you notice about them?" asks Finn.

"Umm, I don't know. They look like ordinary dudes to me."

"What have they got in their hands?" probes Finn.

"Ahhh! I see, Mr Holmes! They haven't got phones; they have good old faithful maps. I see! They have arrived at the same place just as easily as the tech guys. How interesting is that!"

The guy continues. "Yeah, it's so much easier to do it than by trying to figure it out for yourself – you know, like using maps and so on or even not bothering to do anything at all."

"Oh …" says Bronagh knowingly.

The guy tries to reassure them of his confidence in the technology. "The answer to our questions, a word or name, is supposed to appear after the Auto-GPT has been whirring a while, but it's been going for much longer than usual this time. We are not sure what's going on. The bot normally comes up with solutions or findings fairly quickly."

"And what word is that?" enquires Bronagh. "What are you expecting?"

As they are all wondering why it's taking so much longer on this occasion, there is an interruption by the Chat Bot Controlling Council (CBCC). A very formal-looking bowler-hatted gentleman approaches and says to them all, "Now look here, you chaps, this is quite enough of this. Just what do you think you are up to, eh? We've been getting a lot of referrals from the police in various locations about crowds of you people gathering in particular places. Now, it's just got to stop, do you hear?"

The CBCC does its job by using an array of chat bot computers to try to work out which one is telling the truth. They can't rely on one on its own to determine whether another one is true or false in its conclusions and writing. The "man from the Ministry" hasn't got the brains to figure it out either.

They all pile in and gather around the laptop in the guy's car, trying to glean a glimpse from any viable quarter, through a side window or quarter-light. They take no notice of the bowler-hatted man from the Ministry ... they do not hear him; they cannot hear him; their attention is so hyped up as they watch the screen that they are all in a trance-like state. Nothing can touch them, only the long-anticipated, slowly evolving ultimate result that they expect to appear and change their lives, and the world, for ever.

The word slowly appearing on the screen is the word ...

Dominus.

Dominus? Dominus? Yes, Dominus ... that is what they all see ... nothing else.

That is the final answer – the final result.

Dominus: God; the Lord; a master, possessor, ruler, lord.

Dominus is the Latin word for "master" or "owner". Dominus saw use as a Roman imperial title: the Lord, dominus, owner, possessor, erus, Jehovah.

But also let's not forget 24 May 1844.

Samuel Morse taps out "What hath God wrought" in the world's first telegraph message.

The yew tree with the large hollow trunk sheltered poor souls in that early freezing winter. It was their "little place".

The yew tree, still in the churchyard at South Boarhunt, is surrounded by many, many gravestones. The engraved dates, which are still visible on some of them, tell the long history of thoughts and of memories, now long forgotten by many but still lingering here, to those who have seen them or still see them now.

And the word clearly still visible on one gravestone …

… Dominus …

RIP
The Family of Edmund

What is our life? A play of passion,
Our mirth the music of division.
Our mothers' wombs the
tiring-houses be,
Where we are dressed for
this short comedy.
Heaven the judicious sharp spectator is,
That sits and marks still
who doth act amiss.
Our graves that hide us
from the searching sun
Are like drawn curtains
when the play is done.
Thus, march we, playing,
to our latest rest.
Only we die in earnest, that's no jest.
Sir Walter Raleigh, 1552–1618

THE END

Appendices

⣟⣟⣟

1. The background stories of the Thistlethwayte family: Life in their little place

At the outbreak of World War II, the incumbent Squire of Southwick was Colonel Evelyn Thistlethwayte. Living at the mansion house which dominated the sleepy, secretive village, he was quite unprepared for the momentous events that were to alter his family's destiny forever.

The family had owned Southwick Park and its surrounding 8,000 acres for some 400 years stretching back to the dissolution of the monasteries presided over by Henry VIII.

Immediately after the outbreak of World War II, Colonel Thistlethwayte was in the habit of offering a gun on the estate's shoot to Admiral Sir William James. He was the Naval Commander in Chief at Portsmouth.

"I had always been accustomed to taking exercise every day, and during the previous summer I had kept fit by walking along the top of Portsdown Hill every afternoon, but just when I was getting rather bored with this walk, Col. Thistlethwayte invited me to a day's shooting on the reverse side of the hill. That was the beginning of a remarkable shooting season … I owe a great debt to the Colonel. The sirens were screeching nearly every night that winter in Portsmouth, and there was no better refreshment to body and mind than an hour or two in the country with keepers who still thought in terms of wildlife, and talked of the habits of birds and animals instead of the habits of Hitler and his gangsters."

On 11 and 24 July 1940, the dockyard experienced its first air raids, and from then on, irregular attacks were endured to the end of the year. The Navigation School's buildings were especially susceptible to fire, so it was necessary to organise night patrols, which had to be drawn from the teachers and students.

This resulted in a fairly tired set of chaps, many unable to stop falling asleep during lectures. The base captain mentioned the problem to Admiral James, who, in turn, persuaded the good colonel, early in 1941, to allow the officer pupils to spend their nights at Southwick House.

Even here, the air raid sirens caused the officers to retreat to the cellars to complete their night's sleep.

"One night when the sirens had sounded, we dutifully descended to the cellars for shelter. After a lapse of half an hour, during which nothing happened to disturb our peace, there was a sudden clatter in the cellar. We looked up to see Col. Thistlethwayte appear clad in a heavy woolen dressing gown and seated in a wheelchair, being propelled by two manservants. He was protesting loudly at being dragged down to the basement at that hour of the night.

"On another occasion, we awoke early one morning and, looking out of our bedroom window, across the park saw the white tresses of a parachute entangled in a magnificent oak tree on the edge of the lawn to the south of the house. Ah, we thought, a filthy Hun who had been […] shot down by our […] night fighters. We assumed the dark shape at the end of the harness must be his body hanging still and lifeless. Ought we to go and cut him down and report our action to the Commander in Chief's office? On closer inspection the dangling shape appeared too regular to be that of a body. Then the awful truth dawned on us; it was a land mine which had failed to explode – as yet! We washed and dressed, returning to the Navigation School in Portsmouth for breakfast and subsequently heard that the bomb disposal experts came later and removed the offending object."

The land mine story is well remembered by a villager, then a young bar assistant at the Golden Lion pub. She was given a length of the parachute cord and, together with other villagers, shared out the silk parachute material, which was quickly machined into glamorous underwear – most welcome in those days of clothing coupons and rationing!

2. Developments of Southwick Estate: A housing initiative

Homes on the doorstep: Finding them

"The new urbanist philosophy employed at Chapelton, Tornagrain, and on the Paton family's Grandhome project – also planned by Duany – is neighbourhood-based.

"People will get in the car if they are more than five minutes' walk from their neighbourhood centre, so it's about trying to remove the car and promote the pedestrian," Lord Moray says.

"You put the primary school in the middle, so when parents walk their children to school it's less than five minutes, and then there's a coffee shop, too, where they can meet with other parents.

"It's about trying to remove the car and promote the pedestrian."

This is the philosophy behind a new prospectus from the Prince's Foundation for Building Community. *The Landowner's Guide to Popular Development* was launched this week to promote the idea that building a community, rather than just houses, creates a far more valuable asset.

It comes a few months after the Country Land and Business Association called on Sajid Javid, UK Secretary of State for Communities, to consider the opportunities for house building on private landed estates, where the priority is the long term.

"There are a growing number of landowners in the UK starting to take this approach," says Ben Bolgar, the Foundation's senior director. "Getting the built fabric right is a way to unlock the natural, social and financial capital of an area. Getting it wrong will produce a negative impact on people's lives for generations to come."

It is this belief that has turned Mark Thistlethwayte from estate owner to town planner. The local council, ordered to build 80,000 new homes in south Hampshire, identified a patch of land for 10,000 new homes – 80 per cent of which were on the Southwick Estate in Hampshire, which has been in Thistlethwayte's family since 1539. The family objected.

"The scale was completely inappropriate," Thistlethwayte says. "They just wanted homes. Nobody thought about what a community might have looked like." The council compromised and they agreed on a 6,000-house settlement, Welborne, that will cover 6 per cent of Thistlethwayte's land. One of the government's chosen fourteen village developments, it is set for completion in twenty years at a rate of 340 houses a year.

To prepare, Thistlethwayte has already constructed a 200-acre solar park that will produce enough energy to power 16,000 homes. But town-building is an expensive business: the four schools will cost up to eighty million pounds to build and a motorway junction of the M27 another forty-five million pounds. While these costs add up, Thistlethwayte will have to make sure that the properties stay within a reasonable price range for first-time buyers.

"They just wanted homes. Nobody thought about what a community might have looked like."

Homes at Welborne have yet to hit the market. Available properties at Tornagrain start at £111,000 for a one-bedroom flat or £160,000 for a two-bedroom house. Chapelton homes include a three-bedroom semi-detached house with garage and garden for £310,000.

Whether government-backed or not, building a settlement on this scale is a big statement to make. The Duke of Fife believes that being a large private landowner is beneficial to such a venture.

"People don't trust councils to hold developers to account," he says. "The family's involvement is a layer of control that they believe in."

The home

One ordinary afternoon, after work, I was watching the television. A plane had just flown into one of the Twin Towers in New York. My daughter had just walked in the door from school. We both watched in disbelief as the tragedy unfolded before our eyes. I commented, "Life will never be the same again."

Everyone remembers the day as thousands of shockwaves rolled out across the nations: in the USA every airport shut down, rental car companies emptied their lots, schools closed. All Americans suddenly had one supreme desire: to find a way home.

For all its flaws, stresses and challenges, home and family is where we most want to be when faced with a crisis – national, local or personal.

When the weather brings an unexpected snowstorm, where do we want to be? Home.

When work becomes difficult, we can't wait to get … home.

When our kids experience a friend's rejection or disappointment over a failed assignment, they just want to go … home.

Home is both the physical place and the emotional environment God imagined into being when He created the family. Home is the place where every person can know belonging and shelter from all the storms of life.

Update: February 2023

Work on the Welborne site development is visibly going ahead. "These little places" will happen.

3. What happened in Judaea under Roman rule

However, what actually happened in Judaea under Roman rule?

There were clearly thoughts and discussions circulating amongst many communities: "This Jesus of Nazareth … is he the prophesied Messiah?"

The Jewish world was split – some thought he was, some thought he was not.

The Jewish leadership eventually decided that he was not the Messiah. They have had to abide by that decision to this day, but there are Jews today who have decided that Jesus actually was or is the Messiah.

Pontius Pilate, the Roman prefect (governor) of Judaea (26–36 AD) under the emperor Tiberius, presided at the trial of Jesus and gave the order for his crucifixion.

According to the traditional account of his life, Pilate was a Roman equestrian (knight) of the Samnite clan of the Pontii, hence his name, Pontius. He was appointed prefect of Judaea through the intervention of Sejanus, a favourite of Tiberius. That his title was prefect is confirmed by an inscription from Caesarea in ancient Palestine.

Protected by Sejanus, Pilate incurred the enmity of Jews in Roman-occupied Palestine by insulting their religious sensibilities due to his hanging of worship images of the emperor throughout Jerusalem and minting coins bearing pagan religious symbols.

After Sejanus's fall in 31 AD, Pilate was exposed to sharper criticism from certain Jews, who may have capitalised on his vulnerability to obtain a legal death sentence on Jesus (John 19:12). The Samaritans reported Pilate to Vitellius, legate of Syria, after he attacked them on Mount Gerizim (36 AD). He was then ordered back to Rome to stand trial for cruelty and oppression, particularly on the charge that he had executed men without proper trial.

According to Eusebius of Caesarea's *Ecclesiastical History*, Pilate killed himself on the order of the emperor Caligula.

The New Testament suggests that Pilate had a weak, vacillating personality. Would the mob be just as happy if he released Barabbas instead of Jesus on the feast day (Mark 15:6)?

Pilate weakly capitulates. His wife sends him word of a revelatory dream she has had about Jesus and urges him to "have nothing to do with that innocent man" (Matthew 27:19), and Pilate abdicates his responsibility to the emperor. In John (19:7–11), Pilate is depicted as having accepted the Christian interpretation of the meaning of Jesus, and he rejects Jewish leaders' reminder that Jesus has merely said that he is "the king of the Jews" (19:21). On the other hand, John's picture of Pilate delivering judgment from a tribunal in front of the prefect's mansion fits typical Roman procedure. Clearly, as an index of the character and personality of Pilate, the New Testament is devastating, but it is preoccupied with concerns of the nascent Christian communities increasingly making their way among the Gentiles and eager to avoid giving offense to Roman authorities.

Clearly, then, between 36 AD and 312 AD, in Rome and Judaea and elsewhere, the Roman world had gone through much pondering, reflection, guilt analysis and revelations of realisations and ultimately come to a conclusion.

Others in the Roman world, and now Constantine, had reached the same conclusion. The events in Judaea had been a major error and a miscarriage and travesty of justice.

There had been a much bigger significance to the Judaea situation that they had not seen, and the price had been paid.

How did others in Judaea see the events and circumstances in hindsight? Well, the jury remains out on that to this day.

One thing is clear, though – that the followers of Jesus, the apostles, the disciples, remained strident and undaunted and spread the word continuously and widely, gathering momentum as they did so.

In the Jewish communities, convention, dogma and historical interpretations of the Old Testament and its founding translations meant that a much more subdued view was taken of those events.

Meanwhile, Constantine in Rome and the empire, with his new seal of approval on the profound consequences of the Judaea situation, rolled out Christianity in a version known in various forms as the Roman Catholic Church, arising from the newly emerging religious views at that time. In effect, it was the state Church of the Roman Empire.

He saw that this was imbued across the Roman world, including the people of southern Britain, as far as was possible at that time.

Religion in Roman Britain was generally polytheistic, involving multiple gods and goddesses;

in being monotheistic, or believing in only one deity, Christianity was different.

After the collapse of Roman imperial administration, much of southern and eastern Britain was affected by the Anglo-Saxon migrations and a transition to Anglo-Saxon paganism as the primary religion. The Anglo-Saxons were later converted to Christianity in the seventh century and the institutional Church reintroduced, following the Augustinian mission. There remained an awareness among Anglo-Saxon Christian writers like Bede that a Romano-British Christianity had existed.

4. A Ukrainian account of the impact of the Special Military Operation on Ukrainian homes and places

In a quiet monastery hidden away in the mountains of the Zakarpattia region of Ukraine, three nuns are providing refuge for women and children who have fled their besieged towns and cities.

The Retreat House, Monastery of the Congregation of the Sisters of St Vincentia, resides around four hours outside Lviv and makes a welcome difference to the terror many families have been subjected to.

Now, instead of falling asleep to air raid sirens and bombs each night, they hear the sound of the gentle lapping of the river that runs behind the monastery.

There is also a chapel, where they can sit in quiet contemplation. Even if those displaced citizens are not religious, they are still welcome to use the space.

The monastery's most recent residents include Nataliya Povod, aged forty-two, who escaped Mariupol at the end of March with her three children, Nikita, Melania and Vlad, aged eighteen, ten and three years.

Ms Povod explained that on the day they were forced to leave the besieged port city, she had woken at six a.m. as Russian forces started shelling her apartment building. She grabbed her children and a bag containing their documents and ran from the building as it was collapsing around them.

"A Ukrainian soldier screamed at me to take my kids and run," Ms Povod told reporters, shaking as she recounted the horror.

What was even harder for Ms Povod was that her parents lived on the opposite side of the same building. As they were running for their lives, she saw that her parents' apartment had been completely obliterated.

For half an hour she ran down roads with her children, the sound of shelling overhead. She said she was so terrified and physically worn out that she almost "blacked out" and thought she would die.

Eventually, they found a bus that could take them to Lviv and then into the mountains. On the journey to safety, they were taken to a supermarket, where they were given food. Ms Povod said she cried at the sight of fresh apples and bread – items she had not seen in months due to food shortages caused by the Russian occupation of her city.

It took them three days to get to the monastery and, when they finally arrived, they had their first hot shower in over a month.

While this family appreciate the safe refuge provided for them by the nuns, it will be a long time before they can feel truly safe. Ms Povod explained that her daughter now goes to sleep fully clothed, as she is petrified there will be a bomb and they will have to run. Her youngest has started wetting the bed again.

"When the war started, I felt okay at first, like 'nothing is going to happen to me and my family'," Ms Povod said.

"But when I saw holes from bombs in the ground outside, I started to worry."

All Ms Povod has ever known is Mariupol. She only speaks Russian and does not see a future for herself anywhere else, due to language barriers and missing what was her home.

"I blame Russia and Putin for all they have done," she said. "Mariupol was always a Russian-speaking city and we had no problem with that. But we never wanted to be a part of Russia."

5. Continuation of Finn's early life background

Next morning it was just the wife, as the husband went to work. The wife was okay; she didn't say much, just suggested for me to watch TV. I said I wasn't going to stay and just walked out the door without bugging out, as they say. She tried to stop me but wasn't confident in actually stopping me, so I managed to get out of the door. She just stood on the steps outside and watched me, saying, "You have nowhere to go. I'll just have to call the police."

I ignored her and walked off. She didn't follow me or call for me to come back. They're an emergency placement; they have no reason to care. The police caught on to me quickly. I got in the car with them and they asked what I was doing.

I said, "Going back to my foster family."

They knew I wasn't supposed to. Clearly the wife had given them the lowdown. I knew if I said something, it would be taken out of context or I'd be seen as unsafe to others or to myself. I thought I could try and get out of this placement a quicker way, saying, "If you take me back, I'll just smash up their house until everything they hold attachment to is gone."

They looked at each other and one of the officers said, "Why would you want to do that?"

I asked a question back. "Why am I not with my family?"

They couldn't answer, as they didn't know.

"Take me back there and I'll honestly just attack them," I said.

They took me to the police station. I couldn't be bothered trying to make a commotion. I just wanted to go back home, or what I thought was my home. You see, I was unknowingly getting lost in trying to escape, but then to go back to safety when the safety I had, I had tarnished … I guess a ten-year-old doesn't know that yet. It took five hours to get through to someone who actually knew my case and knew the situation.

They called for emergency transport to pick me up and take me to my new emergency placement. Two agency workers picked me up and took me to the location. It was very late at this point. I know it was a fair way – I think over two hours. As I fell asleep, this is where it gets a bit embarrassing … I wet myself while I was asleep. When I woke up, the worker was okay about it. It was blatantly obvious, and I wearing grey joggers.

The lady opened the door. She just said, "I'm going to put you to bed and we will talk in the morning. It is past midnight."

I slept quietly, as I didn't know what I was into. The next morning, I got up and the mum was waiting for me. She took me downstairs and introduced me to her three sons and one adopted son and her husband. The husband was very hyper and had obviously been given a handover by Social Services, as he wasn't shy about making a joke! He said, "No way you're smashing up this house today, boy! We're all going to Bournemouth." I wasn't up for it. I didn't know where I was, but I knew where Bournemouth was, so I did go, thinking I could try and do a runner, but as I brought my bag down to go, the dad stopped me.

"Ah, I see you have plans after Bournemouth. That's strange — I thought you was staying here tonight," he said.

I looked at him and said, "You know I can't let you know I want to go home. Home is where you make it, and I know it isn't here"

"But we can only try," the dad said.

I was confused, because I thought this was temporary — or was I the one making these placements temporary? I didn't want to think about it, so I took my bag upstairs and went to Bournemouth as planned.

Everything came about okay. The dad was very charismatic and funny; he had something about him like a cool dad. I actually never knew one existed … one that showed a softer approach to life. It was again confusing, but I just went with it. The two sons and one adopted one were keeping an eye on me, and they weren't sly about it, walking down to Bournemouth. They would walk me like I was being protected, two to the side of me and one at the back. It was like nothing I knew!

The mum was always very grumpy. I didn't get the contrast between them, as she didn't really find him funny and didn't smile often at him. I didn't like her, and I normally would do; I usually found the father harder to deal with.

We got back to their house late, and the adopted son said he would play Xbox with me, so I entertained it. We chilled for a while, then the other two brothers came in and started to play fight with us randomly. As they burst into the room with a WWE belt round them, thinking they were the tag team champions, it was amusing, and the dad let us continue, but the mum stopped us quite quickly.

I still didn't want to stay there; it was fun-"ish", but it wasn't anything I could be in. I just wanted to escape, but I knew I couldn't do anything. The brother would stop me and was strong enough to do anything, so I thought maybe one thing dangerous enough could make them call for Social Services to get me. I walked into the kitchen, turned all the gas rings on and let the tea towels catch fire, but I made sure it didn't spread. I also put a ball of tinfoil in the microwave before calling for the mum to come and see. She just gasped, sorted it all out and dragged me to the living room really aggressively.

I said, "If you don't call Social Services now, I'll do that when everyone is asleep and barricade your doors." She looked me in the eye and called Social Services.

Not giving me any satisfaction, she made the brothers watch me as she made the phone call. She took a long time and looked exhausted when she came back into the room.

"You'll be locked inside your room, and I'll slide your dinner through. I'm going to take everything out and you can have a mattress to sleep on."

She finished by saying Social Services would be taking me to my new placement tomorrow morning. I'd need to be ready by eight a.m. That that was a hard night.

I remember it well.

The dad opened the door – he was the only one to come and see me at all. He looked me in the eye.

"I don't know why you did it, but I know why you did it. Just keep safe, you hear me? I see fire in you; just don't let it be the fire in the house, please!" He was still trying to make a lighter side to everything! He locked me back inside, and I got picked up in the morning. I wasn't picked up by agency workers.

It was two well-known social workers who were attached to my case. They put me in the car. They were trying to work out why I wasn't settling in any of the placements I'd been to. Social workers like to play dumb constantly – you can tell them the reason one hundred times, you could write it on a brick and smack them with it, and they still won't know, I guess (because they'll be knocked out!), but that's not the point. They said that I had to try and make this placement work. I was taking a lot of resources and time. They reminded me I hadn't been to school in five months.

I didn't care.

"We really need to try and get you back in to education," they said, "and we don't want to make you start at a new school, so we are thinking of putting you back into your previous school. How does that sound?"

Obviously, in my head, amazing!

I guess it was school, but my foster family lived close to the school. I asked excitedly if I was going back to my foster family. They said, "No, but you didn't like it there. You weren't very kind to them towards the end. Why would you want to go back?"

"I love them. That's my home."

They didn't say anything.

6. Publications on the subject of alignments

This line of locations, the St Michael's Line, as well as many other similarly well-documented lines (known as alignments), are also described in the following superb publications:

- *The Old Straight Track*, Alfred Watkins, 1925
- *The View over Atlantis*, John Michell, 1969
- *Mysterious Britain*, Janet and Colin Bord, 1972

All discuss the broader history and concepts too, and in immaculate detail.

These are just three of many excellent publications in this subject area over the years.

7. Recognition of Edmund

There is a tribute song to the death of Edmund at the hand of the Vikings, by Justin Hawkins and the band the Darkness. The song is called "The Barbarian", and it can be heard via YouTube or Alexa.

8. El Niño/La Niña

There was a prominent El Niño during the second half of 2023 and into the first half of 2024.

9. Acknowledgements of research material

- Southwick estate website
- St Nicholas Church, South Boarhunt, website
- Jerome O'Connor, *The Hidden Places of World War Two*
- Wikipedia: Roman History/Constantine/Augustinian mission
- Constantine the Great: History of York
- Encyclopedia Britannica.com: Pontius Pilate – Melissa Petruzzello
- The map room, Southwick House
- Sir William James, *The Sky Was Always Blue*
- Vice Admiral B. B. Schofield, *Navigation and Direction: The Story of HMS Dryad*
- Dartmoor National Park Authority: The basis of the legend of Brentor church

10. This book can be purchased at...
chalkstreambooks.com/molp

www.facebook.com/profile.php?id=61556713946264